Saxon Ba

# Saxon Bane

### Book 7 in the Wolf Brethren Series

### By

### Griff Hosker

Saxon Bane

Published by Sword Books Ltd 2014
Copyright © Griff Hosker First Edition
Smashwords edition
The author has asserted their moral right under the Copyright, Designs and Patents Act, 1988, to be identified as the author of this work.
All Rights reserved. No part of this publication may be reproduced, copied, stored in a retrieval system, or transmitted, in any form or by any means, without the prior written consent of the copyright holder, nor be otherwise circulated in any form of binding or cover other than that in which it is published and without a similar condition being imposed on the subsequent purchaser.
A CIP catalogue record for this title is available from the British Library.

**Cover by Design for Writers**

Saxon Bane

## Contents

| | |
|---|---|
| Saxon Bane | 1 |
| Chapter 1 | 4 |
| Chapter 2 | 15 |
| Chapter 3 | 25 |
| Chapter 4 | 37 |
| Chapter 5 | 46 |
| Chapter 6 | 54 |
| Chapter 7 | 67 |
| Chapter 8 | 79 |
| Chapter 9 | 90 |
| Chapter 10 | 95 |
| Chapter 11 | 104 |
| Chapter 12 | 118 |
| Chapter 13 | 127 |
| Chapter 14 | 136 |
| Chapter 15 | 147 |
| Chapter 16 | 159 |
| Chapter 17 | 172 |
| Chapter 18 | 183 |
| Chapter 19 | 195 |
| Chapter 20 | 205 |
| Chapter 21 | 212 |
| Chapter 22 | 222 |
| Chapter 23 | 233 |
| Epilogue | 243 |
| Glossary | 245 |
| Historical note | 249 |
| Other books by Griff Hosker | 252 |

Saxon Bane

# Part 1

# Lord Lann-Warlord of Rheged

# Chapter 1

**Wyddfa 623**
Myrddyn had been particularly elusive and enigmatic of late. Always mysterious he had seemed to be especially hard to find. I did not mind. I spent more time with Myfanwy, my wife, Delbchaem Lann, my youngest daughter and our grandchildren. Hogan Lann, Nanna and even Gawan had all produced grandchildren for us to fuss about. Gawan's had been the most recent and Arturus was a delight. His wife, Gwyneth, was a perfect mother and we had spent some time with both of them as they began their family. My daughter Delbchaem was at that awkward age when she and her mother argued about everything. Quite often I was a peacemaker in my own home. So it was that I had not really noticed Myrddyn's absences. He had always had a tendency to go off on his own and I just put it down to that. Myrddyn was being a wizard. I know that he spent a great deal of time in the cavern beneath Wyddfa. We had called it the dream cave for when we slept there we dreamed and the spirits of the mountain came to us. It had been some time since I had done so.

That Midsummer Eve he had asked me to accompany him. I had been with him on that special day before. On the longest day, we could watch the sun set to the west and, when we woke, watch it rise to the east. It was a symbol for us of life. The fact that the darkness was so brief made us hopeful.

It was noon when we left the fort that guarded the straits between Gwynedd and Mona. We took no one with us; there had been no danger

## Saxon Bane

since King Cadwallon, the husband of my daughter, had concluded a peace with Cearl, the King of Mercia. It would not last but we had had a few years when our young men did not die in huge numbers. The skirmishes with the Hibernians and the Northumbrians did little to diminish our numbers and merely served to improve their skills. That last battle where I had suffered such a terrible wound to my leg now seemed worth it. The damp made my leg ache and I limped more but that was a sacrifice worth making for the peace we had enjoyed.

We had both aged a little although Myrddyn still seemed to be half my age. Consequently, we took horses to ascend the mountain and we took it steady. My leg still ached from the battle some years ago when I had nearly lost my life. I would never stand in a shield wall again. Indeed, I believed that my days of wielding my sword, Saxon Slayer, were long gone. I had thought to hand the sword on to my son, Hogan Lann. He was young and he was powerful. He was the warrior I had been many years earlier. There was something about the sword, which I had found buried by a Roman ancestor of mine that meant I could not relinquish it. As we rode up the well-worn track it was still strapped to my side. The sword seemed to talk to me. I often felt that there was a being within it. When I fought with it I never worried about losing. That was not arrogance or an innate belief in my own skill but I believed in the sword.

Myrddyn and I were growing old together; we behaved like an old married couple. I was greyer than he was but we both knew each other's ways and could walk for miles without exchanging a word and yet knowing what the other thought. Although I am still certain that Myrddyn could read everyone's thoughts and not just mine. He had an uncanny knack of knowing what someone was going to do.

"We are getting too old to be climbing mountains at our age."

"Hmph!" He snorted, "Speak for yourself. Besides if you feel like an old man you will be an old man. Imagine that you are the same young lad who strode across Rheged fighting Saxons. He is still somewhere buried beneath the flesh you have accumulated of late!"

## Saxon Bane

He was right. A lack of exercise and a rich diet had given me a little more of a paunch that I liked. "Perhaps it is time to relax and enjoy what we have won."

"Have we finished what you started? Is Rheged free?"

He had me there. I had sworn to King Urien of Rheged that I would defend the people of Rheged. As I reflected on my achievements I decided that I had failed to uphold my promise. The Saxons had yet to conquer Rheged completely but all that I had succeeded in was providing a haven for our people in Gwynedd and fighting the Northumbrians whenever I could. The old kingdoms of Bernicia and Deira now seemed to be joined under one banner, Northumbria. However, it was hard to know who ruled. The Saxons had more factions than the court of the Emperor.

We just had to keep on top of their advances and stop them from encroaching into our lands too much. My son, Hogan Lann, was even now raiding the Saxons north of the old Roman fort of Deva the fort the Saxons called Caestre. He would never stop fighting; he was a true warrior but I had been content to build alliances and build up our trade. Our people were richer but Myrddyn was quite right; I had not finished what I had started and my oath still remained unfulfilled.

I had outlived all of those who had begun the journey save Aelle. My half brother still lived but Raibeart had died in his bed the previous year. Pasgen and all the other princes of Rheged were dead and their issue were farmers trying to avoid the attention of Saxons. I had failed. Of course, my wife, my sons, the husband of my daughter Nanna, the King of Gwynedd, all of them would say I had succeeded. The Saxons had been held at bay. That was not what I had intended. I had thought that I would send them back from whence they came. The only one who would speak the truth to me was Myrddyn, the wizard.

"Do not dwell on the negatives, Warlord. Look at what we have achieved and realise that there is still much to do." Myrddyn reined in his horse and pointed to the rocky mountain. "Do you see the mountain? It changes. Each year it looks a little different. When the Romans were here they would have seen a different mountain. When Hogan Lann's great-grandchildren look up at it they will see something different. The changes are slow. But they happen each year. Perhaps it is the rains or the frost or even the mountain itself but it is evolving year by year. I tell you now Warlord that you have been as the small stone tumbling from the top of Wyddfa's crown. You have set in motion an avalanche. It is started and nothing can stop it." He shrugged as he urged his horse forward. "Of course, you will not be here to see the result of what you started but that is the will of the gods."

I hated the way he could do this. He read my thoughts and then left me with more questions than answers. "How do you know all of this?"

"I dream as you do but your mind is now clouded with blood and death. Mine is clearer; I have seen the future." He looked at me and I saw, in his clear blue eyes, real affection for me. "One day a warrior will come from across the seas from the east and he will be of your blood. He will be the one who will restore Rheged. Perhaps it will not be as great as it once was under the Romans, Coel and Urien but it will be free from Saxons."

We continued along the trail and my world was turned upside down. Why had Myrddyn waited until now to tell me of this? I would not succeed but my blood would. A child of mine I did not know would finish what I started. Why could I not be there to witness it? I felt a shiver down my spine. Wyddfa had great power and the spirits of the mountain could read my thoughts. I was not immortal and I served the gods. The shiver down my spine had been my reminder. It would have to be enough.

I recognised the trail we had taken. Many years earlier I had spent some time in a cave along it. I had dreamed and seen my mother. I had dreamed there many times but since my wound, I had not ventured up. The cold and the damp from the dark cavern would have made it ache. I suddenly felt guilty. I had not dreamed and spoken with the spirits since the day I had nearly died. Myrddyn was right to bring me with him. I should have done this myself.

He halted before we reached the entrance to the cave. A large stand of trees hid it beyond the turn in the trail. "I have had men here working on the cave. Call it a fancy of mine if you will. I am planning for a time when you and I are no longer here and we are just a memory."

He had me intrigued. "You always manage to surprise me Myrddyn. I had thought we came here just to dream."

"We will do that but I want you to look at the cave with new eyes."

To say I was surprised would be an understatement. When we turned I saw that the rocks and the entrance had been fashioned to make the head and mouth of a wolf. It only took a little imagination to do so. It looked spectacular.

"But why?"

"This is the cave of the Wolf Warrior. Your descendants may only know that about you. When they come here, they will know."

I was confused. "Know what?"

"Enter and all will become clear."

We tied the horses to a tree and entered. There was still plenty of light from the afternoon sun and the widened entrance, as well as the light from the holes of the wolf's eyes, meant that we could see a little better once inside. I could see, as soon as I walked in, that it was not just the entrance where the work had taken place. There were now a number of shelves and niches cut into the rock at the sides. I could only see those nearest the doors.

Myrddyn went to the middle of the cave and began to light a fire. It was our normal practice. I left him to it and wandered over to the nearest niche. They came up to my chest and I saw that they went into the rock about the length of my arm. The height was also that of my arm. I saw that there were four of them. I wandered over to the other side where I saw that there were just two of them. At the back of the cave, the floor had been smoothed by workmen so that it looked like a large hall. By the time I reached Myrddyn, the fire was burning well and he had a happy look on his face.

"I can see that you have done much work but what is it and what is it for?"

"I would have thought that was obvious Warlord. It is a tomb and it is for us!"

## Saxon Bane

I could not believe what I was hearing. I had had little idea of the function of the cave save as a place to dream but I would never have guessed that it would be a tomb. "You are being a little premature are you not? Or have you dreamed of my death?"

I had asked him the very same question many times and I always had the same answer. This time a sad look came over his face. He nodded slowly. "I know not the time but I know the hand. It is one of your blood who shall do this."

"Can we stop it?"

He shook his head, "Your death is necessary. It has been foretold and is part of the avalanche you began when you found the sword and killed your first wolf. You need to die so that Rheged may live."

I sat down. I knew that I was mortal. I knew I had outlived almost everyone and yet to be told that you were going to die was strange to say the least.

"And you know not when? Next week? Next month? "Next year?"

He shook his head again. "Even if I knew I could not help you. This will happen no matter what we do but if we try to interfere then things may go awry. It is best to let the spirits of the mountain work things out. We are mortal and they are not."

"And your death?"

"I told you before; I dreamed of my death many years ago. I know that I will be there when you die for I have dreamed it. My death will come after yours." He smiled, "I want you to live as long as possible too."

I noticed that the light outside was fading. We would have to unsaddle the horses soon and bring in food and drink but I still had more questions. "You say 'our tomb'?"

"Yes, you and your family will be over there." He pointed to four holes on one side. "And I will be on the other side. There."

"I see four spaces on my side."

"You, Myfanwy, Hogan Lann and Gawan."

"Nanna?"

"I think the tomb of the Queen of Gwynedd might attract rather too much attention and besides she should be buried with her husband." I

Saxon Bane

went to speak. "And Delbchaem will be married too. She should be with her husband."

It was maddening the way he read my mind. "And you will be on the other side?"

"I will."

"And why are there two spaces?"

"For my family."

"But you have none!"

"Not yet! Now go and unsaddle the horses and give them grain while I prepare some food."

As I went about those mundane tasks my mind was in a whirl. Suddenly each moment in the day became important. Suppose my death came on the way down the mountain? I thought of all those I would not have the chance to speak with and say goodbye to. I had not managed that with my brother Raibeart. He had been taken ill by a sudden fever and died even as I was sailing to be at his side. At least I had fulfilled a promise to him. I had taken his wild son Morcar ap Raibeart under my wing and, in the last two years, he had quietened down and become a fine member of my warriors. I put much of that down to my other nephew, Lann Aelle and Pol who had been my squire. They understood the young man far better than an old man like me. He was now my squire and Hogan Lann would decide where best he should serve.

Suddenly many of Myrddyn's actions made sense. He had had Oswald, our priest of the White Christ, create many laws and rules for those living under my sway. I had thought it was because Oswald was becoming old. These priests, like Osric before him, lived a long time but Brother Oswald, like me, was creaking around the edges. As I carried the saddles back into the cave I reflected that it had been at least two years, perhaps three since I had drawn Saxon Slayer in anger. You do not remember the last time you do something. You always imagine that there will be another opportunity to do so.

Myrddyn watched me with hooded eyes as I walked toward him. "Why are you so unhappy? You always said that you wanted to know when your death would come."

## Saxon Bane

"That is because I imagined it would a long time coming!"

"It might be. Do not watch for death on your shoulder. Be the Warlord feared by the Northumbrians and the Hibernians. Be the warrior every young man aspires to be. That way people will remember you."

I took the bowl of food he passed to me. He was right, of course. He was infuriating like that. He was always right! Besides I had always expected to die in combat. I had been fighting since I had been little more than a boy. My brothers had given up the sword when they married but I had continued. I resolved to get myself fit again so that I could, once again be Warlord.

Myrddyn smiled, "There, that is better is it not. Now you are resolved and your dream will be sweeter."

"When I get to the Otherworld I will ask the spirits how it is you can read my mind so easily."

He gave me his enigmatic smile and poured me some of the wine we imported from Byzantium. "And I will ask how you manage to defeat every warrior you face, even when they have better weapons and are stronger."

"Tell me why I must be sacrificed." I held up my hand. "I am not objecting but I would like to know the reason."

"In the old days before the Romans came, the Druids," he smiled, "that was the name they gave for wizards such as me, would ask for volunteers to be ritually killed and sacrificed before a battle. Their heart would be removed and their body plunged into a sacred pool or hole. The heart became a symbol of the sacrifice and would be buried in the centre of the village to protect it from the Romans."

"Did it work?"

"It worked against others like them but when the Romans came there was great slaughter. The Druids became fugitives in their own land. But those priests held them up for a long time. The Romans thought of giving up and returning home so great was the power of the Druids."

"So I may die and it still might not save Rheged?"

"That may happen but I have dreamed and know that your sacrifice will not be in vain. Besides, as you said when we were coming up here, you are old. You will not die by the sword for you are too great a warrior for that. You would not wish to slip away in your sleep like Raibeart would you?"

He was right. I wanted a warrior's death. We sat and talked until the sun had set completely on this, one of the shortest nights of the year. I reminisced about the adventures we had had and the things we had done. No one had been with me as long as Myrddyn and he knew me better than any man.

When the time came to sleep and to dream I was ready. Myrddyn loaded the fire with the herbs and sweet-smelling wood which enabled us to drift off into the land of the spirits. As I succumbed to the magic of Wyddfa I wondered if Hogan Lann or Gawan would dream here as I did. Gawan had already shown that he could dream and the spirits wished to speak with him. Perhaps he would be the dreamer and Hogan Lann the Warlord. Certainly, the injuries my younger son had suffered at the hands of Aethelfrith meant he would never be the warrior that Hogan Lann was. Thinking of my sons sent me into a deep sleep and I fell into a deep dark hole which seemed to have no bottom.

*It was dark. It was cold. I saw Hogan Lann and Gawan trying to reach me but I was falling. I turned and saw a face I knew. I felt a blade sinking slowly through my back and then it was black. I heard my mother's voice, "Come to me, Lann! I am here."*

*I opened my eyes and my mother enfolded me in her arms. "Soon you will be here with me my son but your work is not done. You need to find friends and allies. You need to visit with the Irish; find new friends amongst your foes. Not all Saxons are your enemies. Look to the south. You must risk all for your time in Rheged is brief. You have come so close and now is not the time to falter. Beware your blood!"*

*I fell, down and down. I never reached the ground. I saw a wall of stone and I remembered that it was the Roman wall. I saw warriors hurtling towards me and, with Saxon Slayer held aloft I charged forward. I looked and my hands became claws and I became a wolf. When I looked again the wolf was my son and I was lying bleeding on the ground. I watched as Saxon Slayer was torn from my grip. My*

## Saxon Bane

*enemies fled and I was victorious and then the knife in the dark slashed down and all became black.*

I looked around and saw the first glow of the new day peeping through the entrance of the cave. It lit Myrddyn's face. He was watching me. He nodded. "An interesting death."

"Was it like that when you dreamed yours?"

He nodded. "And now we must put on a face to meet the world and you must prepare answers for the questions we cannot give."

"You mean lie to my family?"

He stood and stretched. "What is the alternative? Do you tell them you are to die and have them worry? Would you have Hogan Lann and Gawan so concerned with watching over you that they die themselves? The dream is a weapon just as much as Saxon Slayer but you need to use it wisely. It can hurt our own people as well as our enemies."

Infuriatingly, he was right, of course. I could not burden my boys with the knowledge that I was to die. "And what of this Irish venture? The last thing we need is an alliance with those unstable wild men. They are great fighters but they have no control."

"The spirits know all."

"And Saxons? Can I ally with Saxons?"

He shrugged, "King Cearl of Mercia appeared to be a reasonable man. He is south of here." He waved a hand as though trying to rid himself of an invisible fly. "The spirits do not lay everything out for us. We are expected to think for ourselves. Our world has changed, Lord Lann. Come and let us eat. Dreaming always makes me hungry."

Myrddyn was a good cook and he soon had some food for us. I decided not to talk about the dream. I did not like the thought that I would die soon.

"We will have to visit with Kay soon."

"Aye. There is an example of the spirits. They did not warn us that Prince Pasgen, his sons and his wife would all succumb to the plague. It is good that Kay rules there still."

"If they had warned us could you have saved them, wizard?"

"Possibly. The books we read in Constantinopolis gave some ideas on the matter. Perhaps when Gawan visits he can read up on the disease." Gawan had shown some wizard-like abilities and soon he would have to visit the east as his brother had.

"Kay is a stout warrior."

"He is, Lord Lann, but the equites were laid low with the plague and they are few in number. It is only the land which stops the Northumbrians from flooding over. Kay is lucky to hang to what he holds."

"Then the Irish plan might just work. We will visit them first and I will see for myself what they are like. They may not be as wild as they once were."

As he packed away the pots and dishes we had used he said, "Perhaps you will be able to give them that control. It could be that all that they need is a hero whom they can copy. Who knows?"

As we stood at the entrance to the cave I asked, "And this tomb of mine, when will I see it again?"

He looked at me sadly, "When you are dead."

Saxon Bane

# Chapter 2

We had a long journey down from the cave for me to prepare my mind for the meeting with Myfanwy. The rest of my family was not at home. Gawan Lann and Hogan Lann were on the borders keeping the Saxons in check along with Lann Aelle. There was just Morcar of my family who was waiting for me. He did not know me well yet. I would just have to deceive my wife. If I could fool Myfanwy then that would give me time to become used to the idea.

This was the first time that Gawan had been away for any length of time. It was that time in a young warrior's life when he has to learn how to be a warrior. Hitherto he had trained and fought in skirmishes but Hogan Lann and Pol would show him how to campaign. He would learn how to keep three horses in the field and to be as prepared as possible to fight. Oft times it was dull work with no action, and that too was part of the process. His maimed hand would not stop him from leading but he could never be the warrior that his brother was. Myrddyn had hinted that he might become a wizard.

Myfanwy greeted me and I could see that was genuinely pleased to see me. "I have missed you, husband."

I laughed, "I was away but one night!"

"I know and that was fine when the boys and Nanna were at home but this hall feels lonely and empty." She nestled into my shoulder and whispered, "My heart aches for my children." Hogan Lann had been the son of my first wife and although Myfanwy loved him as one of her own Nanna and Gawan were special. I knew that, despite what she said, Gawan was her favourite. She and Nanna had butted heads too many times when my daughter was growing up but Gawan had been a delight. He was polite, considerate and courteous. When he had married, Myfanwy had scrutinised every uncia of Gwyneth before she approved. There was nothing to dislike about the personable young Welsh woman and those first years when we all lived under the same roof were a joy. Now, however, Gawan Lann and Gwyneth lived to the north close to the monastery of St. Asaph. My wife could visit but it would be to another woman's home.

I sighed, "I will be away again, my love."

She pulled away and glared at me. "Why? Is it not enough that our sons campaign the whole time? You are an old man and you should be resting at home."

"If I rest I will die and besides I dreamed."

"Your mother?"

"Aye, she told me to seek out the Hibernians."

Her hand went to her mouth. "They are wild people and they tattoo their bodies. They are savages."

"I know all of that and yet my mother's spirit urged me to make the journey. Has she ever given us false information?" She shook her head. "Then I shall trust her still and go but I would be happier if you were with Gawan Lann and Gwyneth. It will stop the pain you feel and there is a new grandchild for you to fuss over. I know that Gwyneth would appreciate the help."

She appeared mollified by that and she kissed me on the cheek. "I still think that you deserve some time to yourself. Just promise me that you will engage in no more fighting! You are too old."

"I shall have Morcar with me."

She snorted, "He is too much in love with himself that one. He likes prettier clothes than any woman."

"Now then. He is the son of my brother and he is a good warrior."

"There is still something about him." She shook her head. "I am getting to be a grumpy old woman. Perhaps I do need to visit with my grandchild."

I found Brother Oswald with Tuanthal in the main hall. They were poring over maps. Tuanthal was still a young man in my eyes but the leader of my horse was now nearly as grey as me. He rose and smiled and I saw the young boy in him still. He asked, "You dreamed?"

## Saxon Bane

Brother Oswald crossed himself. He always did that when the Otherworld was mentioned. He never commented but I knew that he did not approve. He had told me that I was a Christian, I just didn't know it. I was not sure. I liked many of the Christians. Old Osric and St.Asaph had both been good friends of mine but I still believed in the old ways. I was still what the Christians called, a pagan.

"Aye, I did. I would pick your brains. What do we know of the Hibernians?"

Tuanthal shook his head, "They are a wild and ill-disciplined race of warriors. This is fortunate for us for if they could be controlled they would be more dangerous than the Saxons."

I had learned nothing there. I looked at Oswald. In answer, he went to one of the maps he had collected over the years and brought it to the table. He pointed to the island of Ireland and I saw that there were many red crosses dotted about it. Oswald smiled, "They are a Christian people." I heard the snort of derision from Tuanthal. Oswald ignored it. "They have, there, many churches and the church has a great influence on their leaders. The people, largely, grow cereals." He frowned. "You are not thinking of stealing from our neighbours are you?"

"I will do as I see fit, priest. Continue." I noticed that Myrddyn had come in. He and Oswald got on well despite their religious differences.

"They also prize cattle but they raid them from each other. They have few towns but their kings, and they have many of those, live in large ring forts. They are built in much the same style as the one in Stanwyck."

"Good. Now tell me about their kings."

"There are three main families. The Eóganachta rule the south or at least the males of that family contest the south and only join when there is an enemy from the north. Then there is the Uí Néill. They rule in the middle and northern part of the land. They are the same as the Eóganachta in that they fight amongst themselves unless they are threatened."

"You said that there were three families."

"Yes, there are the people of Dál nAraidi who live in the north and east. Of late they have begun to flex their muscles so to speak. They have even raided the Saxons and established themselves in the old kingdom of Strathclyde, where King Riderch Hael held the Saxons at bay for so many years."

"That is interesting." Could this be the connection my mother had wanted me to make? I caught Myrddyn's eye and he spread his arms as he gave me another of his enigmatic smiles. I ignored it. "And who is their leader?"

I am not certain but the family are the Ulaid. As to their present king, I am afraid I do not know."

"Daffydd ap Gwynfor would, Warlord." Myrddyn's mind worked quicker than most.

"Then send for him. Tuanthal, I need some warriors to take a trip with me. Just a bodyguard. We are not going to make war. We aim to make friends instead."

Tuanthal nodded. "We have some young warriors who are keen to impress the Warlord."

"I do not want any headstrong young men keen to show off."

He laughed, "Do not worry they know what sort of warrior you would choose."

"Good and have one of Aedh's riders take a message to Daffydd. I would have him come to us so that I may consult."

After all of the business had concluded and we had eaten I went to my solar. I would watch the sunset, on this longest of days, from my favourite room. Having told my wife of my plans she would be busy packing for her trip to St. Asaph. It might only be a few miles up the coast but to her, it would be like another country.

I sat in a comfortable chair and watched Mona in the distance as it glowed, seemingly green, like an emerald against the gold of the sun. This might be my last midsummer. What if my death were to come in the next few days? I realised how much time I had wasted lately. I had important things to do before I died or rather before I was killed. I now understood Myrddyn's words. I could not look at every person I saw as a potential killer. I had to put such thoughts from my mind and deal with everyone as though they had not changed. Indeed they had not changed. The only change was within me; that had to remain secret.

There was a knock on the door. I sighed with impatience; I wanted to be alone. In an instant, I laughed at myself. Soon I would have all the loneliness I could wish for. "Come!"

Morcar came in. Each time I saw him I was reminded of his father, my younger brother. They had the same build, the same eyes, and even the same voice. The differences were subtle. Morcar laughed less than his father did and when he did it was never with his eyes. He was also far more serious about being a warrior and a leader. Raibeart had never wanted to be a leader such as me. He had been a good warrior but it was not in his blood as it was with Pol, Hogan Lann and Lann Aelle.

Morcar was ambitious and he was a good warrior. His cousins had trained him well. He had been the youngest and they had passed all of their skills on to him. He could ride as well as Pol, use a sword as well as Hogan Lann and a bow as well as Daffydd ap Miach, the captain of my archers. He was desperate to be a captain such as Lann Aelle. The peace of the last few years had not suited him. My captain did not die and there would be no place for him to win honour. He had begged to be allowed to accompany my sons to the border. The simple answer I gave him was that he was not needed there and he still had much to learn from Myrddyn and Brother Oswald.

"I hear we will be going to Ireland soon."

I gave him a sharp look, "Have you been gossiping?"

"No, Warlord, I was asked by Oswald to put some maps away and I saw that they were of Hibernia and then I heard that you had sent for Captain Daffydd." He shrugged. "It seemed obvious to me."

He was an incredibly clever boy. I had thought to send him, as I with Hogan Lann and Pol, to Constantinopolis. It had made them much better leaders and they had learned much about the Roman ways of fighting. However, the intrigues of that Eastern court made me wish to spare the boy.

"Aye well you are right and we will visit with them."

"Shall I come with you?"

## Saxon Bane

"Would you wish to? It will be a peaceful mission. We go not to fight."

He grinned, "Perhaps not this time but may be in the future?"

"We have enough enemies of our own on this side of the water without annoying our near neighbours."

"But Warlord, Saxon Slayer has never tasted defeat."

"And that is because I only choose to fight battles that I can win."

"I heard that the battle in which you hurt your leg was one where you were heavily outnumbered and you nearly died. Did you choose that one?"

"Perhaps not all of them then. But I choose to try to use the peaceful approach when I speak with the Irish."

He could see that I wished to be alone, "I will leave you then Warlord." He paused at the door. "I am learning much from you."

And then he left. He was far more serious about being a leader than either Lann Aelle or my sons had been. They had been keen to be warriors. Hogan Lann and Pol had only become more serious about being a leader when they returned from the east. Morcar appeared driven. Perhaps it was the death of his father which drove him on. I know that the two of them had had words before Raibeart died and they had had no chance to take them back. There would always be the memory of words unspoken for Morcar. You could not unsay cruel words but you could regret not speaking how you felt. Both of my parents had been taken when I was young. My mother's spirit still spoke with me but, as the years went on, I found it hard to remember my father's face and his voice was lost to me. I wondered how Morcar felt about his father.

Daffydd's ship pulled in the next day. He had renamed it **'Gwynfor'** in honour of his father. She had been an Irish ship we had captured years ago. Although she was old, Daffydd looked after her as though she was the most precious thing in the whole world. Each winter she would be hauled onto the beach and all of the weed and sea life removed. Planks would be replaced or repaired and she had a new set of sails each year. The result was that she still sailed faster than those pirates who might try to catch her and she could sail through storms which would keep other ships in the harbour. He usually traded with the kingdoms of the Welsh although he had sailed to Byzantium before now.

He looked expectantly at me as I strode down to the wooden jetty which jutted out into the sea. "You look well, Warlord."

I snorted, "What you really mean is that you are pleased I am still alive."

He laughed, "You sound like my father when he grew a little older. I suppose it will come to all of us that we do not wish to grow old." He saw Myrddyn behind me. "Of course, there are some who will never grow old."

He was one of the few who could banter with Myrddyn. Most feared the wrath of the wizard. He chuckled, "Why grow old, Daffydd? It is better to stay as young as possible for as long as you can."

Since our visit to the cave, I was constantly aware of the passage of time. I needed to get things done quickly. "Walk with us, Daffydd. We need your mind." We left his crew unloading supplies for the fort. "What do you know of Fiachnae mac Báetáin, king of the Dál nAraidi?"

He looked surprised, "Hibernians? You normally shun them."

I smiled, "I know but humour me."

"This Fiachnae mac Báetáin, he calls himself king of the Dál nAraidi but others dispute it. He is one of the few Irish kings who venture beyond their shores. He has raided Strathclyde before now and attacked the Saxons."

I looked at Myrddyn who seemed pleased by the news. "He is ambitious then?"

He nodded, "And more than a little greedy. He loves gold. I am surprised he has not tried to raid here."

"Perhaps he is also clever enough to realise what the result of that would be."

Myrddyn was correct. There were far easier nuts to crack than our well-protected domain. "Perhaps he is."

"I intend to visit with him."

Daffydd looked surprised. "Is that not a risk? Unless you take your army he could hold you hostage."

"The Warlord would want you to make contact with him so that he could visit peacefully. You trade with them, do you not?"

He nodded, "As I say he loves gold and he trades for it whenever he can."

"Does he read?"

"He is a Christian and he has priests of the White Christ there and so I assume that he can."

"Good, then the next time you trade you can deliver a letter." Myrddyn looked at me. "I will go and write one now, eh Warlord?"

He was really telling me what he would do. I would have bitten the head of any other man who did that but he was like another part of me and I waved him away.

When I was alone with Daffydd I said, "How many men could we take on '*Gwynfor*'?" We had other ships but they were busy trading and it took time to gather them together. I needed speed.

"With or without horses?"

"Without."

"We could take twenty but it would be a tight fit."

"Thirteen?"

He smiled, "That would not be a problem."

"And try to think of a gift we could take him which he might appreciate."

"That is simple. Something gold."

"Like a torc?"

"Perfect. It will take me some time to arrange a cargo."

I nodded, "As soon as you can though."

"Aye Lord Lann."

I left my captain to await the letter from Myrddyn. As I strode along the road we had made from the shore to the fort I smiled to myself. I had not completed all that I had wished but we had, at least, made a copy of Rome here under Wyddfa's watchful gaze. Our roads and paths had not been made by Romans but we had used Roman ways. Here the people were safe from raids and Mona produced more grain than we could use ourselves. We traded it all over the seas around Britannia and beyond.

## Saxon Bane

The guards all saluted me as I walked back to my fort. I absent-mindedly returned their salutes. There would have been a time when I knew all of their names but these were the sons of the warriors I had fought alongside. They had grown up with the legend of the Wolf Warrior and his sword, Saxon Slayer. They would fight and die for me and I would not even know their names.

I suddenly stopped and said to the two guards on the interior gate. "What are your names?" It was only later I realised how gruff my voice had sounded. I had not meant it to be. They both looked petrified as though they had done something wrong.

"Er I am Mungo ap Bors."

"And I am Gruffydd ap Llewellyn. Have we done aught wrong, Warlord?"

It was then I realised that I still had my serious face upon me. I smiled and clapped them both on their backs. "No. I just realised I did not know your names. How is your father Bors?"

"He serves on the border close to King Cadwallon's land. He will be pleased you asked after him."

"And you?"

"My father serves with Mungo's father."

"Good. One day you will serve somewhere that does not involve having to suffer stupid questions from grumpy old men."

I left them and I knew that our conversation, mundane and inconsequential though it was, would be repeated in the barracks. It would be analysed and dissected as though it was important. There had been a time when I would not have needed to ask such awkward-sounding questions. I had grown apart from my ordinary warriors.

By the time I reached my hall, I knew what I had to do. I sought my wife. "I will take you to Gawan this afternoon and then I will visit with Cadwallon."

She glared at me. "Then why cannot I come with you and see our daughter and our grandchildren?"

I sighed. I could not do right for doing wrong. "I thought you wanted to be with Gwyneth and her children."

## Saxon Bane

"I can visit with them when you return. You men; unless you are planning to slaughter another army you have not the first idea of how to plan things. We can go directly up the Clwyd and save time!" There was no arguing with a woman and she would have her way. Had I said it the other way around I would still have been in trouble.

I left her and found Tuanthal. "We need an escort to visit with King Cadwallon. When we go to Hibernia I will need ten of your warriors and you. Choose warriors who know how to think for themselves."

"Aye my lord."

Saxon Bane

# Chapter 3

As we rode along the Clwyd it came to me that I had not visited the fort here for over two years. The valley looked different. Since I had brought peace the settlers had flooded in and the hillsides and valley bottoms were littered with prosperous-looking farms. Sheep and cattle dotted the valley sides. I could have come here with just my wife and Myrddyn and been in no danger.

As we passed the fort at the head of the valley I reined in. Bors, the father of Mungo, strode out to greet me. "An unexpected visit, Warlord."

"I am on my way to Wrecsam. How are things here?"

"Dull. The Mercians keep to their side of the border and Edwin's men have learned to avoid us. My men crave action."

I laughed. "Soon, perhaps, we will remind Edwin of our power. I spoke with your son yesterday and Llewellyn's son too."

His face clouded, "They have not given offence have they?"

"No, no, they are fine warriors and crave frontier duty."

He looked relieved. "They still have much to learn. Garrison duty at the fort is never wasted."

We rode over the col at the head of the valley and dropped down to the fertile lands at the eastern extreme of Gwynedd. Many questioned Cadwallon's decision to have his court so close to the Mercians. Many of his nobles thought that he should live in the fort I occupied. It showed how little they knew of the young king. He had been trained with my sons and he had a keen mind. He had made peace with the Mercians but his presence ensured that no one would try to attack his people. His army was almost as good as that commanded by my son and the Mercians were just grateful that the king of Gwynedd prevented cattle raids and incursions from King Edwin and his Northumbrians.

As Warlord and the parent of the Queen, we were quickly ushered into the royal presence. I saw the Steward's panicked look as he took in the entourage. He would be wondering how to feed so many of us. I said quietly to him, "We will be here but one night."

He grinned with relief, "Thank you, Warlord."

He scurried off and Myfanwy linked my arm. "You can be quite thoughtful when you choose."

"I have my moments."

King Cadwallon looked genuinely pleased to see us and Nanna showed how much she had grown over the years as she fussed over her mother. A few years ago they would have fought like cat and dog.

"Let us stroll in my courtyard. I am guessing that you have some news to impart to me." We left the women and the grandchildren.

"I do, your majesty. Morcar, go and see to the horses. We will be leaving at first light." Morcar looked disappointed but he nodded and obeyed. Myrddyn strode to the other side of the young king he had helped to train.

"Now that we are alone we can dispense with this *'your majesty'* nonsense. I would not be king, nor my father before me if you had not made us so."

"How is your father?"

King Cadfan had been wounded in the same war as I had received my injury. "He is as well as can be expected. He is pleased that he is no longer king. His life is much easier." We reached a courtyard lined with trees and we sat on a bench under an apple tree which had the small fruits already growing. "Now please tell me why you are here."

"I dreamed again."

"Ah, that normally means something momentous is on the horizon."

Myrddyn sniffed, "Not always."

Cadwallon laughed, "Perhaps not to you, wizard, but to us mere mortals they are."

"I was told to seek an alliance with the Irish."

I could tell that had surprised him. "I was not expecting that."

"Perhaps it is not that surprising. In the old days of King Urien, there was an alliance of Strathclyde, Elmet, Rheged and Bernicia. In your father's time, we allied all of the kings of Wales. It is the only way to defeat the sea of Saxons."

He looked up at the sky as he took in that information. Myrddyn and I had taught him to reflect when given news he was not expecting rather than dismissing it out of hand. "There is the danger that if we invite them to help us they may stay."

Myrddyn nodded. "It is how the Angles first came to settle. They were invited as mercenaries and they stayed."

Sometime Myrddyn could be infuriating. He was now being what the Christians called a Devil's Advocate. I knew why he did it. He wanted Cadwallon to think more widely about the issue.

"Yes I know but I have thought this through wizard." The ground below my feet was made up of small pebbles of different colours. I took a black one. "Here is King Edwin in the north of the land. He will be in Din Guardi, or as they call it now Bebbanburgh, or Dunelm, possibly, even, Eboracum." I took a reddish stone. "We are here in Wales." I found a brown stone. "This is Fiachnae mac Báetáin in Dál nAraidi. I do not intend to invite him here." I pointed to the red stone. I picked up a white stone and placed it halfway between the black and the brown one. "I intend to invite him to Strathclyde. Once he has begun to annoy Edwin then we can bring your army from here and finally defeat him in his own lands. For too long he has fought on our land and we have suffered. Let us make him suffer."

The time I had spent in the solar had paid off for I saw the nod of approval from Myrddyn.

"I have taught you well."

I laughed, "You arrogant old wizard!"

"Will the Irish go along with that? I know not this Fiachnae mac Báetáin."

"He likes gold and he is ambitious. He has raided the Saxons before now. I intend to travel to meet with him and see if he will ally with us. I have our smiths making a torc for him. It will appeal to his vanity and to his greed."

King Cadwallon smiled and nodded. "Neither of you has ever given me false advice and it would scotch the snake. You know that King Edwin is now thinking of becoming Christian?"

"Aye I know and this Hibernian is too but apparently they only worry about stealing from fellow Hibernians."

There was a pause and Myrddyn said, "And, of course, Aethelfrith's sons are both in Ireland too."

I had defeated their father and his death was laid at my door. They both had a blood feud with me but also with King Edwin. It complicated matters. I shrugged, "I can do nothing about that but I have heard that Fiachnae mac Báetáin also fought against Aethelfrith. Perhaps he will want some more Saxon treasure."

We left the next morning having had one of the most pleasant visits I could ever remember. Perhaps it was a combination of the brevity and my impending doom but I made the most of every moment spent with my daughter and her children. I noticed the questioning looks from my wife and the knowing looks from Myrddyn. It was as though I was leading two lives. I suspected, that after I was dead, my wife would berate Myrddyn for having hidden the truth from her. The old wizard would easily handle that.

When we reached St. Asaph, Gawan was not there. He and Hogan Lann had led their equites on a raid north of Deva. Saxon ships had been seen on the Maeresea. The raid would be a warning to them.

Morcar waited until we were heading back from St. Asaph before he questioned me. "Will I be going with you to Hibernia?"

"Do you wish to? It will merely be a peace mission. There will be no fighting."

"It will do me good to see how the great and the good conduct such business."

Myrddyn snorted and Tuanthal laughed. My cavalry commander said, "I would not call an Irish King the great and the good. They are one step away from being pirates."

"Then why the alliance?"

## Saxon Bane

"Our numbers increase slowly. The blood of Rheged is being thinned. Our warriors cannot continue to bleed for this land or there will be none left for the future. We need allies who can help us to drive the Saxons from our shores." I looked at the eager young man. "If you wish to come then you can but you will have to watch silently."

He nodded happily, "I can do that Lord Lann."

I did not expect Daffydd for a few days and I was able to prepare. I would not need my wolf cloak. Sadly, it was showing its age more than I. I liked to wear it to war for it inspired my men but I would leave it at home. I would take my armour, helmet and banner for they marked me out as the Warlord of Rheged and I had to make an impression on this young Hibernian. Over the past couple of years, influenced by Hogan Lann, we had changed our shields from the round ones we had used to an oval one which was more similar to the old Roman scutum. It was a better shield to use on horseback for it protected the legs better but I missed my old shield. I did like the wolf design which was sharper on the leather-covered oval shield.

I visited with my smiths. I had given them precise instructions. The torc had two wolves cast into it. It was a mixture of gold and copper. The copper highlighted the wolves and the goldsmith had inlaid red stones to form the eyes. It was a beautiful piece of work. Now that I knew my time was growing short I did not worry so much about the cost. If the torc bought an alliance then it would save the lives of my warriors and that would be worth it.

I regretted being unable to speak with Hogan Lann and Gawan before I left. Hogan Lann was my heir and he would be the one who led the people of Rheged once I passed on. I would have to spend some time speaking with both of my sons when I returned. I was aware that I needed the alliance before summer ended. An autumn campaign would catch the Saxons unawares and we could winter on their land.

When Daffydd returned it was with good news. Fiachnae mac Báetáin would meet with me. They had one port, of sorts, on their northern coast and that was where we would travel. Tuanthal was worried about Irish pirates but Daffydd laughed it off. "We have the fastest ship in these seas. Even if they try they will not catch us. Besides they would not wish to incur the wrath of our host. I discovered that he is a powerful king and feared by his peers." He looked at me as though it was I who was the wizard. "This is a good alliance."

We left three days later. Tuanthal's men came aboard. They normally rode without armour but, as we had no horses it was decided to impress our would-be allies. They were all issued with the armour used by Hogan Lann and his equites. We had ten spare sets of armour. Poor Morcar was definitely disappointed that he did not get to don one.

"You get to carry the wolf standard."

He did not take that with the grace that I had hoped. I began to realise that he had much to learn yet. His education was only just begun.

I had raided the central part of Hibernia before now but I had never seen the northern part. We sailed past Manau or Mann as some of the sailors called it. Some of our people scratched out a living there but there were few natural resources save water. It made it less attractive for raiders and so far the Saxons had shown no interest in it. I did not know how we would defend against someone who wished to take it.

As we sailed along the coast I saw how close Rheged was to the island. Some of our people lived there still but it was a parlous existence. They were hardy. I felt guilty about leaving them to their own devices. Perhaps the spirits had told me of my death to make me do something. Certainly, it had made me make this visit and the result might be freedom for many of my people. When we rounded the coast of Hibernia Daffydd pointed to the huge stones made by giants. I found myself in awe of the race that had done that. I wondered where the giants had gone.

To call the tiny place we docked in a harbour was a little like calling a fishing boat a warship. A few stones had been forced into the sea and some trees dropped next to them to stop ships from damaging themselves. That was all that there was to it. I could see a ring fort on the hillside above. No one was waiting at the jetty for us.

I looked at Myrddyn. He shrugged, "They are being cautious. You are not only the bane of the Saxons but the Hibernians too. They frighten their children with stories of the wolf man coming for them."

## Saxon Bane

I laughed, "And the wizard who flies them in."

Tuanthal and the warriors went ashore first. Their armour gleamed in the late afternoon sun. It had been a good choice. Morcar stepped ashore next and he held the banner and watched for Myrddyn. My wizard stepped ashore and seemed to sniff the air. I waited until he gave a slight nod. As I stepped ashore Morcar unfurled my banner and a light breeze set it fluttering above my head. I had no idea how Myrddyn had done it but it had the desired effect. The gates opened and the warriors began to descend to greet us. Morcar stood behind me and my warriors flanked us as we patiently waited for this king to greet us.

I had the time to watch him as he descended. He surprised me. He was not half-naked with tattoos and limed hair. His hair was tied neatly behind his head and he wore a purple cloak over a blue tunic. His beard was neatly trimmed and he carried a sword in a richly decorated scabbard.

His guard was more typically Irish. All of them had bare chests although it was hard to tell because of all the tattoos. None of them had limed hair but they all carried a wild variety of swords. Some had two handed ones and others had wickedly curved ones. They strode arrogantly towards us. The sneers on their faces told Tuanthal and his men what they thought of men who had to wear mail and armour.

Fiachnae mac Báetáin stood before me. I could understand his words as he spoke. "I am King Fiachnae mac Báetáin of the Dál nAraidi. I have been told that you come here to speak of an alliance?"

I stepped forward and held out my hand. It was a crucial moment. Would he clasp it in return? I saw his eyes appraising me and weighing up his decision. The silence was almost overpowering. Finally he, too, stepped forward and clasped my arm. "You are older than I thought you would have been."

I smiled, "I have been fighting the Saxons a long time. It ages a man."

He nodded, "And you must be Myrddyn the wizard." Myrddyn bowed. "I have heard many tales of you and the Wolf Warrior. Perhaps we will discover the truth later." He seemed to notice my horsemen for the first time. "And these are your equites; the famous armoured horsemen who carry all before them."

"No, King Fiachnae mac Báetáin, these are my horsemen. My equites are fighting the Saxons under my son, Hogan Lann."

"But they wear such fine armour."

"When you are successful at fighting the Saxons then you can afford such armour for all your men." When his eyes opened wide I knew that the strategy Myrddyn and I had discussed would work. We would appeal to his greed.

"Come let us walk to my home." He nodded to his bodyguard who formed up behind us effectively cutting Myrddyn and me off from Morcar, Tuanthal and my men. From his wry smile, I think he meant to intimidate me and Myrddyn. It did not work. I would not be killed by his bodyguards and I smiled easily.

"You have a well-positioned fort."

"It has been occupied since before the times of the Romans."

"The Romans never came here?"

He said proudly, "They never even tried to conquer my people."

"But you were visited were you not?"

He looked genuinely surprised when Myrddyn spoke. "Yes, a Roman came."

"And he visited St. Brigid and gave her a ring, I believe."

"You are truly a wizard. How did you know? It was a secret and only the kings knew of it."

"I know you worship the White Christ now but I still speak with the spirits and they told me." He pointed to me. "They speak with Lord Lann too."

There was a subtle change in his attitude from that moment on. He stopped trying to impress us and actually listened to us. "I look forward to hearing how you defeated the Saxons so many times."

As we wound our way up to his sanctuary I began to reassess this Hibernian. I had thought him to be a savage whom I could bend to my will. I saw now that he was intelligent as well as ambitious. I could see how he had threatened the more powerful families further south. It would not do to underestimate him.

The guards on the gate were dressed as the king's bodyguards were but they had a shield which was much smaller than the shields our men used. I also saw that their swords were shorter. It seemed the longer blades were reserved for the better warriors. Once inside the walls and ditches, I could have been in a Saxon village. There were round huts and a hall which was also round but larger than the rest. The king pointed to a hut by the gate. "This is reserved for your warriors."

I nodded and turned. The Irish oathsworn behind me parted and I said, "Tuanthal, our men are to be housed in this hut. Watch over Morcar for me, eh."

"Aye Warlord."

Morcar did not look happy but he had to learn that we needed to abide by the king's customs if we were to win him over.

The king took me to his hall. Inside it was dark and was lit by the fire in the centre of the room. The smoke spiralled up to an opening in the middle. There were torches burning around the inside to give light. Unlike our halls, this was just one large space and I saw the sleeping areas around the side.

The king saw me looking. "You will sleep here with me and bodyguards. You will be safe."

I smiled and nodded. Of course, I would be safe. Myrddyn had dreamed of my death and it was not here. We did not need to tell this king that. At one end of the hut was a large table with chairs around it. The king led us to it and we sat down. He waved his arm and a slave appeared with some beer. It was exactly the same type as we had brewed at Stanwyck. The only difference was a slightly more peaty taste to it. I would ask Myrddyn about that later on.

The king took a large swallow and sat back in his chair which was bigger than ours. "Now then, Lord Lann. Why should I join with you?"

I noticed that only two of his warriors remained. They were the largest of his men and both had long curved swords with wicked looking blades.

## Saxon Bane

They flanked their king. He might trust us but they did not. However, it meant that we could talk a little more freely.

"Before we begin. Here is a small gift, a token of our friendship."

Like the magician that he was Myrddyn suddenly flourished the torc from beneath his robes. I knew we had made the right choice when I saw the jaws of his oathsworn drop. The king touched it reverently as though it would break. He ran his fingers over it. "It is gold?"

Myrddyn nodded, "Mainly gold from the Eastern Empire with some copper and precious stones."

"The wolf, it is your sign?"

"It is. When I was younger I was known as the Wolf Warrior."

He gave me a shrewd look as he put the torc around his neck. "You still are. It is why I am surprised at your age. From your deeds and the fear you inspire I had thought that you would be a much younger warrior." There was no answer I could give to that. "And this sword of yours, Saxon Slayer, is it that which you wear?"

"It is." I slowly drew the blade. I noticed the guards' eyes narrowed suspiciously. I reversed the blade and handed it, hilt first to the king. They relaxed.

The king held it in his hand. "This is well made and it is ancient."

"It is. We believe it comes from the Roman times."

"We have no such blades in this land. I would have swords like this for my men."

"If you join with us you shall."

He handed the sword back to me and I sheathed it. I saw the relief on the faces of the guards. "How so?"

"We buy many weapons from the iron makers of Frankia and Byzantium. We could supply your warriors with them once they have helped us to defeat the Saxons."

"We fight and die before you provide the weapons?"

I shrugged. "The Saxons are rich and we use the treasure we take from them to buy our own weapons. It is how we acquired our own"

"I could just stay here in my own land and become more powerful here."

## Saxon Bane

Myrddyn spread his arms, "Your island is filled with brave warriors and they can gain much honour through fighting but there is little treasure here." He pointed to the door of the hut, in the direction of the gate. "The warriors we brought are not the king's bodyguard and yet each is encased in fine mail."

The king gave a cunning smile, "Then you should be able to defeat the Saxons easily/"

Myrddyn smiled. "You are right, we could but there are many warriors such as yourselves in the land to the north of the Saxons, in Dál Riata." He shrugged, "The Warlord and I thought that you might wish to conquer and rule the land between."

I could see his mind working as he took in this information. It was not new information but he had not associated it with a raid on the Saxons.

"How would we share the spoils of war?"

This was Myrddyn's world. He spread his arms as though giving something to the king. "If you join us then we will be fighting alongside King Cadwallon of Gwynedd. As kings, you two would divide the spoils of war between you."

He looked surprised for the first time. "And you would take nothing?"

"I am the Warlord of Rheged. When Rheged is free that is the reward for me and my men."

"You do not have many men in your army do you?"

I shook my head. "No, the men of Rheged are not numerous but we make up for it by being the best warriors."

One of the guards snorted and the king held up his hand. "Calum, do not show such disrespect." The guard nodded but continued to glare in my direction. "Calum and my warriors think you are all overdressed men who play at warriors."

I stared back at Calum. "Then perhaps it is a good thing that we have never chosen to play on this island."

I knew I had angered the guard and I heard Myrddyn tut. The king laughed. "You are not dull, Warlord. You make for lively conversation. We will continue this on the morrow for I wish to learn more about you and your people. For the present, we have a small celebration. It is a fine night and we will eat outside. My cooks have been preparing our food while we spoke. Come."

Saxon Bane

# Chapter 4

We left the dark, Stygian darkness of the king's hut and went outside into the fresher, brighter air of the evening. The sun had begun to set in the west but the air felt much cleaner than in the smoky hall. There were torches lit flickering around a large table. I could see three chairs at the head of the table and we were led to them. My warriors were summoned and they sat down on one side. The same number of the king's warriors sat opposite. I noticed that Calum sat close to the king. I suspected he was the king's champion. I watched him carefully as we ate.

"What of these stories, wizard? Did you fly the Warlord into Din Guardi and slay Morcant Bulc?" The king did seem genuinely interested.

Myrddyn was used to fending these questions. He gave his stock answer. "I used, what might call, my magic to affect entry into the fortress and there the Warlord slew that treacherous king."

Calum snorted and shook his head. The king flashed him an angry glance. He turned back to Myrddyn and continued his probing. "And another time I hear that you walked amongst the Saxons in their camp and they did not see you?"

"Oh they saw me but they did not see a wizard they saw a Saxon healer. Men see what they expect to see."

"And raising the Warlord from the dead? That is a mighty trick if you can manage it."

"I am a healer and I have studied the works of the Romans. I cannot raise the dead." He smiled. "But I have saved some who are close to death from dying."

The king laughed and clapped the table. "You are a valuable man to have around. Warlord, how much to buy this wizard from you?"

I smiled, "He stays with me because he wants to. I do not pay him and he is his own man. If you wish him to serve you then ask him."

## Saxon Bane

That really confused him. "Truly? I can ask him to become my wizard?" I nodded and gestured with my hand for him to ask. "Wizard, come and be my healer and I will give you your weight in silver."

"A generous offer, King Fiachnae mac Báetáin, but my destiny lies with Lord Lann the Warlord of Rheged. I have served him since I was a young boy and the spirits came to me and told me to follow his banner. I have done so since I walked from Mona to Castle Perilous. As you can see it is out of my hands. It is *wyrd*."

I saw an evil smile come over Calum's face. "So if the Warlord was dead you could serve my king?"

In answer Myrddyn said, "Alive or dead I will always serve the Warlord."

It was Calum's turn to be confused. "I think then that this warlord has a reputation which is not deserved. He has achieved all he has through your trickery and his treachery."

I saw my entire band of warriors stop eating and stare at this giant. I waved my hands for them to calm down. I wiped the food from my mouth and measured my words before I spoke. "Be careful Calum of Dál nAraidi for I do not suffer insults lightly. I have killed many warriors, kings and champions and in fair combat. My sword, Saxon Slayer, has never tasted defeat. I would not offend your king by killing his oathsworn."

Suddenly Calum leapt to his feet. "My lord, I demand the blood rite of combat. I have been insulted!"

The king shook his head. "It is you who insulted our guest first."

Calum glared at his king, "It matters not I have the right!"

The king nodded sadly. He looked at me, "It is true. I am sorry, Warlord, but tomorrow you must face Calum and this will be decided by first blood. Whoever draws first blood is the winner."

Myrddyn looked from one to the other, shook his head and said, "I would reconsider, Calum. You are dealing with a warrior who has a sword with magical qualities. Are you willing to take that chance?"

He laughed, "I am fighting an old man who could be my grandfather. He is the one who should be worried."

## Saxon Bane

I smiled, "Then I have to tell you, I am not." I turned to the king. "And what of the alliance?"

The king laughed, "You are a confident one; if you can still walk after the combat and are not lying in a pool of your own blood then we will have an alliance and my warriors will fight alongside you against the Saxons."

I had won! "Excellent! Then this old man will get to bed, the better to prepare for the morrow." My warriors and Morcar all stood to accompany me. Myrddyn sat at the table still. "I will join your later, Warlord." There was the most subtle of winks and I left.

Morcar said, "Let me fight him, uncle. I will be your champion I am not afraid of him."

"No," said Tuanthal, "I am the leader of the bodyguard, it is my right."

I stopped and faced all of them. "The challenge was to me and I will face it. Do you think the Wolf Warrior can no longer fight because his hair is going white? I will defeat this giant and then we will have our allies. The gods are with us."

I saw the disbelief on their faces. Every one of my bodyguards was willing to take my place. I did not need them to do so but I was touched that they offered.

I was still awake when Myrddyn returned to our hut. I know that my bodyguards had arranged for one of them to be awake during the night. I feared no treachery for the treachery had already taken place. I confirmed it with Myrddyn.

"So Calum has been bought." Myrddyn nodded. "By Aethelfrith's sons."

"Aye, I discovered they are across on the other side of their sea, the one they call Loch nEachach. I think that Oswald has bought Calum."

"Not the king?"

"No. The king is most displeased with this challenge and he fears you will die." He chuckled. "We have made an impression on the young king and he does not wish to lose the chance to go into battle alongside such a noted warrior. The spirits were right to direct us here."

"We will need to watch out for Oswald and Oswiu then."

"It is Oswald who we should fear. Oswiu is just a pup. He barks and he growls but his teeth do not bite. Oswald is his father's son. I have heard that he has even considered converting to Christianity in order to win Irish friends."

"Even his father would not have stooped so low."

"Things are changing in the world, Lord Lann. Sons of kings will do anything to become kings themselves. This giant is overconfident. He thinks to defeat you in one or two blows. His sword looks powerful but is a weak piece of metal. You should have little difficulty in defeating him."

I settled down to sleep. Although my mind was racing with plots and treachery I soon went to sleep as I went through the moves, in my head that would help me to defeat Calum.

I rose later than the others and they all stared at me as I rose. Myrddyn, of course, was still asleep. I shook his shoulder and he awoke. He laughed when he saw them staring.

"Have some faith in two old men will you? Tuanthal, get one of your men to fetch us some food. Morcar, begin to dress the Warlord. When you have done so put an edge on Saxon Slayer."

I smiled as Myrddyn dressed, "And what of you wizard? Is there a potion for me to take to ensure I defeat him?"

"You and I know that there is no need for a potion just so long as you are careful. As for me I shall eat well and prepare to watch you whittle this half-naked giant down to size."

Morcar dressed me in my armour as carefully as any squire I had ever had. He made sure that the leather armour I wore beneath the mail was securely in position and that all of the links in the mail itself were smoothed flat. A mail link out of place could be a potential weakness. He fixed the neck armour into place. Finally, he put my helmet on. The helmet marked me as different. It had been sent to me by the Emperor of the Eastern Empire and was the single best piece of armour I possessed. The padded leather skull cap I wore beneath it prevented chafing and it fastened securely beneath my chin. The last two items were Saxon Slayer, now sharpened and my oval shield. This was the first time I had used one of the new shields and it felt much lighter than my old one. I just hoped it had the same protection.

We stepped out of the hut and the Hibernians were waiting there. The king stepped forward. "We allow no blood to be spilt within these walls." He grinned, "Unless, of course, it is the blood of an enemy. We will go outside to the killing ground." The name sounded ominous.

The king walked with me. "This is the first chance I have had to observe such armour and sword. My men prefer to fight unencumbered. Do you not find the armour slows you down?"

"I have used such armour for thirty years. I am used to it."

He leaned closer to me and said quietly, "You need not go through with this you know. You could nominate one of your men to fight for you. That is acceptable."

"But not to me."

"I cannot intervene for it is the way of our people. Calum is a vicious fighter. He will try to hurt you."

"I would expect nothing less." As we walked towards the ring of warriors I remembered the first time I had had to fight a champion. He had been one of Riderch Hael's men and I had blinded him in one eye. He still became a firm friend. Somehow I did not think that Calum and I would share the same bond when he lay humiliated at my feet.

He was waiting for me. He had decided to forgo armour of any kind. His chest was naked and covered in intricate tattoos. He had his hair spiked high with lime and he held two weapons. One was a long curved sword. It was longer than almost any other sword I had ever seen while in his left hand he held an axe. He meant business.

He pointed his sword at me. "You can dress in as much armour as you wish, you will still bleed."

"And you can shout as loudly as you like, you will still lose. And when you do lose they will say you were beaten by an old man."

The barb took the smile from his face.

The circle surrounded us. My men were on one side and the Hibernians were on the other. The king stood between us. "When I say

## Saxon Bane

'*cease*' you stop upon pain of death!" We both nodded. He strode to the side and, clapping his hands, said, "Fight!"

I knew what to expect and what was coming. The giant would hurl himself at me with both weapons scything through the air almost before the words were out. He wanted to catch an old man unawares. He would try to kill me and not just to make me bleed. I could see it in his wild eyes. This would be a stern test of my new shield. I began to yearn for my solid one which was lined with iron and had a heavy quality I liked. I hefted my new one around. It covered half of my leg.

This would be the first combat since my wound. I was not as mobile as I would have liked and I knew he would soon realise that and take advantage of it. In fact, if he had spoken to Aethelfrith's son Oswald he would know already. I had to assume that he knew.

The word 'fight' had barely left the king's lips when the Hibernian leapt towards me. His sword came from above his shoulder and he swung his axe low at the same time. I held up my shield as I swung Saxon Slayer at his axe. The long sword struck my curved shield and slid down to the ground. The new design of shield worked. Saxon Slayer had been sharpened well and a chunk of wood came from the handle of the axe. He stepped back, seemingly surprised that I had survived. I saw him looking at my shield for signs of damage but there were none. Cunning took over and he feinted with his sword and spun around at the same time. His axe smashed into my shield and I felt my arm shiver. I brought Saxon Slayer over and it struck the axe where I had weakened it. The axe fell into two pieces.

He stepped back and snarled at me. "You are not a real warrior! A real warrior would not need a shield."

I smiled although most of my face was hidden by the face mask. "I need no shield to fight someone such as you."

I let the shield drop to the ground. My left arm still ached from the blow. His eyes widened with excitement. He now had a longer reach. I was well aware of his advantage. He brought the sword back two handed and, striding forward swung it with all of his might at my head. In my youth, I would have danced out of the way. Now I had no such mobility

## Saxon Bane

and I used Calum's own trick. I spun the opposite way and brought Saxon Slayer around. I felt it connect with his back and I pulled back. I did not want to kill him.

I heard a cheer from my men and the king shouted, "Cease!"

I lowered my weapon and watched in horror as he swung his own sword at me. My instinct took over and I blocked it with Saxon Slayer. I was angry and I brought Saxon Slayer, two handed in a wide sweep. He brought his own sword around to block it. Saxon Slayer struck it and the long sword shattered in two. As he stood there dumbfounded I reversed my grip and smashed the pommel into the middle of his head. He fell to the ground, unconscious.

The king strode over. His face was a mask of anger. "That was cowardly from my warrior. I will have his head for this." He drew his sword and put the point to the giant's neck.

"Before you take revenge I think you might ask him some questions about who put him up to this."

I saw the confusion on the king's face. "Put him up to it?"

"He was itching for a fight from the moment we met and from the instant the fight started he was trying to kill me, not just make me bleed. Now I have never met this man before and we have no history so someone else either wishes me dead or you harm."

"Me harm?"

"You do not think that if I had been killed my sons would have idly sat by. You would have had the wrath of my equites to face and believe me few of your men would have survived."

"I can see that you may have grown older but it has not diminished your skills and your mind is as sharp as any."

Calum began to come to and he felt the tip of the sword in his throat. Two of the king's other guards pinned his arms to the ground with their feet. "You failed to stop when I ordered it. You should be dead now but Lord Lann here wishes some answers to some questions. Answer them and your death will be swift. Keep silent and we will let the crabs devour you slowly."

There was hatred in his eyes. "Who paid you to kill me?"

## Saxon Bane

He spat. "Kill me! I will tell you nothing. Put me with the crabs. I can take the pain."

I saw Fiachnae mac Báetáin raise his sword. Myrddyn said, "Wait! Please your majesty." He reached into his satchel and brought out a tiny amphora.

Calum glared at him. There was defiance in his voice but fear in his eyes. "Use your magic! I care not."

Myrddyn smiled and it sent shivers up my spine. This was a cruel smile. Myrddyn had suffered insults from Calum and he was in no mood for mercy. He slowly opened the bottle. "This is not magic. This is a liquid they use in Byzantium. It burns through anything; metal, wood flesh, anything. It is just this magic jar which prevents it from eating all in its path." He tipped a little on the stopper and a tiny drop dripped down and struck the warrior on the back of his hand. There was a hiss and then Calum screamed in agony. "They called it an acidus. Some are weaker than others. This one is a strong acidus."

After Calum stopped screaming he tried to look at his hand. We could see that the flesh had been burned from it and the hole in his hand was growing albeit slowly. The warriors holding him down looked in amazement at the effect of the liquid.

Calum was obviously in pain yet he had courage. "I will not speak."

Myrddyn nodded, "A brave man. Pull down his breeks!"

Another warrior began to pull them down revealing his manhood. Calum screamed like a wild beast. "I will tell you! I will tell you! It was Aethelfrith's sons. Oswald paid me to challenge you and kill you."

The king shook his head; I am not sure if it was anger or disbelief. "Where are they?"

"They are in the lands of the Uí Néill. You cannot reach them."

I nodded to the king who lifted his sword and decapitated his former guard. "Put his head on a spear so that all may see the punishment for treachery."

We began to walk back into the ring fort. This time my warriors stayed close to me. They were taking no chances.

## Saxon Bane

The king looked at me. "A day of surprises. My bodyguard is a spy. You prove to be a remarkable swordsman and Myrddyn drops water which burns. I think I have made the right decision and you will be allies I can learn from."

Saxon Bane

# Chapter 5

Morcar couldn't wait to get to the hut and help me to take off my armour. "How did you know that you could defeat him? he was bigger, stronger and..." he suddenly became embarrassed as he realised what he was about to say.

"And younger?" Morcar nodded. "If you fight a man with no armour and he faces you then you should not lose. Even if he had connected with his sword my armour and my shield were more than a match for him. His sword shattered easily. Do you think it could have breached my armour? As for being younger and stronger well, perhaps I used my mind and experience to win the day."

Tuanthal nodded. "Having good weapons helps. I have never seen a sword do that before. I examined the two pieces afterwards and they had been badly bent from the few blows it had struck."

"If they are used to fighting each other with weapons like that then they know no different. Saxon Slayer is a good sword but you all know that there are swords which have blades as strong."

Morcar shook his head, "There is only one Saxon Slayer."

"How do you know? There may be other blades waiting to be found. When Myrddyn and I studied in Constantinopolis we read of other blades which had been lost; some in Frankia and some in Germania. I found Saxon Slayer because the spirits which rule us wanted me to find it. They needed the change that it would bring. Perhaps another sword is waiting for its time."

Morcar looked longingly at my sword, "I would have Saxon Slayer rather than any other blade."

We spent the rest of the day finalising the details of how the king would aid us. Having seen the effects of my armour and weapons he was keen to acquire some himself.

"I will bring you a gift of a sword, helmet and shield when we begin our campaign. Once we defeat the Saxons then we can use some of their weapons and their armour."

"Is it as good as yours?"

Myrddyn put down his beaker of honeyed ale. "No, but it is much better than that which you use."

The king looked offended. "Are you always this blunt?"

"I always speak the truth and do not dress it in borrowed clothes. Would you rather I told you a lie? You would soon find out when you fought the Saxons."

"Then how do I defeat them?"

"You don't. The Warlord does." Myrddyn gestured with his thumb. "He is what the Emperors in the east call a strategos. He can not only fight he can read a battle. If you watch and learn then you will be the greatest king in this Ireland soon you will rule it all."

"The Uí Néill is a powerful clan. There are many tribes who owe allegiance to them. It is why we cannot go after these men who ordered your death."

I drank my own honeyed ale. It was a pleasant drink but I could not drink too many of them; they were too sweet. "You do not need to. I will deal with Oswiu and Oswald in my own time. So long as they are here they will not cause me trouble at home."

"When will you return home then, Warlord?"

"We have concluded what we needed. We will sail tomorrow."

The king looked disappointed. "I had thought to take you on a wolf hunt. There is a pack in the mountains to the south and as the Wolf Warrior, I had thought to take you."

Morcar looked crestfallen and Tuanthal looked unhappy too. Myrddyn said, "We could leave it one more day. It will not hurt and I can study the holy books which the king has acquired."

Myrddyn had discovered that there was a small chapel in the ring fort and he had some of the holy books of the White Christ. Myrddyn always sought knowledge. I relented. "Very well. We will stay one extra day."

## Saxon Bane

They all seemed more excited than I was. "You will enjoy the way we hunt them. We have wolfhounds to run them down. If we let them they would tear the wolves to pieces but we prefer to finish them ourselves."

Leaving Myrddyn engrossed in his books we rode on the small ponies the king used. It was strange as the wolfhounds were almost as big as the mounts we rode. The king's brother, Fiachra, and his cousins accompanied us. There were forty men who rode south on the fine morning. I did not anticipate either killing or being threatened by a wolf. There were too many of us but I thought that it might do Morcar good to have to face such dangers. It had made a man of me.

Morcar and four of my warriors went with the king's brother and his cousins. They had their own pack. The brothers appeared to have a great deal of rivalry. It had not been that way with my brothers. As he had four of my oathsworn to watch him I did not worry about Morcar however I would have preferred to watch him see his reaction to the hunting of this deadly predator.

The king had men who ran with the wolfhounds keeping them on a leash. They kept up with us on the ponies and I knew that they were fit men. I decided to talk to the king about how he might use such men. Speed on a battlefield could carry the day.

The hounds picked up the scent and we galloped up the slopes of the mountains. They were not steep but they would sap the energy from legs. We had to be careful for there were many rocks and places where you could trip if you were unwary. I began to worry about Morcar. He was not as good a horseman as either my sons or Lann Aelle. I would not want him falling from his horse and injuring himself.

It was at noon when the leading huntsman blew his horn. The wolves were within sight. I drew my spear. I would not take away any of the glory from the king. It was his land and he should be the one to garner the glory of the kill. I rode on his left side. He seemed oblivious to the danger and regarded this as some kind of entertainment. It was not, it was deadly serious.

We had to dismount once the wolfhounds ascended amongst the rocks. Four warriors were assigned as holders for the ponies. I carried my wolf spear in two hands. I noticed that the king just balanced it on one hand. He was going to try to throw the spear at a wolf. If it worked it would be a magnificent kill but you needed supreme confidence to be able to strike exactly the right spot.

The slope was steep and my leg struggled to support my weight and move at a speed which would keep up with the king. The hounds were tugging at their leashes. The wolves were near. I looked to the right and the other party was nowhere in sight. I suddenly realised that we had not seen them for some time. Perhaps they were approaching from the other side of the hill and we would trap the wolves between us.

There was a mighty roar and five wolves leapt from cover. The wolfhounds all pounced on one of them and there was a mass of snarling and tearing teeth as the hounds and the wolf tumbled down the slope. Perhaps the sight of the vicious fight distracted the king for his throw was a poor one and it only caught the wolf in the shoulder. The wolf howled in pain and then tore the spear out with his teeth. In one move it sprang towards the king. He had not even drawn his sword. The rest of the hunters were busy with the other three wolves thinking that the king had killed it.

I could not risk throwing the spear for I might miss and I hobbled up the slope and then launched myself and spear at the wolf. I knew that I only had one chance. I had to strike the head. The Allfather was with me and the spear entered the side of the wolf's head just as its jaws fastened onto the king's arm. The weight of my body threw the wolf to one side and I landed on top of the dying animal. The spear had pinned its body to the ground and I watched it as life left its fierce eyes.

"Farewell wolf brother. You fought well."

I was helped to my feet by the king. "That was a mighty blow. I owe you much Warlord."

I pulled the spear out. "Perhaps you might have your sword ready next time, your majesty."

"You are right. I thought I had him."

"He nearly had you."

## Saxon Bane

The king's bodyguards could not apologise enough. They had failed to save the life of the king. Worse, a stranger had.

The wolf which had been attacked by the wolfhounds had killed two and a third had to be destroyed. It had been a mighty warrior. I was sad that we had ended the lives of such brave animals. As the wolves' carcasses were threaded onto spears the king said. "There were no females and cubs. Perhaps the others found them." He turned to his huntsman, "Padraigh, take the wolves and hounds back. We will seek the others." The chief huntsman nodded. All of his animals had injuries.

We found Fiachra and most of the others just in the next high part of the mountains. They had slain some of the wolves but they had suffered wounds. Fiachra was nursing a leg savagely ripped by a wolf.

"My wizard can look at that."

Fiachra looked a little worried until his brother said, "The wizard can help. He is a healer too."

I suddenly realised that I could not see Morcar and the four warriors with him were missing. "Where is my nephew?"

Fiachra pointed to the south. "A few of the wolves escaped and they took after them."

The king mounted his pony. "Do not worry Warlord. They will be safe."

We rode south and crossed the high trails over the hills. The path took us between scrubby low bushes and rocks. It obscured the way ahead. I felt quite vulnerable despite the presence of Tuanthal and the king's guards. I liked to have Aedh and his scouts ahead of me to warn us of danger. When we crested the rise we found the bodies. There were piles of bodies scattered all around. Two ponies lay dead.

I drew Saxon Slayer and spurred my pony on. I found the first cluster of bodies. It was the four warriors of mine who had guarded Morcar. Around them were spread eight whom I did not recognise. The king dismounted and searched with me. There was no sign of Morcar.

"These are not of our people. I do not recognise any of the clan markings."

## Saxon Bane

I sadly shook my head. "No, they are Saxons. This is the work of Oswald and Oswiu." I stared south as though willing them to come into view but it was empty. I turned to Tuanthal. "Put our dead on the ponies." His face showed his distress. These had been his men chosen by him as being the best of the best. They had died doing their duty but that did not ease the loss.

"King Fiachnae mac Báetáin, where would they take him?"

He looked almost embarrassed. He pointed to the south. "There are forts in the south. They are their heartland."

"Find where he is held for me, please."

"I will send my best scouts. I should warn you, Warlord, that you may never see him again."

I turned and smiled at the king, "Oh I shall see him again and he will be alive."

"How do you know? Do you have the second sight?"

"No. It is logical. Had they wanted him dead they would have killed him here."

"Perhaps they might want to torture him."

"They would want me to see that and to suffer. This is to hurt me. Their father was a treacherous man, a nithing. The sons are the same. I need to speak with Myrddyn and my captain."

When we reached the ring fort Myrddyn did not seem surprised by the actions of the two brothers. "They cannot hurt King Edwin over here and he is their greatest enemy but they can reach you through Morcar. They have something devious in mind, Warlord." I knew that. First, there was the attempt on my life and now this. They had known I would be coming here. The question was, how?

I went to the jetty to speak with Daffydd. "I need Aedh and his scouts here," I told him what had happened and his face darkened. Morcar was a popular lad as was his cousin, Lann Aelle. "We will need more than one ship for we will need horses."

"I will return as soon as possible."

## Saxon Bane

The king was waiting with Tuanthal and Myrddyn when I returned. "You are being calm, Warlord. If this was my nephew I would be raging."

I shrugged, "And what good would that do. It would stop you thinking clearly." I pointed to the wizard. "One thing this man has taught me is that every man has a powerful weapon; it is called his mind. In a battle, you need your heart but before and after you need your mind. When the battle begins you will see my anger. When I can do something to those who did this then you will see anger. Until then I will work out what to do. As soon as your men find out where he is held prisoner then we can plan."

We had a rough idea of where he was by the end of the next day. Four well-armed Hibernians and a young priest arrived at the gate. The priest spoke. "I am here to speak with the one who calls himself the Warlord, the pagan Lord Lann."

If this priest, who had barely started shaving, thought he could intimidate me with insults he did not know me. I strode forward. "I am Lord Lann and what do you call yourself little man?"

I saw him colour. "I am Brother Padraigh."

"Then speak before I give you an early visit to your White Christ."

He became more than a little agitated at that. "I am a peace emissary and a man of God."

"It will not worry me to slay a man of God and as for a peaceful emissary; you, I assume, represent those who kidnapped my nephew. Know this, servant of the White Christ, I am, as you say, a pagan. I do not forgive. I do not forget. I do not turn the other cheek. I remember your face and you should fear me."

The colour left his face and he looked around to the four warriors for support. Their faces remained impassive.

"And I am Myrddyn the Wizard, priest and I do not forget. Remember that I have the power of the darkness and the spirits behind me. Fear me too." Myrddyn seemed to grow in stature as he threatened the priest.

The priest crossed himself. All his arrogance had evaporated and he spilt out his words quickly the sooner to escape. "Prince Oswald holds your nephew and he will remain unharmed. You will pay a ransom of five hundred gold pieces and your sword, Saxon Slayer. If not Prince Oswald will send him back piece by piece."

The priest was less than five paces from me and I whipped out Saxon Slayer and held it to his throat before he could move. The four warriors' hands went to their weapons and I heard Tuanthal hiss, "I have seven arrows aimed at you four. Think carefully about your next move." The swords slid back into their scabbards.

I noticed a puddle beneath the priest's feet. "Here is Saxon Slayer, priest. Tell Oswald that you saw it. Now as to the ransom, I do not carry that amount with me. I will have to send it back to my home for it."

His voice almost broke as he gabbled the last part of his message. "You have ten days." He pointed south. "You are to bring the ransom to the southern end of the Lough. If you bring men then your nephew will die."

I removed the sword. "Next time ask them to send a man who actually has a backbone."

The priest fled so fast that the four guards struggled to keep up with him.

The king said as we returned to the fort. "Will you give up your sword? How will you send for the gold you have no ship."

I laughed, "I have no intention of paying a ransom. Even if the brothers had some honour it would only lead to more kidnapping. You do not give in to this kind of threat."

"Beside," said Myrddyn. "They will kill Morcar and the Warlord when he pays the ransom." Tuanthal nodded his agreement.

"Then why did you agree?"

"To buy time until your men can discover where he is held."

"They said he will be at the southern end of the Lough."

"He will be far from there. That is where the exchange will take place. That is why I have sent for my scouts. No offence, King Fiachnae mac Báetáin, but my scouts are the best trackers in Britannia. They will find him and then I will wreak my revenge on these Saxons."

Saxon Bane

# Chapter 6

It took the king's scouts four days to discover that Morcar was being held in the land of Airgialla and its king Mael Odhar Macha was giving the Saxons protection. Fiachnae mac Báetáin had obviously felt guilty about Morcar's abduction. Certainly, he and his brother had had sharp words about his failure to protect his guests and his brother had left the ring fort. It caused bad feeling between the brothers. Perhaps that had also been part of Oswald's plan to cause dissension between my new allies. The outcome was that the king sent his best scouts and they brought good information.

From the scouts' report there appeared to be thirty Saxons with the sons of Aethelfrith. The Irish had around sixty warriors with their king. The hillfort was not as good a site as the one we were in and relied mainly on twisting ditches, mounds and swamp to protect it. As far as the scouts could ascertain Morcar was being treated well and seemed to be moving freely around the fort albeit with a guard.

King Fiachnae mac Báetáin was not happy about taking on this rival king. "He is not a threat himself and his army are like the rats who scavenge in the ditches but he has powerful connections. I dare not attack him for fear of reprisals."

"I would not ask you to undertake such action. Your warriors will be needed for the attack in the east; the attack against Edwin. My men and I will deal with this."

It was six days before our ships returned. They were both riding low in the water as they approached. Myrddyn and Tuanthal watched with me. I saw Aedh on the deck and also Pol and Lann Aelle. Hogan Lann had sent me warriors who could aid me. I had been happy to do this with just my scouts but Pol and Lann Aelle were reassuringly experienced.

Forty warriors and horses disembarked. I saw that they had brought Nightstar for me. That was good. I would need a reliable mount and

## Saxon Bane

Nightstar was just such a horse. I greeted my nephew and Pol as Aedh ensured that the horses were all safely ashore.

"Have we any news Uncle?" Lann Aelle and Pol were more like sons to me than a nephew and a former scout.

"We know where they hold him. They wanted a ransom which is due in four days' time."

Pol nodded, "Of course, we will not pay the ransom."

"Of course not." I looked up as the horsemen began to adjust saddles. They would be ready to move in an instant. "You brought more than scouts."

"Aye, we brought equites but without armour. We could have brought five times this number for all wished to come."

"We will not need more. There are only ninety warriors and sixty of those are the Hibernians." I lowered my voice. "I have discovered that their swords are of poor quality. They bend and break when struck by our weapons. They appear to have no archers."

Aedh had joined us and heard the last comment. "The eighteen scouts I brought are all fine archers."

I looked up in surprise, "You have left few scouts with Hogan Lann then?"

He laughed. The campaign was almost over and he said he did not need us. He would have come too."

I spread my arm. "This is more than enough." I noticed that there were two spare horses. "Let us ride and we will pick up Myrddyn."

Lann Aelle chuckled, "He will not be happy about being on the back of a horse for four or five days."

Pol shook his head, "Do not let him hear you, Lann Aelle, or I may be taking a small toad home with me."

The king stood with Myrddyn at the gate. "You would go with just these few warriors?"

Myrddyn slowly mounted the horse which Aedh held for him. "They have a wizard with them so they need fear not." He flashed a look at Pol. And I can turn people into more than toads."

## Saxon Bane

I could see the twinkle in his eye but Pol and Lann Aelle took him seriously. They gripped their amulets as though their lives depended upon them.

"We will return when we have rescued Morcar."

"I will wait with my army at the Lough. It marks the edge of the land of Dál nAraidi."

"It is good of you."

We had been told where the hillfort was and Aedh himself led ten scouts out to find it. I was not afraid of being seen. We rode better horses than any I had seen up to now and Aedh would warn us of any warriors we might encounter. As we rode Lann Aelle told me what had happened in the campaign.

"The Saxons did not appear to have their heart in defending the land north of the Maeresea. We lost remarkably few men."

"And King Edwin?"

"There was no sign of him. We heard that King Raedwald was laid low by fever and did not supply any men to help the husband of his daughter."

"And we heard that he finally conquered Elmet."

Pol's news was not a surprise but it was a reminder of what we had had. My brother Raibeart had been married to the daughter of the last king. They had been driven out and had joined me in Gwynedd but I knew that some of the people lived there still. It made my alliance with Fiachnae mac Báetáin even more vital. We had a chance to halt the Saxons and I would not let Aethelfrith's sons get in the way.

It was rolling country through which we rode. There appeared to be few villages. The people dotted the landscape on their farms. The only cattle we saw were grazed close to the hill forts and I had witnessed how they were all brought in each night. Cattle theft was a way of life here. As we rode south I wondered how to use that to our advantage.

The Lough which marked the southern boundary of the land of the Dál nAraidi was a huge piece of water. It was even bigger than Wide Water in Rheged. You could have sailed warships on it. We skirted the water on its western side. The meeting place was due south and I had no doubt

## Saxon Bane

that Oswald and Oswiu would have people watching ahead of the ransom delivery.

It was late afternoon when Aedh and his scouts galloped up. "I have found it. I left two of my men watching it."

He lithely leapt from his horse. He still looked like the young boy who had grown up close to my first fortress home in Rheged even though there was just him and Tuanthal left from those who had left Rheged with me all those years ago. He took out his sword and found a smooth piece of earth. He sketched as he spoke.

"The fort is fifteen miles or so away. A couple of hours riding at most. It is an easy country." He grinned, "After Wyddfa anything is easy." He put a cross in the soil. "The fort is here and we are here."

"Did you see their cattle?"

He looked at me curiously and said, "Yes, here." He put a circle halfway between us and the fort.

"So we have to pass the cattle to get to the fort?"

"Aye. They are easy to avoid for they only have six or seven boys herding them and a couple of pony riders."

My plan was already formulating in my mind. "Now, tell me, have you seen Morcar?"

"Yes. He has two guards. He actually came out of the front gate with them, walked around the fort and then went back inside."

Myrddyn suddenly spoke, "Why do you think that was? Did he pass water or anything like that?"

"No, he just walked with his two guards. It was as though it was a stroll."

Myrddyn never asked irrelevant questions. I tried to read his mind as he read mine. "What is on your mind?"

"He is bait. Those brothers are clever and they want you to see him. They will expect us to take him whilst he is walking around."

"We will get closer and investigate this. We still have a couple of days before they move him."

As we rode Pol and Lann Aelle rode next to me. "You have a plan, Warlord?"

## Saxon Bane

I nodded, "It is still forming but I think it might work." I was acutely aware that Myrddyn was listening and I knew that he would comment if I said something of which he did not approve.

"The cattle are the key. We use Aedh and some of his scouts to get rid of the pony guards and drive the cattle southwest. The boys will return to the fort and this king will not want to lose his property. I am guessing that he will take most of his men and follow Aedh. While they are away we slip in and rescue Morcar."

"Do not forget Warlord that there will still be plenty of Saxons within the hillfort and we would have to assault it."

"There is no wall, just ditches and mounds. They can make it difficult for us but not impossible. When we are close I will have a better idea of how to rescue my brother's son."

Aedh took us by a circuitous route so that we avoided the cattle and we found ourselves in a twisting river valley. The hill fort rose above us some thousand paces or so away. The scouts who had been left behind reported what they had seen.

"After Morcar had returned to the fort we saw some warriors, Saxon and Hibernian, come from those woods over there." He pointed to a small copse of spindly trees some hundred paces below the ramparts.

It became clear that the warriors in the woods were there to ambush us if we tried to rescue Morcar. Someone had a cunning mind. This had been planned well.

Myrddyn smiled, "Then we now have the solution to the problem. We will have men waiting in the woods earlier than those warriors and they can eliminate them as they arrive. When Morcar and his guards emerge the last place they will expect an attack from is that direction."

I could see from everyone's expression that they approved. As I looked at the faces I saw that I could not have handpicked a better set of warriors: Tuanthal, Aedh, Pol and Lann Aelle all led warriors at home and Aedh and Pol had chosen the best of the scouts and equites we had left. They had brought the very best warriors we had. If we failed then no one could succeed.

## Saxon Bane

"Aedh, take ten of your scouts and get to the cattle grounds early. Kill the warriors on the ponies and drive off the boys. Make them think that they are lucky to escape. Drive the cattle towards the southwest. I would think a couple of hours of hard driving should do it. That will exhaust them and then you come due east and find us."

"And us?"

"We will find somewhere south of the woods to hide the horses and then we will spend the night in the small stand of trees. When the warriors come, we will kill them."

Lann Aelle gave me a sceptical look. I sighed and began to explain. "They will have done this every day for four or five days. Tomorrow will probably be the last day. They will arrive expecting the wood to be empty. They will assume that the day will be as the others were; filled with no activity and a slow walk back to the fort." I turned to the scouts who had watched. "How many men will there be?"

"There looked to be ten Saxons and ten of the Hibernians."

Tuanthal nodded, "That would make sense. Oswald and Oswiu would want the majority of their men to be in the fort. Twenty would be enough to protect Morcar if attacked and give the others the chance to fall upon us. Besides, that copse would struggle to hold a much larger number of warriors."

We had decided. We ate while we waited for night to fall and then we led our horses along a route which kept well away from the hill fort. Aedh and his scouts remained where they were. They would leave in the early hours of the morning for their diversion.

We left five men with the horses. Although we had Myrddyn and he was no warrior, we would still outnumber the warriors who came into the small stand of trees. Aedh's best scouts who remained were at the very edge of the trees and they would be so well hidden that even I would not be able to find them. Their job would be to make sure none of those who entered escaped. This would be knife work. The ones who would die had to die without a sound.

I lay with my back against a tree. Myrddyn lay on the other side. "Is there no magic you can use to aid us?"

## Saxon Bane

"This plan is our magic. We are like the travelling magician who visits a village and mesmerises his audience. They will see what they expect to see. Even when we attack them they will not believe it is happening." He chuckled in the dark. "Do not worry, Lord Lann. I have a sharpened knife too."

He could be quite surprising at times. I had thought he would let the warriors do the fighting. He had, of course, briefly fought for me before we discovered his skills lay in other directions. But he had not fought with a blade for many years. It is one thing to kill at a distance but to smell a man and then rip a knife across his throat requires discipline.

One advantage of being a Warlord is that you do not stand a sentry duty and I had a peaceful night's sleep. The sleep, however, was punctuated with strange dreams. Morcar was running away and I was trying to save him. I found I could not move and when I looked around I saw my mother holding on to my cloak to stop me from moving. When I awoke I tried to make sense of it. The only explanation I came up with was that she did not want me to get hurt saving my nephew. Perhaps I was meant to let others take the risks.

It was before dawn when I was shaken awake. We swallowed a mouthful of water and ate some dried meat. Then we waited.

The two scouts closest to the fort gave a low whistle. The warriors were coming. Dawn was breaking to the east and there was light enough to see the gate. We had all had enough time to hide beneath bushes, branches and anything else which would aid us. All of us had smeared our faces and hands with mud. We had even committed the sacrilege of dirtying our blades so that they did not reflect light. We would not be seen. It was brighter outside the copse than within and the twenty warriors who trudged towards us would be coming from the light into the pitch dark. Those few moments of adjustment to the different light would be all that we would need. They would also still be sleepy; they would not expect death to be lurking beneath the branches of the trees. I drew my dagger in preparation.

## Saxon Bane

I heard them talking as they walked toward us. They had no need for silence. "I am glad this is the last day we will have to squat in this midge infested swamp."

"Ah stop moaning, Aelle, you are worse than Egbert. This will be the last time. Just do what you normally do and sleep."

"I would if it wasn't for the insects. I have no idea what they eat when we aren't here but they enjoy my blood!"

And then I saw them. They just had swords and axes with them. They had no shields and their weapons were in their belts. They would have to try to draw them. That would make life much easier for us. We had decided that Lann Aelle, Tuanthal and Pol would be the first ones to strike. They were hidden towards the end of the trees which was nearest to the hill fort. I saw one Hibernian approaching my place of hiding. Before he reached me I heard a scuffle and he looked up. I swept my good leg around and he crashed to the ground. I pinned his head with my left hand and slashed across his throat with my dagger. His life gurgled away. All around me warriors were falling so quickly that none had the chance to make a sound. Two of them made a break for the fort but they were wrestled to the ground and killed by Lann Aelle and Pol. One of them managed a shout and we froze.

From the walls came the shout, in Saxon, "What is happening?"

Myrddyn had the quickest reactions. He shouted in Saxon, laughing as he did so, "It was just Aelle, he tripped up. He is clumsier than Egbert."

The voice, seemingly reassured, drifted back. "Well, keep it down. The scouts found horse tracks yesterday."

It showed how close we were to the ramparts that we could have a conversation and I saw why they had chosen the spot. We all moved closer to the edge of the trees. They would not see anything wrong with warriors in the trees now. They would assume that they were their own men.

"Is anyone hurt?"

One of Lann Aelle's warriors said, "They are animals. One of them bit me."

Lann Aelle laughed, "You were killing him at the time."

## Saxon Bane

"Quiet. Now we wait."

We knew that they would not bring Morcar out for some time. They would wait until it was later in the morning. It was hard to wait within spitting distance of the walls. I began to worry that someone could come out at any time but no one did. The sun rose higher and I was expecting Morcar and the guards to come out every time the guards on the walls walked in the direction of our hiding place. One of the scouts threw a stone to attract my attention and pointed. In the distance, I could see some of the cattle boys running towards the fort. Just at that moment Morcar and his two guards came out of the gate and walked towards my hidden warriors. Their backs were to the gate and they did not see the boys. They began their walk around the walls. The scouts we had sent had said that they walked halfway around and then came back. They never lost sight of the copse for obvious reasons. The men in the woods were their protectors.

Suddenly ponies erupted from the gate. Thirty Hibernian warriors galloped out and rode north. One of the guards on the ramparts shouted, "Tadgh, bring your men out and collect the boy. It looks like they have stolen the cattle."

Myrddyn shouted, "Understood."

It was now or never. The news of the cattle raid could never be precise; Aedh had to strike when he could. "Pol, Tuanthal, fetch the horses. We will have to get Morcar now."

This was less than perfect. The ponies could be recalled quickly. They were still less than a mile away. We had to rescue him now. The two guards had heard the noise and were bringing Morcar back. There was no time for deception. I just had to hope that they would take us for their own men, at least for a few moments.

The two guards were briefly taken in as we ran towards them. When we were just twenty paces away they saw that we were not the men they thought we were. They grabbed Morcar and ran for the ramparts. They shouted as they did so, "We are under attack!"

They would have been better keeping their hands free rather than trying to hold on to my nephew. Lann Aelle and one of his warriors reached the two guards and, even as they tried to fend off the attack, they were slain. I saw men pouring down from the fort. I recognised Oswald immediately. Then I heard the thunder of hooves as our horses galloped towards us. With the exception of Myrddyn, we were all experienced riders. As we mounted our horses those who had been holding them loosed arrows in the direction of the advancing warriors. We headed east away from the ring fort. My aim was to put as much distance as I could between us. I knew that the riders on the ponies would be recalled and it would become a race to the Lough and the border. Our advantage was our superior horses. Their advantage was numbers and knowledge of the land.

"Lann Aelle, watch over your cousin!"

Morcar's voice drifted from behind, "I do not need help, uncle."

I turned to look at him. Considering he had just been rescued he did not look happy. Perhaps he had hoped to emulate me and escape himself. He was desperate for some kind of glory. I had no time to indulge him and I concentrated on watching for the enemy. We gradually turned north to head toward the Lough. We had fifteen miles to go and anything could happen.

I shouted to those who were ahead of me and to the west, "Watch for Aedh. He will be joining us soon." One advantage of the recall of the warriors was that Aedh and his men would not be pursued. We did not thrash our horses to death. It was important to keep a steady speed up. If we had to we would be able to move faster than ponies so long as we were on the flatter areas.

Tuanthal shouted, "Warlord! Look to the west!"

I turned and saw the pursuing ponies. They were heading to cut us off. "How far are we from the Lough?"

One of Aedh's scouts was with us and he shouted back, "It must be nearly five miles!"

I gambled that we would reach the Lough before they caught up with us. "Keep the same speed but be prepared to kick on if they close too fast." I was suffering from my old wound. I had not ridden as far in a long time and my leg ached so much it felt as though someone was burning me with a brand. I was getting too old to campaign.

"Warlord!"

I looked to where Tuanthal was pointing. The ponies were closing. They were riding them to death in an attempt to reach us. "It is time to show them what the horses of Rheged can do!!

I kicked Nightstar hard in the flanks and the mighty horse almost unseated me with a burst of speed. I was soon outstripping the others. There was little point in reining in. The others would be close behind me. I saw the sunlight glistening off the water ahead. We had made it. I glanced over my shoulder and saw that my warriors were strung out. Myrddyn was struggling at the back and Pol had stayed with him. Morcar and Lann Aelle were in the middle. The warriors pursuing us were now close enough to see their weapons. It would be tight.

As I turned around I suddenly saw twenty Saxons running from the Lough. They had been at the ransom exchange early. Hearing the noise of hooves they must have left their place of concealment. We would be caught between the ponies and those on foot. They were less than thirty paces from me. If I swerved I would lead my warriors into the pursuing Hibernians. I would charge them! I drew Saxon Slayer. This was not my death. This was not my dream.

"Wolf Warrior!" Instead of veering away, I rode directly at them. They had been so keen to get at us that they had lost all order. I leaned forward in my saddle and, swinging my blade from behind me, slashed the first Saxon from his groin to his throat. The spear he held brushed my shoulder as he stabbed at me too early. I tugged the reins and Nightstar responded. We swung towards a knot of men with spears. As we headed for the next warriors I heard the crack as Nightstar's hooves smashed into the skull of an unfortunate Saxon who had come too close to us. One Saxon showed more sense than the other. He knelt before me and planted the spear into the ground. I urged Nightstar on and we soared over the surprised Saxon. I swung my sword as Nightstar's front hoof clipped the spear and Saxon Slayer split the man's head in two.

## Saxon Bane

There were no more warriors before me, just the sparkling waters of the Lough. I wheeled Nightstar around and saw that my charge had split the waiting Saxons. My warriors were laying about them and the field was filled with death. The ponies were closer but I judged that we would just make the frontier. I hoped that the king would be waiting for us.

I slowed Nightstar down and my warriors gradually joined us. I was about to say 'well done' when there was a cry from the rear. Myrddyn had fallen from his mount. Pol reined in and grabbed the horse's reins. Myrddyn lay still on the ground. I could not leave my old friend and I led my warriors back. The Hibernians seized the moment and charged us on their sturdy ponies. We were outnumbered. I led the warriors towards the ponies. Morcar and Lann Aelle had joined Pol and were trying to get Myrddyn back on his horse.

We thundered towards them. All of my warriors had bloodied swords and our mounts were also blood-spattered. Unlike the Saxons, the Hibernians had no armour and few helmets. Even so, this would be hard for they outnumbered us.

I saw the leader who urged his men on. I charged him. He threw a javelin at me. I tried to duck out of the way but it stuck in my shoulder. I reached with my left hand and pulled it out. The bloody tip showed me that it had managed to penetrate, mail, leather and skin. I threw it, left-handed and it struck a pony. The leader had drawn his sword and he came at me, eager to finish me off. He swung his sword at the same time as me. They met and there was a crack. My sword carried on and hacked into his shoulder penetrating through to his chest. The two halves of his sword fell from his lifeless fingers.

Suddenly arrows began to fall amongst the Hibernians. I looked and saw Aedh and his men. My captain of scouts had used his head. His warriors were all experts with the bow and soon the Hibernians had had enough and began to fall back. I saw that Myrddyn and Pol were heading north and we followed them. Once we reached the northern shore we stopped so that I could examine Myrddyn.

He shrugged his shoulders to make me release my hands. "Get off me, Warlord. I am fine. It was just an animal hole and that stupid horse stumbled."

"But you were not moving, Myrddyn!"

"I was merely winded Pol." He glanced up at me. "But you have been wounded again, Lord Lann."

I put my finger up to my shoulder. There was a tiny trickle of blood. "It is nothing, the armour took most of the impact."

King Fiachnae mac Báetáin rode up. "We saw! That was well done."

I pointed behind me. "If you send your men to the Saxons they can get weapons and armour as good as any." He looked dubious. "Those we defeated are busy running back. I would advise you to get some decent weapons."

He nodded and sent his men to collect the Saxon arms. We headed back to the safety and security of the hill fort.

Saxon Bane

# Chapter 7

We rode back to the coast in silence. We had been more than lucky. My new wound ached a little but it was not life-threatening. Lann Aelle rode next to Morcar while Pol watched over our wizard. We watched our own. The lack of discipline shown by the king's men when Morcar had been abducted was a warning of their frailties.

Our farewells were rapid for I wished to find out from Morcar what had happened to him. "We will send a message to you when we are ready for the attack. Until then prepare your men."

"I will Lord Lann and I can see that we have much to learn from you."

Daffydd ap Gwynfor was also glad to be away. "I saw too many sails on the horizon for my liking. There seemed to be Saxon ships everywhere. I am pleased we are travelling back with so many of your warriors."

The captain's words disturbed me. We had plied the seas and traded successfully for some years. The Byzantine ships had also begun to return to trade. If the pirates and Saxons were in the waters of Britannia then it did not bode well. We might well return to the dark ages of a few years ago.

Much to Morcar's annoyance Myrddyn had insisted upon examining him.

"I tell you I was treated well! I am not a child anymore!"

I hid my smile for, at that moment, he seemed like a petulant child refusing to go to bed.

When Myrddyn had finished and nodded we sat at the prow of the ship. Myrddyn watched as Lann Aelle and I spoke with Morcar.

"Tell us all you can of what happened. It might prevent it from happening again."

He shrugged as though the whole incident had been blown out of proportion. "The hunt was going well. The king's brother had killed a wolf and we saw some wolves escaping. One of the king's men shouted for us to chase them and we did."

Myrddyn frowned, "Did he lead you after the wolves?"

"Aye, he did. He led us as though he was a hound himself. He seemed to know where they were going."

"Did you see the wolves again?"

He frowned as he thought back. Then he shook his head. "No, for we were ambushed by the Saxons. We stood no chance."

"And the warrior who led you, was he slain along with the rest?"

He thought for a moment. "I do not think so for I was bound face down but I seem to remember him fleeing north."

Myrddyn looked at me. "It seems that the king has more than one traitor in his midst. Calum was not working alone."

It was a worrying thought now that we had King Fiachnae mac Báetáin and his men as allies. If Oswiu and Oswald had a spy in our host then we had a problem. We would consider that when we returned home.

"Carry on Morcar."

"They took me to the hill fort and asked me my name. I told them and they seemed pleased. I was assigned two guards. The men you slew when you rescued me. I expected torture and death but they treated me like an honoured guest. They allowed me to walk around the hill fort each day and the two guards played games with me."

Myrddyn suddenly asked, "Did you like the two guards?"

For the first time, he seemed uncomfortable, "They treated me well. They treated me as a warrior."

"And the Saxons, Oswiu and Oswald?"

"Oswiu was kind. He was only a little older than me. He made me laugh with his stories."

"You were lucky then. They could have treated you worse than they did."

He looked thoughtful, "I know. Tell me what the ransom they demanded was?"

"Gold and Saxon Slayer."

## Saxon Bane

He looked genuinely surprised. "So that is why you affected the rescue. You could not hand over the sword. I thought you did not think me worthy of ransom."

"Know this, Morcar, I would not pay a ransom, not even for Myfanwy. If you pay a ransom and give in to such demands then it leads to more tragedy."

"You mean that, do you not, Warlord?"

I nodded. "I have dealt with Saxons like Oswiu and Oswald all of my life. They are not to be trusted and they will use devious and underhand means whenever they can. They have learned long ago that we are better warriors and they have to resort to tricks to achieve their ends."

I left Lann Aelle with his cousin as we headed south. "What do you think Myrddyn?"

"I think there are doubts in Morcar's mind. He is not sure if you value him. He has also been duped by the Saxons. He does not see them as his enemies. We will have to watch him. The story he told came out too easily. We will need to treat him with care."

"I will assign him to Lann Aelle."

"I would not do that. He would see that as a slight. It would confirm his view that you do not value him. Keep him by your side and win his mind once more. I will watch him."

We had much to plan once we returned. King Fiachnae mac Báetáin would land with his army at the estuary close to Civitas Carvetiorum. He had promised to bring as many of his warriors as he could. I would need to send my own warriors there to help him to land and to protect his men while they were ferried from the land of the Dál nAraidi. Kay had some warriors who could help but the plague had thinned their ranks considerably. I would need to send men from the south. It would take many days to move King Fiachnae mac Báetáin's army to the mainland. King Cadwallon and I would need to move north long before then to be able to meet him. I had hoped to make the attack by the end of summer but Morcar's abduction had made that unlikely. I would have to meet with my captains and make a decision before we spoke with King Cadwallon.

## Saxon Bane

We landed close to St. Asaph. Hogan Lann was there as was Myfanwy. I knew that she would be worried about Morcar. There was no jetty at the Clwyd and we had to clamber over the side. Tuanthal and Aedh stayed on board to offload the horses at The Narrows.

We wound our way up the path to the small fort which guarded the monastery and the crossing of the Clwyd. It was only small but it was well placed and had prevented any Saxon incursions. It also protected our route to Wrecsam and that, too, was important.

I saw the concern on my wife's face as she waited for me with Hogan Lann and Gawan. She threw her arms around Morcar. "Did they hurt you?"

He shook his head, more than a little embarrassed to be cuddled like that in front of his cousins. "No, I told uncle that I am fine."

She wagged a finger at me. "I told you the Hibernians could be trouble."

I put my arm around her and laughed as we entered the fort. "And it was the Saxons who kidnapped him and not the Hibernians."

I looked up at Hogan Lann, "Oswiu and Oswald."

My eldest son nodded. Hogan Lann was now a mature warrior. Brother Oswald often said how much he looked like me when I had been his age. It pleased me and saddened me at the same time. It was as though he had become the man I was. Where did that leave me?

"Shall we deal with them now, Warlord?"

"No. It is more important to use our new alliance to go on the offensive against Edwin. Besides they only have a handful of men left."

Myrddyn's voice sounded ominous. "Their danger is not in their numbers but in their influence. They managed to sway Hibernians to their side did they not? Do not underestimate them."

I did not ignore Myrddyn but I pushed the words to the back of my mind. I suppose it was a mistake but at the time I was too concerned with other matters. "You managed to clear the Saxons from our borders then?"

"We did. There are none to the west of the mountain divide."

## Saxon Bane

That was music to my ears. It meant they had been driven from the land of Rheged south of the land of the lakes. It confirmed my decision. "Good. When we leave here I would like to see all my captains so that we may plan our campaign and then I will go to see King Cadwallon."

It was good to see my children and grandchildren again. Myfanwy fussed over me, especially when she discovered I had been wounded again."

"It was barely a scratch. It was a lucky throw and the javelin found the tiniest of chinks in my armour."

"And that is how it will end, through a chink in your armour. I told you before that you do not need to fight."

It was then that Morcar told them of my fight with Calum. He ignored the shaking of my head and gave me all of the details. Myfanwy paled and then reddened as she became angry. "You do not need to fight!" She glared at Myrddyn and Morcar. "And I thought you, old man, would have had more sense than to let my husband risk his life over a challenge."

Myrddyn smiled and said, "This is why I have never taken a woman, Warlord. They seem to want to run men's lives for them."

That did nothing to mollify my wife. I tried to explain. "I had no choice. He challenged me and if I had not accepted then we might not have had the alliance and besides, he would have found another way to get at me. He had been paid by Aethelfrith's sons to kill me; he told us that. Better to face him with a weapon than risk a knife in the back."

She seemed a little happier at that. "I am just grateful that you emerged unscathed."

"Next time I will come with you, father, and I can take up any challenge."

It was at that moment that I realised that Hogan Lann would have disposed of my enemy far quicker than I had. He was just as I had been, twenty years ago.

We left Myfanwy with Gwyneth and the rest of us rode down the coast road to The Narrows. We were well guarded for Hogan Lann had most of his equites with us. Morcar asked, "Hogan Lann has the best warriors in the land. When we conquer Rheged will he become king? Or will you Lord Lann?"

"I am the Warlord of Rheged and I have no desire to be king, nor the right. The descendants of King Urien and Prince Pasgen still live in the north. They might not be kings any longer but the blood of kings still courses through their veins."

"But they have done nothing to deliver Rheged from the Saxons."

It was Hogan Lann who answered. "We are the protectors of the land and the people. We were appointed. We swore an oath and we will not be foresworn. A warrior who is foresworn is to be despised."

Morcar began to become angry, I put it down to his abduction. "But only Lord Lann took the oath. You could become king, Hogan Lann. You have the warriors. With the equites behind you, there is nothing to stop you from conquering the whole of Britannia."

"Enough Morcar. Your father never desired to be king and I do not desire to be king. We have enough honour just being protectors of Rheged. If you wish to serve me still put such thoughts and words from your head."

My two sons could not understand Morcar. I could see that in their faces. They saw that what they did was important and they understood it. They had both studied with Brother Oswald and knew about the Roman warriors who had come from the far ends of the Empire to defend Britannia. It was only when they left that the barbarians descended. To Gawan and Hogan Lann they were continuing a tradition of which they were proud. The sword was a visible symbol of that. The sword had been hidden by one of my ancestors and I knew that he had been one of those warriors. That was why I had been guided to the sword all those long years ago. In a way, it was my fault or perhaps Raibeart's. Morcar had been brought up as a rich spoiled nobleman. Raibeart had been well off and able to indulge his eldest. Both my sons had served as warriors from an early age. It had been bred into them. Perhaps I would send Morcar back to his mother. Not everyone was cut out to be a warrior. Morcar had the skills but did he have the heart?

## Saxon Bane

Tuanthal had followed my orders and my captains awaited me at The Narrows. It was no secret what I had planned but I knew that they would be excited. It would be almost three years since I had led an army to war. What they did not know was that I expected it to be my last.

Brother Oswald had anticipated my return and I could smell the food cooking as I entered the gates. I knew that I would have clean clothes laid out and the baths would be at the perfect temperature. Since he had worked out how to use the hypocaust we had had warmth in the winter and hot baths whenever we wished. As much as I loved my wife I knew that the evening amongst my warriors and sons would be a rewarding one.

I went to my solar when I had bathed, trimmed my beard and dressed. I poured myself a chalice of the heavy wine from Lusitania and looked to the west. When I died I expected to have a view like this throughout eternity. I believed I had done enough to be rewarded by the gods. I had always enjoyed a sunset and a western view. That would be reward enough for a life fighting Rheged's enemies.

As I drank my second chalice of wine I realised that was the difference between Morcar and me. I had been brought up a shepherd boy on a windswept ridge above the valley of the Dunum. He had wanted for nothing. I, along with my brothers, had had everything taken from us. Morcar's only loss had been his father and that when he had grown up. I wondered if the death when he was older had had a more profound effect upon the young man. I decided that I was being too harsh on him and I would give him one more chance to prove himself.

We ate, that night, in my main hall around the oval table I had made so that we could all see each other. Many of the captains had their names carved on the table and there were names from warriors now with the Allfather; Miach, Garth, Aiden and Mungo. Others, like the faithful Einar, had no name there but his sword on the wall was a reminder to all of us of his deeds.

The walls themselves were now more colourful. Brother Oswald had found that he enjoyed painting and he had painted tableaux and murals on the walls. He had wanted to paint images of the White Christ and his mother but my warriors said that it had to be the scenes from our defence of Rheged. Some were now finished and they looked impressive. I had advised him on some of the detail and they brought back emotional memories for me.

My sons flanked me at the table and then Myrddyn while Brother Oswald sat next to the wizard. They were an incongruous pair. On the other side of Brother Oswald sat his recently appointed assistant, Carac. The others: Tuanthal, Pol, Lann Aelle, Daffydd ap Miach, Daffydd ap Gwynfor and Bors were seated opposite. I frowned when I saw that Morcar had sat so that no one was on either side of him. He was still sulking over the lack of support from his cousins for his ideas. He would have to learn.

The food was superb but having just spent many days eating rough fare at the court of King Fiachnae mac Báetáin, anything would have tasted good. I watched my intake of wine and was pleased to see that my sons did the same. They had learned well. The other captains quaffed copious amounts. We chatted easily over the meal. I filled in the details of our new ally and my experiences in Hibernia while they let me know of the warriors I would be commanding.

"What is the size of our army now?"

"There are the one hundred equites I command and the one hundred squires who support them. Gawan here has fifty equites and fifty squires. Tuanthal has his one hundred horsemen; Daffydd ap Miach his one hundred archers. Bors his two hundred spearmen and Aedh his twenty scouts."

Over the years we had adopted the Roman idea of hundreds and tens. It meant we could use our natural leaders to command smaller sections. Hogan Lann had the most powerful force for he had Pol and Lann Aelle with him.

"Before we talk of this in public how many men will that leave us to defend our homes and our people?"

"Small garrisons only; twenty men in each fort."

"That is not enough. Bors can use one hundred of his spearmen to bolster the forts. We will have King Fiachnae mac Báetáin's men."

## Saxon Bane

"How many of those are there?"

"He can field over two hundred and fifty but I suspect that he will leave some to guard his home."

"And are they reliable?"

"Do you mean will they fight? Yes but if you mean will they obey orders and do as they are bid then I do not know. I am gambling that the extra men will swing the battle in our favour. They are an uncertain element. If we do not know what they will do then King Edwin will be even more confused."

I noticed that all eyes were on the three of us. I stood. "Forgive me friends for speaking with my sons for so long. We had much catching up to do." I nodded to Brother Oswald and Carac who stood and unrolled a map which they placed on the table. It had been begun by Brother Osric and added to by both the wizard and the priest. It was as accurate a map as we had of Britannia but there were many places in the east which were just brown, empty areas. The towns and forts were marked in red and the Roman Wall in black.

I stood. "We are going to retake Rheged!" I waited as they all banged the table and cheered. They had not been as restrained in their drinking as my sons had. "I will outline what I think we ought to do and you can voice your opinions." It was the way we normally worked. I often wondered if their acquiescence was because they really agreed or because I was Warlord and old.

King Fiachnae mac Báetáin will meet us at Civitas Carvetiorum and King Cadwallon will march with us. What we have to decide is when to go and which route to take." They nodded and all of them stared at the map intently.

"I propose to go before the end of the month and take the western route. King Edwin will not expect us to attack this close to autumn, and the western route, thanks to all of you, is free from Saxons. We can march north undetected."

That set a conversation off. I sat down and noticed that Myrddyn did the same. He looked at me and spread his hands as much as to say, 'what is there to discuss?'

## Saxon Bane

Hogan Lann said, "I like the idea of the attack from the west, it will surprise them but I cannot agree that now is the most propitious time. We have just had a campaign against the Saxons and, whilst we did not lose many warriors, it has taken its toll on the horses and equipment. We would have to stay in Rheged over winter and the winters there can be harsh. We are relying on the Irish and we do not know how they will cope with winter. I suggest we go in the spring."

I could see that most of them agreed with my son. The exceptions were Morcar and Myrddyn. I found myself agreeing with Hogan Lann but he did not know that my time was running out. I had to get so much finished before I died.

"Edwin will not expect an attack and all of you have weakened them considerably. By the spring he will have recruited more men. And it gives him longer to find out about our attack and prepare."

I could see that my words had been thought-provoking. We were almost back at a stalemate. Myrddyn chuckled, "Unless, of course, we let him know that we are coming so that he can prepare."

Everyone looked at the wizard as though he had taken leave of his senses. Bors just said, "What?"

"We plant information which tells him that we will attack but not where. We then let him discover information from his spies which makes him think that we will attack one place when, in fact, we are heading for another. Surprise will be all. Imagine if he withdrew his armies from north of the wall to meet an attack further south. We could take…"

Brother Oswald finished his sentence for him, "Din Guardi!"

Myrddyn clapped the priest on the back, "And we all know how hard it is to take that if it is garrisoned."

Tuanthal said cheekily, "Unless, of course, you know how to fly there."

They all laughed and I saw Hogan Lann smile. "That might just work. How would you do it?"

Myrddyn swallowed off some of the heady wine. "I just came up with the idea. We will work it out over the next few days."

## Saxon Bane

I allowed silence to descend so that each man could ruminate in his own head. "What say you? We will have to keep silent, even before our own men but I like Myrddyn's refinement." I put my sword on the table.

"I say, Aye." Hogan Lann did the same and soon the table had our weapons all laid out. We were agreed. We would go in the spring. We would plant information which might suggest a different time and place; I wanted Edwin to be confused. Had I been a dictator then we would have left before the end of the month. I believed that my way was a better one. Hogan Lann had disagreed and we had refined his plan. It boded well for the future. In addition, it gave Brother Oswald and Carac more time to plan the supplies we would need. We had been successful in the past because we had more and better weapons than our enemies.

Brother Oswald and his assistant remained behind when the rest had gone. "We will need as many carts and wagons as you can manage to acquire. We will need plenty of arrows and I would like to take as much food as possible."

The old priest smiled, "It is good that you listened to the others, Warlord, we could not have managed that in a month." He nodded towards Carac who was busily making notes on a wax tablet. "Luckily I now have an assistant with energy who can run around more than this old priest."

"How do you like it here Carac?"

The young man had only been with us for three or four months. He had been washed ashore having been in a ship attacked by Hibernian pirates. He had shown himself to be a literate and hard-working young man and Brother Oswald had pounced upon him as an assistant. It was he who took on the duties of travelling to St. Cybi and dealing with the traders and captains. It extended the time that Brother Oswald could stay at The Narrows. This was the first time I had had to speak with the young man.

"I am grateful that my life was saved. It is good having a purpose in my life. With all of my friends and family dead I can now make new friends and Brother Oswald is like a father to me."

I was pleased that it had worked out so well. Brother Oswald was a lonely old man and I believed that Carac brought companionship into his life.

"Good. I am pleased that you can take some of the burden from Brother Oswald's shoulders. There will always be a place for you here."

Saxon Bane

# Chapter 8

Myrddyn and I concocted our plan alone the next day. All of my captains had much to do. Brother Oswald had lists of weapons and supplies which would be needed. Spring might be some time away but winter storms kept ships in port and we needed to be prepared. We sat in my solar and worked out what to do.

"It seems to me that we need to keep King Edwin looking to his southern borders. We know that he has the support of King Raedwald but King Cearl is an uncompromising enemy. We need to enlist the aid of King Cearl and make Edwin believe that the attack will come up the eastern side of his kingdom. He will strengthen his defences and use his influence to get King Raedwald to help him."

"How do we get the Mercians to help us?"

"Penda is a rival to King Cearl; he is a cousin. If we offered to take Penda off his hands he might be inclined to listen to our proposal at the very least."

"Why would Penda wish to help us?"

"He hates the Northumbrians and Aethelfrith in particular. His father was killed by Aethelfrith and Cearl inherited the kingdom as a result. He is a bitter man. He wants power."

I could not fault that argument. "We will visit with Cearl when we have spoken with Cadwallon. We need to send a message to King Fiachnae mac Báetáin. Tell him that we will not be attacking until spring. I hate to deceive our new ally but I thought to tell him that we would launch one attack with him and some of our horsemen from the north after we had started an attack on the eastern side."

"It would not be a deception for when we arrived with our whole army in the north then we could say you changed your mind."

"Aye, and it gives our new ally more time to prepare his men. You think that the word will go from Hibernia to Edwin?"

## Saxon Bane

"I can guarantee it. There is still a Saxon spy at the king's court. I doubt that the king will have uncovered him."

"But he is Oswald's spy. They hate Edwin."

"But they are pragmatic. They might offer the information to Edwin to win his favour. I am certain that the news will travel to Edwin. If we can plant doubts in his mind then we have already won." He walked to look out at Wyddfa. "Edwin will know already that we plan to attack him. Hogan Lann's success in the west has shown him that we are on the rise again."

I joined him and we both stared at the holy mountain. "He did well."

Myrddyn looked at me and there was sadness in his eyes. "He is ready to be Warlord. That is why the spirits spoke with you. It is why we dreamed your death. It is time for a change. Rheged and Gwynedd will be safe in his and Gawan's hands."

It suddenly became clear. "Then the spirits have decided that my time here is at an end and I have done all that I can."

"Perhaps or it could be that your death is needed to ensure the final victory. It may be that you are the sacrifice." We sat again. "Before the Romans came our people would often sacrifice a man before an important battle or decision. He would go willingly to his death. It would be an honour to do so. The Irish did the same although, for no reason, they liked to throw their victims into a bog. Your death might be just such a sacrifice. You would give your life for Rheged would you not?"

"Of course. Every time I fought for King Urien I expected to die. It is just…"

"It is just that you wanted it as a surprise rather than anticipating it?"

I nodded, "Not a surprise but in battle." I shrugged. "I am a servant of the spirits of Wyddfa and I will do as they wish."

Myrddyn nodded, "And I too serve them but, if it is any consolation, I wish they had not chosen to take you. You have been my only friend and I shall miss you." I saw that he meant every word and I was touched. We sat in silence reflecting on our time together. Somehow I felt more at peace as we left to begin our preparations.

## Saxon Bane

I spoke with Hogan Lann before I left. "I want you to visit with King Fiachnae mac Báetáin and tell him that we attack in spring. Tell him there will be two attacks. His will be the smaller one with Gawan to aid him and ours will be from the south through the land of Elmet." He gave me a strange look. "Remember when we were in Constantinopolis? That is a sophisticated version of what you will find in Dál nAraidi. You will need all your guile in Hibernia. There are Saxon and Hibernian spies at his court. He knows not who they are or even that they exist. This way we deceive our enemies."

"And our friends?"

"No, Hogan Lann, for we will attack from the north. He will not be left alone to face the Saxons, we will fight with him. And another reason I wish you to go is to get to know him and his men. I believe they will be valuable allies for us."

"You are not thinking of abstaining from war and staying with Myfanwy are you?"

"Of course not. I am just using your abilities to help our people."

I took Lann Aelle and Morcar with me to King Cadwallon. I thought Lann Aelle might help to build bridges with my nephew who had seemed a little distant since his abduction. Certainly by the time we reached Wrecsam they were laughing and joking together.

King Cadwallon was taken into our confidence. We told him all that had occurred and all of our plans. He was too good a friend for anything else. Lann Aelle and Morcar spent time with Nanna while we spoke. It was not that I did not trust them but they were young men and might be indiscreet without meaning to be.

"I can fortify my land which borders that of Northumbria. It is good that you will speak with King Cearl for I would not want him to think I was planning to attack him. Our people have prospered in the peace we have had."

"What can you tell me of this Penda? Myrddyn says he has a claim to the throne so why is King Cearl allowing him to live?"

"The king has no children and Eowa, Penda's half brother, is a little, shall we say unstable?"

## Saxon Bane

"Unstable?"

"Aye, he has a tendency to lose his temper. He has beaten slaves to death with his bare hands before now. Penda is seen as the sane one. Cearl keeps trying to father children but he has little luck. He gets his women with child but either they die or the child does. Penda would make a good king but he is ambitious. Cearl just worries that he might wish to take the throne sooner rather than later." He looked at me shrewdly.

Myrddyn said, "Well I shall leave you now. There are some maps in your fort I wish to study. Our knowledge of the land to the east is woefully poor."

When he had gone I smiled at Cadwallon. He had his father had been as sons to me. They had both been my squires and I was pleased that Cadwallon would be my daughter's guardian after I had gone.

"There is something different about you, Lord Lann. I cannot put my finger on it."

I smiled and looked away, "Put it down to my age."

"I served you as my father did and you know I trust you completely. Cannot you trust me as completely?"

I looked him in the eye. "You know all there is to know. Neither my sons nor my wife knows more."

"I dare say the truth will out one day." I could see that I had not convinced him but he still respected me too much to bring it out into the open. "My army will be ready by the spring. I should be able to field fifty horsemen, a hundred archers and two hundred spearmen."

"You will still leave enough to guard your land?"

He nodded and smiled, "Nanna and your grandchildren will be safe." He saw Morcar and Lann Aelle approaching. "I assume your confidence was for my ears only?" I nodded. "You play a dangerous game, Warlord." He smiled, "Life is always interesting around you and Myrddyn. I shall get Dai to provide a guide for you to take you to Cearl. When will you leave?"

"First thing in the morning. We might as well make use of this fine weather and lighter nights. Soon the nights will draw in."

## Saxon Bane

Afon, who had volunteered to accompany us, was a serious warrior. He said little as we headed for Tomtun, Cearl's capital the heart of Mercia. Myrddyn gradually drew out from the warrior that his people had lived in the borders and he was the only survivor of a raid by the Mercians before the peace. I wondered at King Cadwallon's choice of guide. I did not want our guide to start a war. We only had ten lightly armed warriors with us. More than that would have constituted an aggressive stance.

I found the land to be peaceful. We found few fortified towns. I suspect that the accord between the two neighbouring kings contributed heavily to that. The first few miles were over rough tracks but then Afon found Wæcelinga Stræt, the old Roman Road, which ran to the south coast we found the going much easier. When we asked Afon how far was the journey to be he shrugged, "Two days."

Myrddyn grimaced when he heard that. We were both used to a comfortable bed at night. Our days of sleeping on the ground were a distant memory. Lann Aelle smiled when he saw our reaction. "Perhaps we should have brought a cart for you, Uncle."

It was late afternoon when the armed warriors emerged from the top of a nearby hill. There were twenty of them and they were led by a mailed warrior. Morcar carried my banner and I knew that the Mercians would remember it from the last time we had fought.

"Keep your hands away from your weapons." Afon looked nervous.
"Do not worry Afon, they will speak with us." The confidence was in my voice but not my head. I had many enemies amongst the Saxons. I had slain too many kings and princes for it to be otherwise.

They were not mounted and they trotted down the hill in a defensive formation. Their spears prickled out of their shields and they looked for all the world like a hedgehog. Their leader had a full-face helmet on and I could not see his expression. We were riding without helmets. I smiled, "I am Lord Lann, Warlord of Rheged and I seek an audience with King Cearl of Mercia."

The warrior took off his helmet. "I know who you are Lord Lann for I fought against you at Wrecsam." He pointed at my leg with the tip of his spear. "I was there when you nearly lost your leg and your life." He pointed to the skies. "The Allfather watched over you that day or perhaps this Necromancer with you."

I could see that Myrddyn did not appreciate the comment. "You know our names, Mercian, what is yours?"

"I am Penda the king's cousin."

So this was the man who would be king. I saw a man a little older than Hogan Lann. He was stocky and Saxon from his blond hair to his blue eyes. His golden beard was flecked with a few wisps of grey. He was a warrior from the bands on his sword to the scars on his arms. His armour and weapons showed a warrior who cared for his weapons.

"So, shall I take you to my cousin or shall we fight here?"

Only Morcar reacted with an angry flash of his eyes and a jerk on the reins of his horse. "Nephew, it is a reasonable question. We are in Mercian land and we are armed." I smiled at Penda. "I would prefer to visit with your cousin but we are happy to oblige you with combat if you wish."

He laughed, "I like you, Warlord, not least because you brought about the death of my enemy, Aethelfrith. We will take you to my cousin. If we step out we can be there by dark."

I looked at Afon. Why had he said two days? "Afon, we have our guide now. You may return to the king and thank him for his help. Tell him that you saw us on our way."

Flashing an angry look at Penda, Afon nodded and said, "As you wish, my lord. But I would sleep with a knife beneath my bed."

He rode off and Penda chuckled, "There is a man who does not like Saxons."

"You understood him then?"

"Aye, it pays to speak their language when you live close to the Cymri."

"His family were slain by Saxons. You can understand his feelings."

"Aye, we have all lost someone." I noticed that they were not out of breath as they walked beside us. We had gone into two long lines. It gave

## Saxon Bane

us mutual protection. "And you, I believe, have slain more Saxons than most. What do you have to do with Cearl?"

I noticed that he did not give him his title. "I have killed few Mercians. My enemies are the men of Bernicia and Deira; the ones who now call themselves Northumbrians."

"Well, there we have an agreement." He was persistent. He wanted an answer to his question. "And what do you seek from Cearl?"

Although we had not expected to meet Penda, Myrddyn and I had prepared ourselves well for the next few days. I would be honest with Penda; as honest as I could be at any rate. "I need to tell King Cearl that we intend to attack Edwin in the spring."

He looked up at me with surprise on his face. "Isn't that a little dangerous? You could be inviting an attack from Mercia?"

"I believe that King Cearl is an honourable man. If he gives me his word that he will not do so then I will believe him. If he tells me that he will attack Gwynedd in our absence then we will not attack Edwin."

"That would be a pity. I should like to see Edwin knocked from his little hill."

Myrddyn, who had been listening to every word, chirped in, "If you wished, Penda son of Pybba, you could join the Warlord. I am sure he would welcome any ally to fight against the Northumbrians."

That really surprised Penda. "You would fight with a Saxon?" I nodded. "Then you are a remarkable man. I heard that you hated Saxons and just wanted to kill them."

"I have only ever wanted one thing; a Rheged free from Saxons. When we have reclaimed Rheged then I will sheath my sword."

He spent the next few miles, each one marked with the Roman milestones, asking me about my sword and the stories of Myrddyn and myself. I allowed Myrddyn to reply to his many questions about his magic. He knew how to weave a story better than I did.

As the afternoon wore on he asked, "Where did you envisage sleeping this night?"

"Our guide said we could camp by the road."

## Saxon Bane

"Then your guide is a fool. These are still dangerous lands. My men and I patrol the road to protect travellers. There are still bands of rogue Saxons and Angles who steal cattle and kill those who use this road. And there are Cymri who disobey their king and steal also."

"Would that all men were as honourable as the ones we lead."

He nodded, "Besides we can reach King Cearl if we push on."

Lann Aelle was at the front of our line and he suddenly held up his hand and stopped. He was just three riders ahead of me. Penda looked up at me and I said, "He would not stop without reason. Come let us see him." We walked up to Lann Aelle. "What is it, nephew?"

"My horse's ears pricked up." He nodded at the stand of trees and bushes some fifty paces away. "The wind is coming from the south-east and I too picked up the smell," he shrugged apologetically at Penda, "of Saxon."

I looked down at Penda. "Have you warriors waiting there?" His eyes flashed anger. "I am not suggesting treachery but I trust Lann Aelle's nose and his horse's instincts."

"No, Warlord of Rheged, we have no men there. Whoever it is they mean no good."

Myrddyn said, "If I might suggest walking into this trap then."

Penda laughed. "Aye let us do that. My men are ready for a fight. They are disappointed that we did not cross swords with you when we met."

"If your men stay on our right they will be protected from those on our left. The trees to the right are closer. As soon as we are within ten paces we charge."

"That sounds good to me."

I turned and passed the word to my men. They were good warriors and would not panic. They could have their weapons drawn in an instant. Our left sides were already protected by our shields which hung from our shoulders. Only Myrddyn had neither weapon nor shield but he was a wizard. It would be a foolish bandit who attacked him.

I could smell the men now. The breeze was quite strong as was their smell. I knew that I could draw Saxon Slayer quickly but I slipped a

## Saxon Bane

dagger into my left hand just in case. When we were at the edge of the tree line I shouted, "Now!" and kicked my horse on.

Our sudden charge resulted in spears and arrows being loosed prematurely. There were Saxons hidden in the trees and bushes. It looked to be a small warband, perhaps thirty or so warriors. I drew Saxon Slayer as a spear was thrust up at me. I hacked down and the head was severed from the shaft. An eager Saxon tried to rip me from my saddle. I could not swing and so I used the pommel to strike him in the eye. He fell clutching the bleeding orb. The warrior behind me leaned forward to finish him off. I could see that they had planned on using their bows to attack us and they were struggling to grab their shields and their swords. I watched as a warrior ran towards Myrddyn, his sword poised to strike the weaponless wizard. I urged my horse on knowing that I would not be in time. Myrddyn reached into his satchel and threw some dust in the warrior's eyes. He fell screaming to the ground as though they were on fire.

Morcar had not been trained to use his banner as a weapon and he was just watching the attack impotently. Lann Aelle in contrast was laying about him to such effect that the Saxons began to flee. Lann Aelle and my riders took off after them. I turned to see how Penda was doing. He and his men had despatched their assailants even quicker.

I went over to join Myrddyn who was with the warrior he had blinded. The warrior was whimpering, "I am blind, I cannot see."

Morcar rode up and looked in horror at the reddened mess which had been the Saxon's eyes. I watched as Myrddyn washed his hands in water.

"What was that Myrddyn?" There was awe in Morcar's voice.

"Just something I picked up in Constantinopolis. It makes the Greek Fire we use to burn a little longer. I always keep some in my satchel and today it came in handy."

"Will he see again?"

"On no, he is blinded for life now and he may well die. That will teach him to try to kill a wizard."

Penda had joined us. "Were they bandits then? Rogue warriors?"

## Saxon Bane

"They were rogue alright. They are Northumbrian." He pointed to the amulets which were clearly Northumbrian.

"Oswiu and Oswald."

"That would be my guess."

Myrddyn nodded, "Afon, it would appear, has questions to answer."

Penda nodded at the blinded Saxon as Lann Aelle returned with the horsemen. "Shall we ask him then?"

"We might as well. Who sent you?"

"My eyes, I cannot see."

Myrddyn's voice oozed sympathy. "I can ease the pain if you answer our questions."

"Anything. Help me I beg you."

"I will get the salve while you answer the Warlord's questions."

"Who sent you?"

"Oswald the son of Aethelfrith."

"When did he send you?"

"When we failed in Hibernia. Please help me."

I nodded to Myrddyn. He applied some white paste. The relief on the Saxon's face was obvious. "Thank you, healer."

"What did Oswald want you to do?"

There was a little more confidence in the Saxon's voice now. Perhaps the salve had emboldened him. "Why to kill you, of course."

I looked at Myrddyn who shrugged. "The paste kills pain but it also acts like heady wine it loosens the tongue."

"What will he do now?"

"The brothers are buying an army and they will come to reclaim their throne." The pain must really have worn off for he laughed. "They have spies everywhere. They will know exactly what you are doing at any time."

"Where did they get their gold?"

"Their father was rich. Edwin stole the throne but not the treasury. Aethelfrith hid it."

Suddenly he let out a scream and his body went into spasm. He shook violently and then lay still. He was dead.

Saxon Bane

"The powder must have burned down to the brain." He said it as though it was an interesting fact rather than the horror we had just witnessed.

Penda shook his head, "Remind me never to cross you, wizard."

## Chapter 9

There was an urgent pace to our step as we headed for Cearl's capital. Penda did not think that there would be more of Oswald's men waiting but he was taking no chances. All of us were exhausted as we stood before Cearl's gates.

"Who is it?"

"Aella, if you do not recognise me then I will have to assume that you have been drinking."

"Of course I recognise you but what are you doing with the men of Cymru, the horsemen of Rheged?"

"They are come in peace to speak with my cousin. Now have the gate open before I lose my temper."

The gates creaked open and a dozen warriors had their spears levelled at us. Penda drew his sword. "Lower those spears now. I will vouch for Lord Lann."

As soon as they heard my name the warriors took a step back. In the dark, they could not see my smile. Mothers had been terrifying their children for years with the threat of Lord Lann coming to get them. These were grown men but they still feared me.

I turned to Morcar. "See to the horses."

A brief moment of annoyance flickered across his face and then he dismounted and complied. The Saxons parted and Penda led me to the hall at the far end of the fort. He shook his head at the spearmen who backed away from us. "They are typical garrison warriors; frightened of their own shadow. It must be the same with your warriors eh, Warlord?"

"We rotate our men so that even our equites have a spell walking the walls."

"That might explain why your horsemen are so hard to beat and your forts impossible to take."

"And I take it you have tried?"

## Saxon Bane

He laughed, "Of course!"

The leader of Cearl's bodyguards, Aelfraed, stood in the doorway. This was not a frightened sentry, this was a warrior who would die rather than let any harm come to his king. He just glared at me and then Penda.

"This is Lord Lann of Rheged and Myrddyn the wizard. They seek an audience with the king."

"I can see who they are. I was at Wrecsam when the Warlord was brought back from the Otherworld. What I cannot understand is why you brought them here."

Penda shrugged, "We are at peace and he has something interesting to tell the king."

Aelfraed looked defiantly at me.

Myrddyn shook his head, "If you are afraid of two old men and a handful of horsemen then the tales of Mercian bravery must be exaggerated."

"Then give me your sword." He held out his hand.

Myrddyn shook his head, "That is Saxon Slayer. If you were to touch it then you would be cursed and never be able to touch a weapon again." It was a cold, calm and chilling voice that Myrddyn used. I saw that it had an effect on Aelfraed who stood aside.

"I will be watching both of you. At the first sign of a trick, I will have you cut down."

Myrddyn smiled as we passed. "Unless, of course, I had flown out of the hall already."

I knew he was teasing and I think Penda knew it too but the guards at the gate took it seriously and I saw them clutching at their amulets and charms. Myrddyn had a reputation which transcended people, tribes and kings. He was unique.

It was some time since I had seen King Cearl and he had aged. He looked even older than I thought I looked. He was, however, courteous. "Welcome, Myrddyn and Lord Lann. This is an unexpected visit. Sit down and break bread with me."

## Saxon Bane

He was very old fashioned and we went through the ritual of breaking off a piece of bread from a loaf, eating it and drinking some ale to wash it down.

He glanced at Penda. "Well cousin, would you begin the tale?"

"I was patrolling Wæcelinga Stræt when I met the Warlord. He said he had some news to impart to you. I brought him here." The king nodded. "However we were attacked on the road." I looked around the faces. All appeared to be surprised but the blinded warrior had told us of spies everywhere. Penda and I had worked out there must be some at Cearl's court. I could not detect who they might be.

"Bandits or Welshmen?"

"Neither, they were Northumbrians sent by Oswald and Oswiu."

"Where are they now, these Northumbrians?"

"Feeding the carrion."

"So Warlord you risked death to bring me news which I might like. I am intrigued." He turned to Aelfraed, "See to the Warlord's men. Make sure they are fed. They will be staying the night." I was not sure whether we were guests or prisoners. The distinction might prove crucial in the morning. He waved a hand at me so that I might continue.

"I have met with King Cadwallon. We intend to invade Northumbria in the spring."

"And what has this to do with me." I waited. "Go ahead; I bear Edwin no love."

I nodded, "It is partly a courtesy, as we intend to move east and then north. We did not wish you to think that we were breaking the peace and threatening you."

The king smiled and nudged the newly returned Aelfraed in the leg. "You see these Welshmen and the men of Rheged have manners after all. And what else, Warlord?"

"We would like assurances that the peace would not be broken in our absence."

Aelfraed snarled, "You insult my king!"

"No, I do not. I trust your king which is why we are here. I like to look a man in the eye when I ask him a question whether he be my friend or foe. I know King Cearl to be a man of his word. I just want to hear it from his lips as he heard the question from mine."

King Cearl smiled, "It is a reasonable question, Warlord." He shook his head, "I think that Aelfraed spends too much time with that hothead of a brother of yours, Penda." He looked at me and stood. He held out his hand. "You have my word, Warlord that I will not attack King Cadwallon's lands while he is away." I clasped it. "I will go further. While you are away I will ensure that his borders are safe. I like this peace of ours for our people to prosper. Mayhap this will make it stronger."

"And that is my deepest wish too."

"While you are in such a generous mood cousin could I crave a boon?"

The king's face smiled but not his eyes. "Ask away, cousin, I can only say no."

"I would like to accompany the Warlord with my oathsworn when he ventures against Edwin and Northumbria. I would learn from him and I have a score to settle with the Northumbrians."

The king nodded, "That you do. I cannot see a problem although I never thought that I would live to see the day when a Saxon fought alongside the Warlord and Saxon Slayer."

Everyone looked at me. "Perhaps, King Cearl, the world is changing."

Despite our misgivings, the evening went well. I hoped that Lann Aelle was watching Morcar. He was a headstrong youth and I did not want him to say anything which might jeopardise our plan; so far it was working.

I sensed, with King Cearl, that he felt a certain frustration that he had made Mercia so powerful and yet he had no heir. When he died it would pass to someone else. I had no throne to leave but I knew that Hogan Lann would not only be a warlord when I died but a better one than I was. He had the experience of travelling the world. When I was his age I had only seen Rheged. I would be leaving Rheged in safe hands. I knew that Myrddyn would watch over him.

## Saxon Bane

As I watched Myrddyn, telling King Cearl how he had walked amongst the enemy unseen, I could not see him ever dying. He looked as young now as he had thirty years ago. The rest of us aged but not Myrddyn. His mind was sharper than ever. I felt happy that he would be there for my sons. They would not be alone.

Penda sidled over to me. "I will just bring my oathsworn with me, Warlord."

"I saw them fight today. They will be more than enough. Bring them to Wrecsam a month after Yule. We will not leave until spring but it is as well to be prepared. Besides, it will help to train with our warriors."

I found it easy to talk to Penda. I think he felt isolated from the other Saxons and we found that our differences were not as great as we had once thought. I discovered that he was driven by a hatred of Oswiu, Oswald and Edwin. It even surpassed his hatred of us. I found myself wondering about this, seemingly unnatural hatred of all things Saxon. It had been the Angles and Saxons, who had come to Northumbria and destroyed Rheged, whom I hated. I had no idea what lay in Mercia before the Saxons came but I knew that Rheged was still Roman and I wanted that to be returned.

King Cearl gave us an escort back to the border. He did not want the peace to be jeopardised by an attack on our small column. Sadly it was not Cearl who escorted us but Aelfraed. He was an unpleasant man who hated us unremittingly. He said nothing at all until we reached the scene of the ambush. The blinded warrior lay where he had fallen but birds, insects and animals had used his burned-out eyes as a way into his body and his was the most ravaged corpse that we saw. Penda's men had told everyone else about Myrddyn's magic and even Aelfraed looked at my wizard with fear written all over his face.

When he left us at the border he rode his horse close to mine, "As far as I am concerned, Welshman, this is merely a truce. When Eowa is king we will fall upon your lands and tear you apart. This I swear."

"Then be ready for a world of pain Aelfraed for I have never lost to a Saxon and that includes every king, prince and champion I have fought. Think about that!"

Saxon Bane

# Chapter 10

We did not spend long with King Cadwallon; just long enough to assure him that his borders would be safe. "However, I would make sure that you keep more men at home than we take with us."

I knew that we would visit with them in the depths of winter. Myfanwy always liked to see her children and grandchildren at Yule. The days of all of the family gathering with us were long gone.

We were about to leave when I suddenly remembered Afon. "Your guide, Afon, did he return?"

Dai, who was standing close by the king frowned and said, "No, when you told us what happened we assumed he was killed in the ambush."

Myrddyn shook his head, "We believe that Afon was part of the ambush. We were attacked close to the place he had said we would camp."

That made Dai frown even more. "With horses, you could have made the journey in a day."

I nodded, "I know. In fact, we did so. I would not like to judge him but all the evidence points to him being a traitor. He is your man Dai and I dare say you will deal with him."

"If he turns up we will question him closely. You may be assured of that."

"The one survivor told us that Oswald and Oswiu have spies in all of our camps. They used the treasury of Northumbria to pay for them. We will be examining all of our men when we return."

"Thank you for that information. I will look for warriors who have suddenly acquired better weapons and armour."

As we headed back along the Clwyd Valley I realised that this next Yule, if I lived that long, might be my last. I would not complain about the journey in the cold and the wet. I found myself smiling.

Lann Aelle, who was next to me asked, "What is so funny uncle?"

## Saxon Bane

"Oh, nothing. I was just reflecting that we have a good life nephew. Despite the problems of Edwin and Aethelfrith's sons, we are lucky."

He nodded, "My father has told me what it was like growing up in Rheged and you must be right. I cannot imagine what it must have been like to survive with so many enemies around you. He still talks of how you came back for him and Uncle Raibeart. He cannot believe that you risked all to rescue them. I am certainly grateful."

I shrugged. "It is family, Lann Aelle. We do it all for our family. Rheged is just the larger family. That is where many kings go wrong. They are so worried that their family will stab them in the back that they lose sight of their real quest; to protect their family and their land." Morcar was at the back with Myrddyn who was explaining how he used his special powders and spells. "Speaking of family, how is Morcar these days?"

"He is a strange one. I had expected him either to be angrier or happier about his abduction but he will not talk about it. I know it is on his mind for he is more withdrawn and speaks less."

"Do not let him hide within himself. Take him under your wing. You can teach him how to fight whilst carrying my standard. I noticed he did not know how to do so when we fought the men sent by Oswald."

"I will do so." He laughed, "My body was black and blue when Pol taught me."

When we reached St.Asaph we collected my wife and headed back to The Narrows. I hoped to see Hogan Lann there. I was keen to get his opinion of Fiachnae mac Báetáin. My eldest son was a good judge of character. Gawan accompanied us. I had seen little of him of late and I think he wished to talk. He and I rode at the head of our snaking column while Myfanwy had the comfort of the wagon.

"You should not risk yourself so much, father."

"You sound like your mother."

"Perhaps she is right. You have done more than any other man, and that includes King Urien and King Coel."

I snorted, "And how do you know that? You never even met King Urien."

## Saxon Bane

"I know for Brother Oswald has written it all down and I have read the writings of Brother Osric. You have earned the right to take it easier now that you grow older. Hogan Lann and I can shoulder more of the burden."

"It is no burden. Besides I do not feel old."

"You always told us to be honest with you. I have seen you wincing when the wounded leg aches. I have seen you struggle to mount a horse. You should be honest with your sons. Unless you do not trust us."

He was right of course. I did suffer pain from the wound. I suddenly felt guilty. "Of course, I trust you but getting old means that I have to make sure that my work is complete before I go to the Otherworld."

He snapped his head around to stare at me. "You are not ill, are you? Has Myrddyn seen your death?"

I cursed my own tongue and covered my indiscretion with a loud laugh. "Don't you think I would have told you? No, you are right, I am getting old and that is why I am preparing for the end of my life. Hopefully, I will have many more years ahead of me and I will be able to teach your sons how to wield a sword as I taught you and Hogan Lann."

His eyes searched my face for a lie but I had learned, over the years, how to mask what was in my heart. The only one who could penetrate my armour was Myrddyn. I did worry that Gawan, who was more like Myrddyn than anyone, might soon be able to see behind my mask.

"Even so, we would wish that you take it easy. When Hogan Lann returns from Hibernia let us plan the attack on Edwin. The winter always causes your leg pain; we can take on the task of speaking with Brother Oswald and King Cadwallon."

"Very well but the two of you will need to sit down and speak with Myrddyn and me first. This is not a simple attack or a raid. This is the beginning of the end of Northumbria. Any mistake on our part could cost us the whole of Rheged."

"You can trust us, father, we are family and we will never let you down." That reassured me. My family was not treacherous. I had seen how ambition could tear a family apart.

## Saxon Bane

Hogan Lann was waiting for us when we reached home. Lann Aelle and Morcar had travelled over to Mona to visit with their families. When Yule was over both would be busy beyond words. Even though Hogan Lann was not Myfanwy's child she greeted him with as much affection as if he was and she fussed over him. She told him he needed to eat more. His wife always ensured that he did so but he promised that he would just to please his stepmother.

The four of us sat in my solar. I found myself being scrutinised by my sons. It was disconcerting but I chose to ignore it. "What did you make of Fiachnae mac Báetáin?"

"Not what I expected. His men were as I thought they would be; brave, wild and uncontrolled. Their king, however, seems more like, well, one of us."

"That was how I saw him. Was he worried when you said we would be having our major attack from the east?"

"No, you seem to have made quite an impression on him, the two of you."

"I am not quite ready to be put out to pasture then?"

Gawan spoke, "We just want the best for you father. You and Myrddyn are both getting older and we should do our share."

"And just because you have learned one or two spells and a little healing young Gawan does not mean that you are ready to take over from me yet!"

Gawan laughed, "I will never be able to take over from you Myrddyn but you do need to take things easier."

"Why? Because we have lived longer than you? That is a good thing. We have more experience. When we think you have learned all that there is to know then the two of you can take over."

His voice sounded harsh but his eyes twinkled. Hogan Lann and Gawan were as near to sons as he would ever have.

I told them of our alliance and then the disturbing news about spies. "We have none amongst our men. I can swear to that."

"Can you, Hogan Lann? I am sure that Dai and King Cadwallon would have said the same thing but we nearly lost our lives because of a traitor.

Until we can be certain then only tell your warriors what they need to know."

"I do not like that idea. We have always been honest with our men."

"I did not say lie. I only said to tell them what they needed to know. The plan to dupe them by feigning an attack up the east goes no further than this room."

"But Lann Aelle, Morcar, Pol, what of them?"

"They need not know. They just need to concentrate on preparing our men for a campaign which will rid the land of Northumbria. All else is irrelevant."

I could see that we had upset the two of them. I was keeping a secret from them and I knew how hard it was. If they had known of the prophecy then they would understand. They would, however, worry so much about me that they would not be able to perform as they should.

"Kay will need a visit too."

Gawan spoke quickly, I think before his brother did. "Then I will make that visit."

I smiled as did Hogan. "Of course. You will need to assess their ability to provide warriors."

Hogan Lann shook his head, "When I visited there last year they were still recovering from the plague. They had barely twenty equites left. It is all they can do to defend their forts from the Saxons. Their biggest concern is keeping their sheep and cattle safe from Saxons and Hibernians."

"And the men from Strathclyde."

Hogan Lann looked at me, "Strathclyde? I thought that they were friends."

"They were but that was in the past. The new kings of Dál Riata are pushing out from the coast and devouring all before them. The Roman Wall may still be needed to slow them down."

Myrddyn had appeared to be asleep for his eyes were closed but he showed that he had been paying attention when he said, "If we block up the gates then there will be no thefts."

Gawan laughed, "Not a bad idea."

Hogan Lann took it more seriously. "When you visit with Kay, take enough men to block up the gates on the eastern side of the country. We do not need to use the gates as the Romans did to collect taxes. It will give us one secure flank at least."

"I will do that."

I was pleased. My sons were working together. Their minds were as one. I saw Myrddyn's eyes open. He winked at me. The old wizard could read my mind.

"When we do attack, will we advance up the Dunum Valley?"

"No. We strike at the heart of Northumbria. We go to Din Guardi. It will be a much shorter journey. Our horsemen could reach it in two or three days and our foot could make it in four if we pushed. The key is our deception. I want Edwin's eyes to the south and not the west. I want the attack in the last weeks of winter. He will not expect that."

"But you have told our allies that it is to be spring."

I smiled at Hogan, "And I am telling the only four men whom I trust that it will be earlier. We will tell King Fiachnae mac Báetáin a week before we need him and we will tell King Cadwallon when the attack begins."

"You do not trust Cadwallon?"

"Of course but I still worry about Mercia and the spies in Cadwallon's court. Penda will be here a month after Yule. I need him here early in case he has any treacherous tendencies. We can control this fortress. This way we leave Gwynedd with as much protection as possible and continue the illusion that we advance up the east coast. Even if there are no spies in Cadwallon's court there will be spies in Lindsey and the borders of Gwynedd. By keeping the men there until the last possible moment we give us the best chance."

"But that means attacking with just our men and King Fiachnae mac Báetáin's."

"Yes. We use speed and the fact that we have the finest army on this island. You said yourself, Hogan Lann, the Hibernians are brave and wild. They also move with the speed of the wind over the land. We will fall upon them before they know we are over the mountains."

## Saxon Bane

Myrddyn stood and stretched. "I need to research some of the maps." He looked pointedly at Gawan.

Gawan had a mind as sharp as any, "I will come then wizard so that you may impart some more of your arcane knowledge."

"And hopefully you will have improved since our last lesson."

Myrddyn had been subtle. He had left so that Hogan Lann and I could speak. "This will be my last campaign as Warlord." As soon as the words were out I regretted the way I had delivered them. His face showed both shock and concern in equal measure.

"You are not unwell, are you? Lann Aelle had said you were behaving strangely."

I smiled to show that all was well. "No, of course not but in Hibernia and Mercia I found my leg caused me pain and restricted my movements. When I fought Calum he was alone and had a weak weapon. When I fought Oswald's men they were poorly armed and ill-prepared. What happens in Northumbria when I come up against some of Edwin's oathsworn?"

"You can stay towards the rear. We will fight at the fore."

"That is what I mean; if I am there then I will have to lead. The Warlord must be the one who faces the enemy. If I am Warlord then I must put myself in danger."

"Then do not be Warlord. I will take over now."

There was decision in his voice and in his eyes. I shook my head. "No, for this is my alliance. It is the last alliance I shall make as Warlord but I must lead. King Fiachnae mac Báetáin will expect it as will Penda and Cadwallon. I am the one they spoke with and it was my word and hand that they took. You can see it can you not?"

He nodded slowly, "That does not mean I have to like it."

"Then you must become me." He cocked his head to one side quizzically. "All I shall do for this winter is play with my grandchildren see more of my wife and plan for the war against Northumbria. Everything else is in your hands. You will forge closer links with the captains and other leaders. You will send Aedh out to scout the terrain. You will be Warlord."

"What of the others? How will they take the news?"

"Why are you afraid of a rival?"

"No, of course not but…"

I could see that he did not want to be seen to be usurping me. "Very well; when we have the next meeting of the captains I will tell them of my decision. I will insist that they keep the secret for if it were to get out then it might encourage our enemies to begin to move against us." I added, "It is right that the men we lead know what we do."

He looked happy and gazed out towards the west. Suddenly his head whipped around and I saw his gaze fall upon Saxon Slayer which lay on a stool. "And the sword?"

"The sword does not belong to me. It belongs to the Warlord. When you become Warlord then you take the sword and I shall learn how to tend a garden and bounce children on my knee."

He looked at the sword reverently. "And I will care for it as though it were my child."

Of course, I told Myfanwy. That was only right. Her reaction was predictable. "And about time too. Why not now? Do you not trust your son?"

"Don't be silly, woman." I then gave all the reasons I had given to Hogan Lann.

She nodded her approval. "It makes sense and you might end up a cripple."

"What do you mean? I am not a cripple yet?"

"No, but I have seen you struggle with your leg in the morning and when it is wet and when it is cold. Your body says it is time to give up the way of the sword. It is just your heart which cannot hear."

We held the meeting the week before Yule. They all knew that something was in the air. This was especially true as Myrddyn had disappeared into the mountain with some slaves. This time I had an idea what they were about but the effect was to make the air in the room heady with anticipation. They did not know what the pronouncement would be but they knew it would be important. I thought back to the day when King Urien had announced my appointment as Warlord. I had never thought to hand on the title. I had thought to die defending Rheged.

The family members of the council, Hogan Lann, Gawan, Lann Aelle and Morcar all sat together. The older captains like Aedh and Tuanthal sat together while the younger ones formed the third group. They were not in factions but they were with those with whom they were most comfortable.

"Friends and those closest to me, I have brought you here to make an announcement. When we have fought Edwin and conquered Northumbria." There was a cheer from the younger captains and Morcar. "When they are no longer a threat then I will give Saxon Slayer and the title of Warlord to my son Hogan Lann."

Both Hogan and I were gratified by the cheers, the applause and the general good atmosphere of the room. However, I had had my eyes watching all of them and there was one who was not happy. There was one whose praise was muted. I had the winter to worry about that reaction and to try to get to the bottom of it.

Saxon Bane

# Chapter 11

As this was our last Yule I hoped to make it one to remember. Lann Aelle and Morcar returned to their families but Hogan Lann and Gawan brought theirs to stay. Myfanwy made much of it. She was determined to impress the two women my sons had married. Everything was cleaned and polished. She had ordered, through Carac, new bowls from Frankia. She had spent a small fortune on spices from Constantinopolis. For many days before the festival, she had the cooks and the slaves working every hour. Even Brother Oswald and Carac became enlisted.

Carac proved to be the most useful. It turned out he had skills as a cook and Myfanwy came to depend upon him. Delbchaem, in contrast, proved to be obstinate and refused to help at all. She had been recently given a puppy by Lann Aelle, a descendant of the original Wolf. She had named him Lupus and just wanted to play with him. When she refused to help Myfanwy I was called upon as mediator. This time, however, my efforts proved to be in vain. Delbchaem was sent to her room and forbidden to leave it. I could have told my wife that was no punishment for she was able to play with the puppy. She had won. Sometimes you had to step away from the problem.

The day of the Yule feast dawned cold and icy. Snow fell on Wyddfa and we did not mind. We had fires roaring and Brother Oswald's hypocaust kept us all warm. Whilst the women were helping Myfanwy and Carac to finish the preparations for Yule I went to my solar with my sons. This might be the last Yule I would spend on this earth and I wanted them to remember it.

As we sipped our favourite Lusitanian wine I took out two small boxes. I gave one to each of them.

"What is this?"

"Just a little something. I am pleased with the way that you have both grown this year and the duties you have taken on. I am proud of you."

## Saxon Bane

Even as I said the words they sounded stiff and formal to me. I had tried to be casual but failed.

They opened the boxes. I had had a fine dagger made for them. I had sent to the mines further south for the blue stones we prized so much and had them cut for the hilts. They were fine pieces. In the box, too, were two identical stones.

"The spare stones are for you to use." I shrugged, "Perhaps on your swords, or scabbards. I don't know. It seemed a good idea when I put them in but now I do not know."

They both rose and embraced me. Hogan Lann grinned at Gawan. "I will have one put in my sword and work out if I ought to give the other to my wife."

Gawan nodded, "I will keep both of mine until I can think of a suitable mount." He held up the dagger. "This is beautiful work father."

"The blades came from Iberia. They have ways there, of toughening the metal. I am not sure how good they are at swords but their daggers are excellent."

We talked of weapons until a servant came for us. "The domina says the food is getting cold."

I knew that it was not. My wife would want us at the table long before the food was served. "We will come." I shook my head. "Are your wives the same?"

Hogan Lann nodded, "Identical and we would not have it any other way."

When we reached the hall I could see that there had been words. Delbchaem was seated alone, stroking her dog. Myfanwy glared at me. I confess I had had one too many goblets of wine else I would have thought about my words.

"Your daughter is willful and disobedient!"

I noticed that when she was in trouble Delbchaem was always my daughter. I sighed, "What has she done now?"

"She insists upon having that animal in the hall while we eat!"

"That animal, as you call him, is my best friend and if Lupus cannot be here then I shall leave too."

## Saxon Bane

This was my last Yule and I wanted it to be a harmonious one. "No one is leaving. The dog will behave or I will throw it out myself!" I suddenly realised that I was shouting.

Hogan Lann put his arm around my shoulder. "I am sure the dog and my little sister will behave." He gave a wink and Delbchaem smiled. She had a real soft spot for my eldest son.

Myfanwy snorted and said, "Well let us sit then and we can eat!"

The meal was not turning out as I had hoped. Hogan Lann and I sat on either side of Delbchaem. That way we could control both her and the dog. Carac led the servants in with the food. Brother Oswald followed and took his place next to Myrddyn and my wife. Carac ladled out the food. It smelled delicious. We were about to tuck in when Brother Oswald said, "I know that this is a pagan home but at this time of year we celebrate the birth of the White Christ. Would it be possible, Warlord, for me to bless this food? It will not offend your gods or Wyddfa I promise you."

I caught the sight out of the corner of my eye of Delbchaem slipping a large piece of meat to Lupus. If her mother had seen it then it would have led to another row. I looked at Myfanwy and she nodded.

"Very well Brother Oswald but do not expect to convert us!"

"I gave up on that long ago, Warlord." He stood and put his hands together. "Oh Lord, bless this food that we eat and make us grateful for the food on the table and a fire in the hearth. Amen."

He looked at me questioningly. I smiled, "You are right, priest, that would offend no one. Now can we eat?"

Before we could start Lupus began howling and biting at himself. He threw himself to the ground and began foaming at the mouth and then he was still. Delbchaem screamed. I could see Myfanwy getting angry and I held up my hand. "Myrddyn, come and look at the dog."

He shook his head, "I heal humans and not animals!"

"Myrddyn!"

Something in my tone must have alerted him and he raced to the dog. He sniffed its mouth. The pool of white foam lay next to it. He went to the fire and took an unburned twig. He dipped it in the foam and sniffed it. "Arsenicum! The dog has been poisoned!"

Delbchaem began to point at Myfanwy and then Hogan Lann said to her. "You gave the dog some meat did you not?"

Her expression changed to one of horror as she nodded. I took a dagger and speared a piece of meat. I put it on the bread platter. Myrddyn sniffed the meat. "This has been heavily spiced but I smell something beneath the spice. Let us go to the kitchens."

Leaving the women with the children we went to the kitchens where the servants were preparing the next course. Brother Oswald said, "Where is Carac? He prepared the wild boar did he not?"

One of the cooks said, fearfully, "Aye Brother Oswald. We browned the meat and prepared the vegetables and then he laboured with the spices my lady sent for."

I looked around. "Where is he?"

The cooks and servants looked around. "He was here until just before you arrived."

Brother Oswald paled, "There may be a rational explanation."

Myrddyn shook his head, "Or, more likely, Carac is another Northumbrian spy sent to kill us all in one fell swoop."

I know there was no evidence but it made perfect sense to me. "Find him!" We all left the kitchens. We would give him the opportunity to explain but the evidence was damning already.

"Close the gates!" At Yule, we kept the gates open for any unfortunate who was without food and shelter. The guards looked down at me. "I said close the gates. No one leaves!"

I moved as quickly as I could to the main gate. "What is wrong, Warlord?"

"Has anyone left here in the last hour or so, Gruffydd?"

"No, my lord."

"Go around to the other gates and find out if anyone has left."

Suddenly I heard a shout, it was Gawan and he was by the stables. By the time I reached him Hogan Lann was there. They both held their new daggers before them. I saw Carac with his back to the wall. In his hands, he held a spear. "Come near me and you die!"

I did not doubt that we could overpower him but I did not want to risk either of my sons being hurt. Brother Oswald huffed and puffed his way in. "Why Carac? Did we mistreat you?"

"You foolish old man! You were so easy to dupe. Did you really think I had to go to the port every single week! The worst part was having to listen to you sing the praises of this family of murderers and killers."

Hogan Lann stepped forward. "You cannot escape you know. Every gate is closed and there are five of us here."

He nodded. I was warned by his evil little smile that he was about to do something. In a blur, he hurled the spear at me. I managed to fall to the side and it flew over my shoulder. As I fell I saw Hogan Lann and Gawan race to him but before they reached him he put something in his mouth and swallowed. His face contorted and he fell to the ground even as my sons reached him. He began to foam at the mouth and then he was still.

Myrddyn knelt down. "We knew already but this confirms it. He used the poison to kill himself."

Brother Oswald dropped to his knees and began to weep, "I am sorry, Warlord. Your family nearly died and it would have been my fault."

I shook my head and raised him up, "We were all taken in and had you not said that blessing then we might all be dead. You saved my family, priest and we are grateful."

"Aye old man, it was not your fault." Hogan Lann kicked the dead body. "This murderer was sent by Aethelfrith's sons. We need to be even more vigilant and watch for the spy in our midst.

When we returned to the hall I was expecting it to be full of tension. I was more than pleasantly surprised when I saw Myfanwy cuddling my weeping daughter. The death of the dog somehow brought them closer together. Something good came from the death of that innocent creature.

When we had time to talk we realised that our plan would now be in the hands of the brothers. The question was how would they use it? I decided to attack sooner rather than later and hope to catch them off balance.

All was well in place for our attack by the time the last of wintery storms had ended. When the snow disappeared from the foothills then we knew that spring was not far off. Brother Oswald had worked tirelessly to acquire all of the weapons we would need. Since Yule, he had worked every hour that there was in an attempt to make up for his assistant's murderous attempt on our lives. We knew that we had to have the best arms and armour for we would be outnumbered. Gawan had prepared Kay and he and his contingent left for Rheged while winter still gripped the land. We had decided to send our armies little by little. There may be other Caracs and this way would lessen suspicion.

I selected Gawan to be the one to tell Fiachnae mac Báetáin of our new plan. His brother had already met the king and it was important that both of my sons understood our ally. Daffydd took all the ships we could acquire so that he could start to ferry his men across and Gawan could secure the landing site. Gawan had already blocked up, with stones, many of the gates from the north. If Dál Riata tried to take advantage of our attack then they would, at least, be slowed down. Pol visited with King Cadwallon and told him of our changed plans and he returned to our fort at Deva with Penda and his men.

I was already there with the rest of our army and Penda was intrigued with the changes we had wrought. "I remember when we held this. We had thought it good enough as it was but you have made it impregnable."

Hogan Lann, who had done most of the work, nodded modestly. "All we did was clear and deepen the ditches and put a few bolt throwers on the walls."

"And I have seen those before now. They care not for the courage of a warrior. I watched one bolt carry four men to the Otherworld."

"Aye, Penda, the Romans were a clever people."

There were just four of us walking the walls. Myrddyn had joined the three of us. "But tell me, Mercian, how do you see yourself?"

Penda turned round as though Myrddyn had read his mind. I knew the feeling. "What do you mean, wizard?"

## Saxon Bane

Myrddyn shrugged as though the comment was not important but I could see from his eyes that it was. "Are you a Saxon, a Briton or a Mercian?"

He seemed to quail beneath Myrddyn's searching gaze. "I would have Mercia be the dominant Saxon kingdom."

"And what of Gwynedd and Rheged?"

All three of us stared at Penda now. Although Hogan Lann and I knew how to read a man we both knew that Myrddyn would know if he lied. "Cymru and Rheged are not the kinds of land my people seek. We like flat lands and the mountains frighten us. There are spirits within them. Icaunus is our god."

When Myrddyn nodded then I knew that he was satisfied. "I think that we can work together when this is finished. I believe we both have a single aim. We both wish to defeat Northumbria."

Hogan Lann smiled, "Just for different reasons." He looked at Penda. Although they were of an age my son towered over the Mercian. "And then we will see what kind of neighbours we are."

Penda stared back at Hogan Lann and they both nodded at each other. That was the moment I realised that Hogan Lann would be a powerful Warlord. I could go to the Otherworld knowing I had left the kingdom in safe hands. The Rheged royal family might be a memory but the Warlord would still protect the people.

The fort at Deva was big enough to house all of our men but the horses grazed outside on the fertile grass which surrounded it. Although still winter there was enough food to ensure they would make the journey north to Wide Water and not suffer too badly. This had been another reason why I had wanted an earlier start than we had planned; not only would it prevent news of our attack from leaking out it would also mean we had recovery time when we reached the wall.

King Cadwallon came to see us off. It was like watching my son and his equites as he and his bodyguard galloped up. He only had twenty such warriors but they were all dressed the same and all sported the dragon on their shields. They reminded me of Prince Pasgen and his riders of Rheged.

## Saxon Bane

All of the captains and even Penda bowed to the young king. Whatever we did would be in his name. The Northumbrians had clerics who wrote down what they did, chroniclers, they would not write down that Lord Lann the Warlord led the men of Rheged to make war on Northumbria. They would write that King Cadwallon of Gwynedd led the men of Britain to oust the invader and that suited me. I did this for Rheged and not for me.

He grasped me to his chest. He was no longer the frail youth I had trained to be a warrior; he was a powerful leader who was as big as Hogan Lann. "Are you sure you wish to take this risk? Already Edwin is moving men towards the old Roman forts which lie south of the Dunum. As soon as I move my army towards his border he will take the bait."

"That is why this is not the risk you think it is. His eye will be fixed on the east and the south. It will not be his best warriors whom we face. I will send messengers when you are to leave. Remember to leave enough men to protect your borders. King Cearl might be a man of his word but King Raedwald is a supporter of Edwin." I lowered my voice so that only he could hear. "I have learned from Penda that they fear our forts. Have your ditches deepened and they will fear you."

"I will and I will see you again, on the Wall."

We headed up the Roman Road which led north. There were neither towns nor settlements on the route we took, just isolated farms and houses. The people of this land led a lonely existence. They were not Saxons and they were not Britons. They were survivors. Armies and dynasties came and went and they eked out a living. They were to be admired. As I watched Hogan Lann and Penda talking to each other at the head of the column I realised this could not have happened a few years ago. Even last year it would have been unthinkable. The dream in the cave had, indeed, begun an avalanche of change.

Myrddyn rode next to me. I had missed him in the depths of winter when he had been in the tomb. "Were you not cold in the cave?"

He shook his head. "It was as warm as my room in the fort. The men who worked there with me were happy to be there out of the wind, snow and rain. And you, Lann," he had lowered his voice although the warriors assigned by Pol to protect me kept a decent distance, "how is your mind?"

"My mind?"

"I know that my news upset you and it changed you a little. The attempt on your family could not have helped. Now you seem a little more like your old self."

"It was a shock but, as you say, I am over that particular obstacle. All men die and I have lived longer than most. My father, Aideen, King Urien, Pasgen and Raibeart all died without saying goodbye. What made me think that I would be different? The change you see is that I know what I must do before my time." I nodded at the guards. "You didn't say anything to Hogan Lann, did you? These guards are a new addition."

"No, I said nothing but you have given him more responsibility. Perhaps he has second sight too."

"Perhaps."

We were approaching the river called the Lune and I saw some movement at the front of the column. I spurred Mona on. She was not a warhorse but she was a good travelling mount. I reached Hogan Lann as Aedh was reporting to him. He turned to look at me as I approached but I gave him an irritated shake of the head. Until we reached the Saxons this would be Hogan Lann's column to lead.

"We have found a defended settlement. It is on the other side of the river on a low bluff overlooking the estuary. It guards the crossing."

Hogan Lann looked at me and Lann Aelle who had joined us. "We have to eliminate this threat. Even if we could get by them they would send word to King Edwin."

They all looked at me. I sighed and said, wearily, "I agree. It needs only Bors and Daffydd."

Hogan Lann grinned. "We are of one mind Warlord. Bors, take fifty of your men and fifty of Daffydd's. Aedh, take your scouts and stop any escaping from the settlement."

As Aedh turned to leave I said, "I will accompany you Aedh. I need to get a feel for war again."

They all stared at me. "But you have no need, father."

## Saxon Bane

"I know and that is why I will do it. You do not think me too old do you, son?"

He gave me a rueful smile. I had outfoxed him again. "No, Warlord, just be careful."

"Of course and I will not need your warriors, Aedh and his men are more than enough protection for an old man." I saw the scouts sit a little straighter in their saddles. Praise was never wasted.

Morcar kicked his horse forward. "No, Morcar. I need no banner. You remain with Myrddyn. Lead on Aedh, I will try to keep up."

We headed upstream. It was a pleasant wooded valley and I could see the attraction of the site they had chosen. I rode next to Aedh. We did not ride quickly. Although Daffydd had his archers mounted, Bors and his men were afoot.

Aedh pointed upstream. "We found a ford and we will cross there."

"Does the settlement have a palisade?"

"Aye Warlord, and a ditch too. It looks to have been built on the site of a Roman fort."

When we had travelled south to settle in Gwynedd we had not touched the coast. We had kept to a route away from all roads and settlements. Prince Pasgen and his people had been a powerful force when they had left for Rheged. They would not have been bothered by one fort. We had to destroy it.

The water was icy and came up to my knees. Bors and his men would have a soaking. I knew they would curse the fool who ordered them through the water. They would have mail to clean and oil when this day was over. I lifted Saxon Slayer and its magnificent scabbard above my head. I could, at least, keep my weapon dry.

We waited on the river bank as Bors and his men struggled across. The archers helped them and many of Bors' men hung on to the saddles of the archers. It made life a little easier.

We spent a short time drying off and tightening girths on saddles. Aedh pointed downstream. "The village is just three miles down the river." He did not insult either captain by telling them how they ought to tackle the walls. "We will spread ourselves out east of the walls. We will pick up any who try to escape."

Bors snorted, "Then you will have little to do for none will escape."

Bors looked like a younger version of his father Mungo. He was the biggest warrior in my army and like his father, before him, he carried the mighty war hammer favoured by the men of Strathclyde. It looked like a child's toy in his mighty hand.

"Do not be overconfident Bors. The spirits are watching!"

He looked suitably abashed. "Sorry, Warlord."

When a hundred warriors had left us we looked like a pitiful handful. There were just twenty of us in total and I was the only one in armour. I was not worried. Aedh and his scouts were amongst the best warriors I had. They could hide in plain sight, ride faster than any and find tracks on rocks. When it came to fighting they could kill silently and against great odds. They had no armour but they had skill and speed. I was not afraid of any Northumbrians who might come our way.

Aedh held his hand up. I smiled. It was not for his men it was for me. I dismounted and we walked up a dome-shaped piece of ground. Aedh circled his hand and four men took the reins of the horses and led them away from the skyline. The rest of the scouts bellied up to the edge of the low rise. There, some eight hundred paces away, was the settlement. We were able to look down on it and see everything.

It was larger than I had thought. The gates were open and the Northumbrians were not expecting trouble. I saw some stables, recognisable by the horses being attended to outside. It looked to me as though there might be two hundred people living there. I wondered why until I saw the cross on the top of the building. It was a church of the White Christ. Then it struck me that this was a smaller version of St.Asaph. This was a monastery. The supporters of the White Christ were very sociable and liked to gather around their crosses.

Aedh drew my attention to my advancing men. The archers and Bors' warriors were filtering up through the trees which lined the river. They were heading for the open gate. I saw twenty archers and warriors detach themselves and head north towards the northern gate. We were too far to

## Saxon Bane

hear anything but we watched as Daffydd's archers took out the warriors who were on the walls. Bors led the charge to the gate and we saw a furious battle ensue as the defenders tried to close the gates. It was futile and the huddle of Northumbrian bodies in the gateway told their own story.

Aedh said, "Let's get mounted." He pointed to the northern gate. The warriors had not reached it in time and eight men rode out.

I clambered onto Mona's back. I took my shield from my saddle and put it over my left arm. There had been a time when I could have done that in a moment when dictated by action. Now I needed to be prepared.

Aedh led the line of scouts to cut off the Northumbrians. We were hidden below the skyline although Aedh could still see them. I took my place at the end of the line. Aedh and his men knew what they were doing. I was just becoming familiar with combat once more.

We dropped into a dell and then, as we galloped up the other side I saw the Northumbrians. They were just a hundred paces from Aedh. The Saxons were better armed but Aedh and his men had a variety of weapons. As I watched, Aedh drew a javelin and hurtled towards the leading rider. It seemed that they had not seen us until that moment. I watched as panic set in. The first four riders tried to turn north. Two wheeled their horses around to head back to the fort but it was the last two who attracted my attention. They both jerked their horses' heads around and headed for the rear of our line. Most of Aedh's men were riding swiftly and the move caught them by surprise. The scout in front of me hurled his javelin but he hurried his throw and he missed. The two warriors aimed their horses at him. He drew his sword to defend himself but the force of their attack threw him to the ground.

As soon as I had seen them I had drawn Saxon Slayer and, even as the scout was falling to the ground, I was swinging my sword. I launched Mona at the nearest rider. I slashed down and the razor-sharp edge of Saxon Slayer sliced through his arm close to the elbow. He involuntarily jerked his mount's head around and they fell to the earth in an untidy heap.

## Saxon Bane

The other rider spurred his horse and it leapt away. Mona was no warhorse but she was one of the best horses we had and I allowed her to open her legs. She began to eat up the ground. The Saxon had a head start and I think he hoped to be able to outrun me. I was the only one close enough to catch him for Aedh and his scouts were busily chasing the other Northumbrians.

The ground was undulating. On the downhill sections, the Saxon held his lead but Mona's strength paid off on the uphill sections and each rise brought me closer and closer to the Northumbrian. I saw that he wore a full helmet and was wearing mail as I was. I saw that his sword was a typical Saxon sword, it was short and broad. If he fought me I would have the advantage of length.

I saw his bearded face as he turned to gauge the distance. He must have seen that I was alone and would soon catch him. We reached the top of a rise and he turned his horse to face me. I wondered as I tightened my shield if he had ever fought from the back of a horse before. It was not as easy as it might have looked. When he swung his sword at me I knew that he had not. His swing almost took his horse's head off. I nudged Mona forward and she pushed against the Northumbrian's mount. His was a horse for riding. It had not been trained as well as Mona.

I swung my sword overhand and brought it down onto his shield. There was a loud crack and I saw a long sliver of wood slip from the middle. He had learned his lesson and he brought his sword around in a long sweep as he attempted to do the same thing to my shield. Mine was a well-made shield and he looked in horror as his sword banged into my leather coated shield and made not a mark. I kicked hard again and Mona pushed forward. He was finding it hard to control both his horse and his shield. I saw the gap and stabbed forwards. My blade punched into his mail. Some of the mail rings cracked and the tip struck his leather byrnie. He tumbled backwards from his horse.

I dismounted, somewhat awkwardly I must confess. I noticed that his horse ran away but Mona just stood patiently waiting for my command. The Northumbrian struggled to his feet. He had held on to his sword and his shield was still attached by his shoulder strap. He was a young warrior and he must have seen my greybeard as an invitation to finish me off swiftly. The fact was that I was not as mobile as I had been but I knew I was a better swordsman with a superior weapon.

He launched himself at me, hitting my shield with a flurry of blows. All he succeeded in doing was blunting his own weapon. I allowed him to waste his energy and, when he paused to get his breath I sliced horizontally at his shield. There was already a vertical crack going from the boss and when Saxon Slayer struck another chip flew from his shield and a second crack appeared. His defence was weakening.

He changed his attack and began aiming for my head. My Byzantine helmet was the best that there was and the inner padded leather cap also gave me protection. Even so, I blocked his first blow with my shield. He feinted for his next blow. I anticipated that he would try to hit my sword arm and I parried it with Saxon Slayer. I felt his arm shiver as tiny fragments of metal flew from his blade. I was tiring now and I needed to end this. As he closed with me a second time I hit his shield with all of my strength. The shield shattered into two pieces leaving him holding the boss in his left hand. I did not give him time to recover and I head-butted him with my helmet. I heard the crack as his nose broke and he fell to the ground. He was helpless and I skewered him through the neck. He bled his life away on that hillside still wondering how an old man had got the better of him.

I heard hooves behind me as Aedh and four of his riders rode up. Aedh was grinning. "That is a silver piece you owe me Dai."

I saw a warrior throw a coin to Aedh. "What is that all about?"

"I bet Dai here that you would not only catch your Saxon but kill him too."

"How is the young warrior who was hit?"

"He is more embarrassed than anything. He has a broken arm and hurt pride. He will be relieved that you live still. He, too, was convinced that you had gone to the Otherworld."

I mounted Mona which Dai held for me. "Not yet, Aedh, not yet."

Saxon Bane

# Chapter 12

When we reached the settlement the bodies were being placed on a pyre for burning. As I had hoped our attack had caught them by surprise and no word had got out of our presence. The ones I had pursued had been the only ones to escape. There were prisoners; most of them were Northumbrian. I had Bors assemble a party of warriors who had been slightly wounded and they would escort them to Deva and then return north.

There were, however, six others who had been enslaved by the Northumbrians. Two of them were older women whose husbands had farmed to the north and their menfolk had died at the hands of the invaders. Four of them were young women three of whom had come from Rheged but one, Morgause, had been taken from Mona during one of their raids. She had been cruelly treated by both the Northumbrians and the other women. I wondered why for she was stunningly beautiful with hair the colour of a sunset over Mona.

My attention was drawn to her by Morcar who had found her cowering in a hut, fearful for her life. "We should return her to our home, Warlord. My mother could take her in and look after her."

It was a thoughtful gesture. "You are right nephew. She can return to Deva with Bors' men."

"No! She will be mistreated. You cannot let a young girl be alone with warriors. She can accompany us. She is a healer too."

Myrddyn suddenly took an interest. "How do you know?"

"She told me. She knows about herbs and the remedies from Mother Earth."

Myrddyn always had a soft spot for the followers of the Mother cult. Some called them witches and perhaps that explained why the others did not like her. "She may be useful. An extra healer is always welcome."

## Saxon Bane

"Very well but you two look out for her. I have no time for distractions."

Morcar looked delighted. It was as though someone had brought him a puppy. Morgause, for her part, was also overjoyed and the two became inseparable. They were good for each other and Lann Aelle and I noticed the difference in our relative. He was now more like the Morcar before the abduction.

We pushed on north. The other former captives would be returned to their homes. They came from the area just south of Wide Water, on the coast. I had never visited there but they told Hogan Lann that the river which flowed from Wide Water finished by their village. We decided that it might be a better way to Kay's fort at the head of the lake. We reached their village as the sun began to set and the rain started to fall. The villagers withdrew, fearfully, behind their flimsy walls. They would not have withstood an attack. Hogan Lann showed his qualities when he persuaded them that we were friends and we were welcomed. We did not eat their food for we had brought our own. We knew that these people lived a hand to mouth existence. We did however learn much about the people there.

They were the last remnants of the people who had followed Prince Pasgen north. Whilst the equites who had survived had join Kay at Wide Water the rest of the men had taken to farming, hunting and fishing. Some of the older men came up to me and told me that they had served with me on the island of Mona and in the early campaigns. It made me feel my age for all the ones who did so were old men fit only for mending nets and herding cattle.

Prince Pasgen's dream had been ended not by the sword but by disease and that was not the way a warrior should die.

The rain made the journey up the river valley an unpleasant experience but we knew that we only had a few hours of discomfort before we would be in Kay's fort. He had been warned of our imminent arrival by Aedh's scouts and we hoped that would ensure comfort, for a few hours at least.

## Saxon Bane

I noticed that Myrddyn now travelled with Morcar and Morgause. He seemed quite taken with the young girl. If it had been anyone else I would have said that he was attracted to her but Myrddyn was like the priests of the White Christ and did not think of such things. It was her mind and her skills which appealed to him. He quickly discovered that she truly was a healer. She even had one or two potions of which he was unaware.

Morcar was definitely attracted to her and I think the feeling was mutual. It was good to see my nephew regaining his humour. I rode at the fore of the column now with Hogan Lann and Lann Aelle.

"It seems Morcar is smitten eh?"

Lann Aelle chuckled, "He is, Hogan Lann. Perhaps coming back to Rheged will return the warrior we lost in Hibernia."

I nodded to Hogan Lann. "Hogan was abducted as was Cadwallon. It did not make them morose."

"Do not be hard on our cousin father, we are all different warriors. I knew that my father would find me. Morcar's father was not there for him."

Perhaps they were right. I was being a little hard on Morcar. He was a man but a young man. He had not had the training that these two had. I decided that I would make allowances for him. But I had looked into his heart and it worried me.

Kay had grown in stature since he had come north. He had been the reason we had returned to Rheged. He had told Prince Pasgen that the people of Rheged still yearned for their own ruler. Sadly that had not lasted long for Prince Pasgen and the devastating plague they had suffered had hit Kay and his warriors too. I was pleased with his greeting. There was genuine relief that the Warlord had returned.

He knelt before me. "We have long waited for this day, Warlord." I raised him to his feet and his face looked anxious. "You will be staying?"

"I promise you that we are returned and we will hold what we take." He suddenly saw Penda and his Mercians. He frowned. "These are friends, Kay. These are allies, Mercians and not Northumbrians."

## Saxon Bane

Kay shook his head, "Strange times are come to pass then." He waved his arm behind him. "Where are my manners? Your quarters are prepared and we have a feast for you. There is a field yonder for your men and their mounts. We cannot accommodate them within our walls."

The feast was a lively one. The men of Wide Water were lucky. There was plenty of game and fish, even in winter. The only thing they wanted was grain but, as we ate that night, Kay told me that some farmers had begun to sow rye in the northern valley just beyond the fort. "Soon we will rival Mona for its bread."

"Good. We will leave on the morrow and meet Gawan and the Hibernians."

"I will bring some of my men."

I looked at him in surprise. "You do not need to. I know that the plague killed many warriors."

"This is our land. If we allow you to fight for us then it will be as it was before you returned. We should own the defence of our land or we are not men. I will leave Wide Water well defended but we will bring a hundred warriors." He smiled and toasted Penda. "If the Saxons and the Hibernians fight for us then our people should too. This land is worth fighting for! We will not lose it a second time"

The feast was the first occasion where our men had supped together and it surprised me how well it went. Hogan Lann and I had worried that it would result in drunken fights which might disrupt the harmony of the army. It did not and warriors found that they had much in common. I thanked the spirits again for their advice.

Perhaps the gods had watched our celebration for they gave us a sunny morning as we headed north for Civitas Carvetiorum. The first part was as hard as I remembered as we snaked our way along narrow passes with precipitous drops and threatening rock falls. However, it brought back the happy memories of serving King Urien and holding back the first invasions of the Saxons.

Penda commented on the land. "I see why it appeals to your people. You tend sheep and you like mountains. I cannot understand why the Northumbrians are willing to bleed for it."

Hogan Lann smiled, "Oh we have made them bleed over the years and that is why they are a little more cautious these days."

Our horsemen reached Civitas Carvetiorum before dark. Gawan had left a small garrison of twenty men and we were welcomed. It was very late when the weary spearmen dragged themselves into its walls and collapsed into the barracks which had been there since the time of the Romans. The bright sunny day had turned into a chilly night and we were all grateful for a roof over our heads.

Aedh and his scouts left early the next day to await Gawan at the estuary. Myrddyn and I left the others to find Osric's cell. We had hidden there before now when threatened by Saxons and so it was a place of safety for us both. More than that, it was the depository for all things valuable. We went alone for we knew where the secret chamber lay. Brothers Osric and Oswald had told us that it went back to the time of the Romans and that the legions based there had secured their treasures in its vaults. We used them now, ourselves. When we discovered a fort we looked for the secret vault and used it. We had treasure in every Roman fort we found. Hogan Lann would be given that knowledge when he became Warlord.

I had not been here in many years. I was not sure if Prince Pasgen had taken anything from it. I left Pol to guard the door and then we opened the secret door leading to the chamber. Myrddyn had a candle and it flickered in the musty subterranean air. There were four large chests and one smaller one with a carving of one of King Urien's equites upon its lid. I did not remember seeing it before. We lifted the small one out, for it was locked and then opened the larger boxes. The first contained bracelets, jewels and torcs. Some looked ancient and some looked Saxon. They were worth a fortune. The second one was filled with gold and silver coins. Many of them had the heads of Roman Emperors upon them. The final chest had the biggest surprises within. There were maps, all written in Osric's hand, and plans for weapons like the ballista and onager.

Myrddyn chuckled. "Osric had more foresight than any man I ever knew."

## Saxon Bane

We clambered out and dusted ourselves down. Myrddyn examined the small box. It was locked. He stroked his beard and then reached into his satchel. He had various keys. He tried them one by one. The third one worked and it popped open. Inside there were the bones of a hand, a ring and a folded piece of calfskin. Myrddyn carefully took out the calfskin and laid it on the table. He unfolded it as though it might tear. We both saw the signature at the bottom and looked at each other. Osric was speaking with us.

*I write this record knowing that my death is close at hand. I have served my masters well: I devoted my life to God, I helped King Coel and King Urien to protect the frontier and I kept alive the Roman ways. I have done my duty.*

*To that end, I have hidden the treasure of Rheged in the old Roman fortress of Luguvalium. The map will help someone to find it. I believe that God will direct some unborn hand to this end. I have buried it with St. Brigid's hand and ring as a way of telling the finder of the treasure. If the hand is not with this map then the barbarians have won and the treasure of Rheged is lost forever.*

*I go to God with a clear conscience,*

*Osric of Rheged*

"But why, Myrddyn, did he leave the small casket here? Surely it should be somewhere else ready to lead the finder here."
"He must have died before he could do so but we can hide it for him." Myrddyn searched around for some ink and a scribe.
"What are you doing?"

"Osric is not the only one who can tell the future. Find me some calfskin. Osric always kept some hidden about the place."

I rummaged around the drawers and cupboards which had been torn open by thieves hoping to find treasure. They had not known how close they were to a treasure greater than any other. I found a few pieces of usable skin and returned to Myrddyn.

"Good, now while I write I want you to go into the chamber and bring up enough coins to fit in this. Make sure it is a mixture of all types." He handed me a leather purse.

I was not sure what he was up to but I knew him well enough to trust him. By the time I returned he had finished. He held up the second piece of calfskin and it looked identical to the first. "Why have you made a copy?"

"Read it and you will see it is not an exact copy."

*I write this record knowing that my death is close at hand. I have served my masters well: I devoted my life to God, I helped King Coel and King Urien to protect the frontier and I kept alive the Roman ways. I have done my duty.*

*The barbarians are coming and I fear that the Warlord will not be able to hold them back forever. I believe with all my heart that there will come a hero as Lann of Stanwyck came from obscurity to hold back the Angles and the Saxons. It will not be in my lifetime.*

*To that end I have hidden the treasure of Rheged in the old Roman fortress of Luguvalium. The map will help someone to find it. I believe that God will direct some unborn hand to this end. I have buried it with St. Brigid's hand and ring as a way of telling the finder of the treasure. If the hand is not with this map then the barbarians have won and the treasure of Rheged is lost forever. The priests in this church know not what I do and when I return north they will still be none the wiser.*

*The true hero will be from the same stock as Lann of Stanwyck and, in him, is the hope for Britannia.*

*I go to God with a clear conscience,*

*Osric of Rheged*

"Why?"

"I am gambling on the future. I hope that we will win and free Rheged but if not then we know that we will not be here to remedy the situation. Either your son, or one of his children or grandchildren will grow to be a warrior and if he reads this he may see his own destiny."

"But you cannot be sure."

"No, I cannot. Think on this. What have we got to lose? A religious relic, a ring and a bag of coins? It is nothing but if it leads one of your descendants here then he will discover the treasure and that may save the land in the future."

I folded the letter and put it under the bones, the ring and the coins. I closed the box and gave it to Myrddyn. "You will need to guide my sons when I am dead. They will need to know what they must do for their sons. This knowledge must be passed from father to son."

As he took the box Myrddyn said, "I swear that I will watch over our sons and their children so long as I live. And when I die then my spirit will guide them."

"Thank you."

A sudden thought hit me. "And what of my spirit? Shall I be able to guide them?"

"I know not. The spirit is strong in you but perhaps it runs on your mother's side. Your mother was a follower of the Mother cult. That goes back to the Druids and beyond. Perhaps it will be from the mother's side."

"You mean Nanna or Delbchaem."

He nodded, "Or perhaps Hogan Lann's daughter."

"Then they must be told what to do too."

He sighed, "You are giving an old man a great deal of work." There was a twinkle in his eye. He was the one man in the whole world I could trust to watch over my children. He would not let me down.

Pol stared at us when we emerged. "I thought you had gone forever. What did you find to do in such a small room?"

I smiled at Myrddyn, "Save Rheged!"

Saxon Bane

# Chapter 13

Myrddyn took the box and went away to secrete it somewhere safe. I knew he would make sure he placed it in a church where it could be easily found. Hogan Lann and Lann Aelle sought me out. "Perhaps we can go and inspect the work of my son's warriors. Gawan had told me that his warriors had worked hard to block the gates."

All of us were keenly aware that we were in danger of being surrounded if the men Dál Riata decided to fall upon our flank. The three of us took Pol and twenty of his squires as an escort. We did not think that there would be enemies but it paid to be careful.

As we were leaving Penda asked us, "Could I accompany you? I have heard of this mighty wall. I am not sure that I believe it."

I smiled, "It is real but come and see for yourself."

Parts of the wall had fallen into disrepair, especially close to the fort but Gawan's men had made them good. However, they did not look as awe-inspiring as they were closer to the high ground. They were as high as two men and five men could have walked abreast along it. Even so, Penda found the scale of the wall beyond belief. He looked at the mighty structure rolling endlessly eastwards. "Men must have toiled for lifetimes to produce this."

"No, Penda, the legion took less than ten years to build it." I pointed to the blocked up gates. "Those gates were there to allow people through but they were people that Rome wanted. They stopped cattle raids and slave raids. They allowed the Romans to tax all who passed in and out of their lands."

He nodded. "Perhaps I will speak with King Cadwallon. It would be in both of our interests to build such a barrier between our kingdoms."

*Wyrd*! The spirits were moving men's minds. I knew not how they did it. We rode for twenty miles and were happy about the condition of the wall. To save time we came along the Roman military road which ran south of the wall. Once again Penda found himself admiring the work of the Romans.

"I cannot see how they were defeated."

Hogan Lann and Pol had both been in Constantinopolis and knew the story. "The problem lay in the cities which became corrupt and their rulers who became greedy. The soldiers and warriors on the border still fought for their country but they were let down by their leaders."

Penda looked from me to Hogan Lann and back. "I cannot see your leaders ever making that mistake."

I smiled at Hogan Lann. He would not understand my words but once I was dead Myrddyn would explain them. "So long as our blood courses through our veins then Rheged will always have hope."

The first of the ships arrived six days later. It gave us time to recover and to ensure that the horses were fit. It took a day to unload the ships but by the third morning, we were ready to begin our eastward march. Aedh and his scouts left before dawn had even broken. They would operate deep in the heart of the Northumbrian kingdom. Aedh knew it well and no one would find him unless he wanted them to.

Tuanthal's men led followed by the archers, then the spearmen and finally the equites. We had sent the message to King Cadwallon as soon as we had arrived and the day that we set off I knew that he would be heading up the road to join us as soon as he received the message. He had fewer men and would be able to make better time.

Our plan was to reach Hagustald and take that important crossing of the Tineus. That would give us a base from which to delve deeper into Northumbria. At the same time we would send the equites to capture the crossing at Chesters. That was the site of the battle against Aella where Aelle, my brother, had lost his arm. If we held those two crossings then we would divide Northumbria in two. There we would await the arrival of King Cadwallon. We wanted the impact of the flag of Cymru along with the wolf standard and the dragon banner to terrify the Northumbrians. Our numbers were less than the army which King Edwin could field but we hoped to dazzle him with the enemies he would face.

## Saxon Bane

The Mercian standard might be the one which would worry him the most.

Aedh's scouts reported back each day. We had spare horses but I wondered at the endurance of these remarkable horsemen who could ride all day, seemingly without sleep. They reported a small force of Northumbrians at Hagustald guarding the crossing of the river.

We reached Hagustald and Aedh himself met us. He looked exhausted and exultant at the same time. "I rode as far as Din Guardi. Edwin has emptied his land and headed south to face King Cadwallon. The fortress has a skeleton garrison."

I shook my head, "I have been inside that fortress. I could hold it with twenty men."

Morcar chirruped, "Myrddyn could fly us in!"

Everyone laughed but Myrddyn and I knew the truth. That still might aid us. "We will cross that bridge when we come to it. That is two battles away, at least. What of Hagustald?"

"There is a garrison there. No more than forty warriors. There appears to be the beginnings of a church and they are robbing stone from the wall to build it."

"Can it be taken easily?"

Aedh had not been to Constantinopolis but he had a good mind for strategy. "We could take it as we did the monastery on the Lune. We would need to use archers and spearmen."

Daffydd and Bors looked at each other and nodded. Bors said, "Aye, we could do that but are we worried if the word is out about where we are?"

Hogan Lann shook his head. "Now that we are here then the need for secrecy is gone. King Cadwallon will be here in a day or so. If any escape then they will report a couple of hundred archers and spearmen. It will not alarm them. When we strike at Dunelm and Din Guardi then they will know that we are coming but by then it will be too late. It is a long march from the borders of Mercia to here. Remember the Northumbrians do not use horses. They will have to march." He nodded towards me, "The Warlord has thought this through well, Bors, have faith!"

We camped at the old deserted Roman fort they had called Broccolitia. There were no roofs on the buildings but the walls sheltered us from the wind. It was built on little bumps and mounds and Myrddyn chuckled when I commented on that.

"The Roman soldiers had a sense of humour for the name Broccolitia means Badger Holes."

The warriors were all busy preparing themselves for the attack the following day. Although only a couple of hundred of the seven hundred or so warriors we had with us would actually be attacking we all knew that we might have to defend as soon as we had taken the two crossings. We still did not know for certain that Edwin had taken the bait.

I sat with Myrddyn, Morcar and Morgause. I had had little time to talk to the young girl with whom Morcar was besotted. She had prepared the food and I found that she was a good cook. Her skill with herbs and wild plants meant that the mundane meal I had expected was enlivened by strange new tastes. I was a little worried, especially in light of Carac but as she ate at the same time as us my fears were allayed. I was becoming cynical. She was but a young girl.

After we had finished and we sat by the fire listening to the warriors sharpening blades and oiling armour I asked her about her capture. "Tell me Morgause, where did you live on Mona?"

"We lived in a cave above Trearrdur."

I frowned, "That is not far from the fort at the bridge."

She nodded, "We did not bother the warriors and they did not know we were there. My mother did not like men."

"There was just you and your mother then?"

"No, there were two sisters too, Morwenna and Morgana. They were older."

"And how did you come to be taken?"

"We had gone down to the beach at Porthdafarch to collect shellfish at low tide. It was before dawn and the Saxon ship was lying off shore. We did not see the men until it was too late. They silenced us and took us on board their ship."

"The warriors did not see them."

She shook her head. Morcar said, "It sounds to me like they were scouting the defences of the fort."

"I agree and I like it not. When we return I will enforce patrols of the beaches at night. Go on with your story."

"They took us to Hibernia." She hesitated and began to weep uncontrollably.

Myrddyn put his hand about her shoulder and took up the story. "Her mother was abused by the warriors and she threw herself into the sea. The followers of the Mother cult choose when they will have a man. They live apart from men. By forcing her she could not live with herself and by throwing herself into the sea returned to the Mother. Her daughters understood. It is a powerful religion and its roots run deep."

Morgause nodded. "The warriors were shocked and they tied the three of us so that we could not do the same. We were taken to Hibernia and we feared that we would share the same fate but the chief and his brother were kind men and he ordered us to be spared that ordeal. He discovered that we followed the Mother cult and knew that we would be healers for his men. The three of us were sent away. I was sent to the place where you found me and I know not where my sisters went. That was the last day I saw them."

Kind men and Saxons did not appear to go together but I ignored the statement. Perhaps they saw what they expected to see. "When was that?"

"I had been in the village for three summers. The people were afraid of me but more afraid of upsetting their leaders."

This story was becoming more intriguing with each word. "And these Saxons lived in Hibernia?"

"I think it was Hibernia; it was west of Mona for we saw the sun rising to the east and we landed on a beach in the west."

"It could be the island of Manau. We know there were Saxons there."

## Saxon Bane

"Aye Morcar, and they were the followers of Aethelfrith who escaped after Wrecsam." I turned to the girl. "What was the name of the kind man who spared you?"

She shook her head and her eyes filled with tears. She began to become distressed. "I know not, sir. We were only there one night and we were too upset over our mother's death to ask."

"But surely the people in the village you were taken to must have referred to him by name?"

She began to become agitated, "They did not speak to me in the village. They feared me and called me a witch. They only spoke to me of their ailments."

Morcar put his arm around her and cast me a scolding look, "She is upset Warlord! Leave her alone! She has told you all that she knows!"

"I am only trying to discover who this kind Saxon was."

Myrddyn stood and stretched. "It may be a new group of warriors whom we do not know. We will have to wait until we return to Mona to question those we captured."

As we prepared for bed I began to regret sending the captives away so quickly. I had been so keen to head north that I had not questioned the presence on the west coast of a settlement of Saxons. As I lay down to sleep it nagged and gnawed at me. Suppose there was a colony of Saxons on Manau or even in Hibernia; I had left my lands thinly protected assuming that any attack would come from the east. That night my dreams were filled with demons and Saxons who terrorised Mona and I awoke in a sweaty fit well before dawn.

I went to stand on the nearby wall and I stared out towards the west. It was as though I was trying to see across the hundreds of miles. I had thought Oswald and Oswiu had been dealt with. We had killed most of their men but suppose they had more on Mona and in other villages on the west coast of Rheged? Carac and Afon were two spies we had identified but there might be others. It would make sense. They would be able to build up their strength and then the brothers could retake their father's kingdom through Rheged; a Rheged I had left undefended.

Suddenly Myrddyn was beside me. "The girl's words worried you?"

Saxon Bane

"You must have known the import of her story. Why did you not tell me?"

"Your mind is filled with this attack on Edwin and on your own death. I did not want to burden your mind with more fears." He smiled. "The fact that you are walking the walls instead of sleeping is proof that I was right. Besides I was teasing out the information little by little. I believe she does know the name of the Saxon leader but she does not know that she knows it. By gaining her confidence she might relax and then spill the information inadvertently."

"But what of the threat?"

"We left enough warriors to protect our home. We travelled up the west coast and we found but one village. I believe that this is a plan of Oswald and Oswiu to retake Northumbria but they have not the strength as yet. We can scotch this snake and then turn our attention to those two vipers."

Hogan Lann led the equites towards the Roman fort called Chesters while I went with Bors and Daffydd. Penda and King Fiachnae mac Báetáin accompanied me. Both men were keen to watch my men as they fought the Saxons. We rode horses but kept well behind the advancing archers and spearmen.

"Your archers ride horses?"

"Aye it gets them to battle quickly and they can be extricated quickly if attacked."

Penda rubbed his beard. "I never worry about archers." He banged his shield with his hand. "My shield protects me."

I smiled, "Then watch how we deal with that."

There was a low ridge which was some half a mile from the walled settlement. I could see the church which Aedh had identified. King Fiachnae mac Báetáin pointed to it. "Will your men attack the church?"

I did not get a chance to answer for Penda said, "Of course. There are always riches within their walls."

The king nodded, "Many of my men will not attack such places."

"That will not be a problem. There will be more than enough Northumbrians for them to dull their blades upon."

## Saxon Bane

We saw the skirmish unfold before us. Bors led the spearmen towards the gate. The Northumbrians had built the settlement with two gates. One faced us and the other led across the Roman Bridge below us. Our attack had effectively sealed the fate of the village. The only place they could escape would be across the bridge and Pol waited on the other side with his equites. We had chosen not to attack across the bridge. That would be a killing zone.

I saw commotion within the settlement as my men were spotted. Daffydd's archers began to rain arrows upon any who stood on the walls. As Penda had predicted the Northumbrians held their shields above their heads. As soon as they protected themselves, then Bors and his men leapt across the ditch and his axemen began to hack a way through the wooden walls. When the defenders tried to hurl their spears at Bors and his men they were skewered by a well-aimed arrow. Gradually the defenders fell one by one.

Penda shook his head sadly. "They have no chance."

"No chance indeed and look."

I pointed to the bridge which suddenly filled with refugees fleeing the attack which had now breached the walls. Pol timed his attack to perfection and he led his squires across the bridge once the refugees had reached the halfway point. They hurled themselves from the bridge into the quickly flowing river. I am not sure if they thought they could swim to safety but their clothes and the icy waters of early spring dragged them all to a rocky, watery death. Soon there was just the white-capped grey water of the Tineus and there were no more refugees. Within the hour we entered the settlement and Hogan Lann sent the word. He had captured Chesters too. We had achieved our objectives. We had secured the crossings over the river and now we awaited King Cadwallon.

While we waited I rode with Gawan and Morcar to inspect the land around us. Tuanthal gave us twenty warriors to watch over us. We found a few farms but the people hid when we approached. "This is good land, Gawan, you have never seen it before have you?"

"No, I have just had the description from you and Hogan Lann. It is a shame that we lost it."

"We lost it because of the treachery of a king?"

Morcar asked, "A king?"

"Morcant Bulc slew King Urien and then I slew him. That ended the last alliance. We must make sure that this alliance lasts longer."

Gawan sat upright in his saddle and drew his sword. "I swear that I will do all to ensure that it does."

I realised then that Gawan had not been given as much responsibility as Hogan Lann and that was unfair. He was such a kind and thoughtful young man that he was often overlooked. I decided to give him a role.

Saxon Bane

# Chapter 14

Three days after we had captured the two crossings King Cadwallon reached us. He and his men had made good time. He greeted me warmly. "Have you lost many men, Warlord?"

I shook my head, "None to speak of." I waved King Fiachnae mac Báetáin forward. "This is our ally King Fiachnae mac Báetáin."

King Cadwallon gave one of his broadest smiles. "Welcome to this alliance against Northumbria." He gestured towards me. "Lord Lann is the only one of us to have fought in the last alliance against the men of Northumbria. I hope that this new alliance of Ulaid, Mercia and Gwynedd can be as successful."

"And I hope so, too, King Cadwallon. We have heard of your fame and that of the Warlord. Already I have learned much."

Myrddyn stepped forward. "Perhaps, your majesty, you might address the armies." He pointed to the huge bowl on the opposite site of the river. "This is one of the places where we can gather them."

King Fiachnae mac Báetáin nodded, "It is a good idea, your majesty, for the men of Dál nAraidi have not seen you before."

We gathered the warriors together and King Cadwallon sat astride his white horse, Wyddfa. He was encased from head to toe in the armour of a cataphract. When the sun peered out from behind the clouds it made his armour sparkle and gleam as though it was gold. Even before he spoke I saw the awe on the face of the men of Dál nAraidi and even Penda's Mercians looked to be impressed.

"Warriors of the west, today we have our alliance of the finest warriors in this land to oust the dark forces from the east. We will wrest this land from the greedy fingers of Edwin and his robbers; we will free the people of Rheged. Today we begin the road to peace and prosperity."

There was a huge cheer but I noticed that the men of Dál nAraidi were less than thrilled at the prospect of peace. They had come for plunder and

## Saxon Bane

I hoped that the spirits had been right to invite them to join us. I would have to speak with Myrddyn later. I decided that we had to take one step at a time. First we had to capture Din Guardi and then destroy Edwin and his army.

"We will go to the lair of King Edwin and become the first army to take that stronghold of the east. Let us go forward and fight under the banners of the dragon and the wolf and let us be led by the Warlord of Rheged and Gwynedd, Lord Lann!"

If the cheers for the first part had been muted when King Cadwallon had finished there was a cheer and an acclamation which could have been heard in Dunelm far to the south. That evening there was a boisterous and optimistic mood around the camp. It felt as though we were on the threshold of something great. We needed to keep the momentum going. This alliance would not falter as the other had; not if I had anything to do with the matter.

We headed west the next day. This time the scouts of Aedh ranged far ahead while Tuanthal and his horsemen formed a mobile screen before us. We would not be surprised. The kings and the leaders rode with Hogan Lann and me at the front. Myrddyn rode behind us with Lann Aelle, Pol and Penda. I glanced around me and I was reminded of the days of King Urien when I was about the same age as Lann Aelle. The future then had been hopeful but that had been before the treachery of Morcant Bulc. I wondered if all the hearts which headed east were as true as that of King Cadwallon. He had put great faith in me to bring his retinue so far north from his land and fight for Rheged. I felt humbled.

Hogan Lann nudged his horse next to me. "You are quiet."

"I am an old man remembering the days of marching here with Ywain and Pasgen. The last time I was in Din Guardi I ended the life of the traitor who stabbed my king in the back."

"That was a noble thing to do."

"It was but it cost us Bernicia. Remember that my son. The consequences of our actions are like a stone thrown into a pond; the ripples go on forever. We are now going back to finish what I should have done all those years ago."

## Saxon Bane

Before we began to head east I summoned Hogan Lann, Tuanthal, Aedh and Gawan. "Perhaps I am tempting *wyrd* but I believe that we will triumph at Din Guardi."

Hogan Lann nodded his assent. "I believe so too."

"With that thought in mind I want Gawan here to take a column of horsemen south to find King Edwin." I saw him flush with pride. "Take your squires, twenty of Tuanthal's men, five of the boy riders and five of Aedh's best scouts." I saw Aedh smile, "Not you Aedh, I need you with me." His elation was replaced by disappointment. "Well Gawan, are you up to the task?"

"I am." I saw the hesitation on his face and then he turned back to me. "Just to make it clear what do I do when I find King Edwin?"

"Send one of the pony riders to me with the news and then shadow him. You will have the better horsemen. You will be able to evade him."

"Thank you for this honour, Warlord."

I saw Hogan Lann nod his approval. They would work well together when I was gone and that pleased me for Ywain and Pasgen had become enemies when their father died. This would not happen to my sons. We need the harmony within the family else the balance of nature would be upset. We had learned the lessons of family discord and we had paid a high price for the lesson.

Our horsemen and our scouts dispersed the few Northumbrians they encountered so that we reached that mighty fortress perched perilously on the cliffs without loss. Of course, the riders took the news of our arrival and every Saxon within miles would be hiding within its mighty walls. We saw the high walls bristling with standards and with warriors. Only Myrddyn and I had seen the fortress before and I heard the sharp intake of breath from all of the leaders and kings as they beheld the seemingly impregnable fortress.

We sat on our horses on the high ground some half a mile from the castle. It afforded us the best view. You could even see within and beyond its walls. I pointed out the features as I described them.

In ancient times the castle had been built on a rock. I suspected that someone with knowledge of Rome had had a hand in its building. There was plenty of stone work as well as wood. A winding path twisted from the beach to the only gate. An attacker would have to endure missiles and rocks whilst negotiating the steep ramp. The side away from the castle was open and the sharp teeth of rocks awaited anyone who fell. Once they reached the gate an attacker could not use a ram because there was not enough space to wield one. As if that was not enough the path to the castle could only be accessed at low tide. At other times the sea gave it a natural and, at times, a wild moat.

King Fiachnae mac Báetáin shook his head. "It is impossible! No one could capture that without losing all of their warriors in the attempt."

Myrddyn chuckled, "It would appear so but the Warlord and I know another way in, unless, of course, they have blocked it up."

The kings looked to me as did Hogan Lann. "We need your warriors, King Fiachnae mac Báetáin, to go with the wizard at low tide. He will gain you entry into the fortress." I smiled at his open mouthed expression of wonder, "Then you can let loose your wild Hibernians."

He seemed genuinely happy about that. "Good because we have watched and waited too long. My warriors are eager to fight. We will show you what we can do."

Myrddyn wagged an admonishing finger. "We want warriors who win and not just fight. They must obey orders. As I will be leading you and your men they must be my orders which are obeyed!"

"Do not worry wizard. My men will obey orders!"

I turned to Hogan Lann, "The horsemen will be spectators today. If any flee then your men can run them down. I want a circle of iron around the castle. They have no ships here and the only escape will be through your men." I turned to Penda. "I will lead some of the men of Gwynedd, Rheged and Mercia. The warriors who have not fought yet will have their chance."

"No, Warlord, I cannot allow you to lead the attack." I could see the concern mixed with anger on my son's face.

"I must. If Myrddyn and the men of Dál nAraidi are to have a chance to gain entry into the castle then we need the attention of the whole fortress on the front gate. They will see me and my wolf shield. It will make them desperate to kill me. Whoever commands these walls will bring all of their force to bear on me. Do not worry. Daffydd and his men will be able to cover us with their arrows."

"I cannot allow it. It is too dangerous."

I made my voice as hard and commanding as I could. I did not want to demean my son but I had to assert my authority. He would command soon enough. "I am Warlord yet. There will come a time soon, my son when you can put me out to pasture but so long as I am Warlord, I command."

The air of tension remained until Myrddyn shrugged and said, "He will not die beneath the walls of Din Guardi. He defeated King Morcant Bulc here and the spirits watch over him still. I swear to you that the Warlord will not die here."

It was either a brave or a foolish thing to say. The effect was that the warriors who went with me believed that we would not die. That gave the warriors more confidence. I wondered at Myrddyn. He had dreamed my death. He had seen the knife in the back. Had he seen more that he had not told me?

We were up early. The tide would allow Myrddyn and King Fiachnae mac Báetáin the chance to get inside the fortress but we needed to be prepared to go while the waters still surrounded the rock. Morcar and Lann Aelle helped me to dress. I saw the concern on Lann Aelle's face but Morcar just seemed excited.

"Remember Morcar you have to stay behind me and keep the standard high so that all may see it, friend and foe. Use your shield well for they will drop rocks and stones upon us."

"Do not fear, Warlord. I will not let you down!"

Lann Aelle shook his head as he fitted the armour around my neck. It effectively protected the vulnerable part of my body beneath my helmet and above my mail. It was a little fiddly to fit. "It is not about you today, cousin, you bear the standard and you are the rallying point. Remember you will march at the Warlord's back. You will protect him with your shield whilst keeping the banner high. Trust me, cousin, it will take you all your time to keep your feet in the press of warriors who will be around you." He stepped back. "There it is done. This one piece of armour is the hardest to fit."

I nodded, "It is but it is the most important for it protects the neck. I have forgotten how many warriors I have despatched with a blow to the throat or neck."

"And you, cousin, will need to learn how to do this. Remember you are the Warlord's squire now."

Morcar handed me Saxon Slayer. "I know and I am honoured."

"I will not ask if it is sharp I know it is."

Morcar laughed, "To show you how sharp just feel my chin. I shaved with it this morning."

"That is no test cousin; put some milk on your beard and the cat could lick it off."

I smiled until I saw that Morcar had taken it seriously and had reddened. "Do not mind Lann Aelle, Morcar. Pol and Hogan Lann both teased him the same way. It is what happens when you are new."

"One day I will not be new. One day I will lead armies. Just you watch. Then no one will mock me!"

"Of course, you will cousin. Do not listen to me." Lann Aelle had only been bantering. It spoke of the state of mind of Morcar. He had yet to prove himself. Until he did he would be sensitive to all comments. And of course there was Morgause...

The chosen warriors waited eagerly. They had all been chosen because they had good mail and sound weapons. Bors and Kay led the men of Rheged and Penda those of Mercia. I was happy with their choices. While we waited we practised marching in formation. None of the warriors I was leading had fought with the others. This would be a baptism of fire.

We could see, in the first light of dawn, the sea as it began to recede. I gathered the warriors behind me on the sandy shore across from the gate. The sentries inside the Northumbrian stronghold had seen our movements and I watched warriors beginning to line the walls. That was a good thing. We had their attention.

Bors and Kay stepped in front of me. "You can lead Warlord but not in the front rank. That honour goes to Kay and me."

I noticed that Bors wielded his war hammer. He meant business. "Very well."

Penda said, "And I will have my warriors with axes close behind, Warlord, just in case they do not open the gate for you when you knock." My warriors all laughed. Penda had a sense of humour and they had already forgotten that he was a Saxon.

We formed up with Kay, Bors and three men before me. Two of Bors' men were to my left and two of Kay's men on my right. Morcar was tucked in behind me and Penda and a warrior were to his right while two other Saxons were to the left. I hoped that all would see the trust I had in Penda and his men. It would be simplicity itself if the Mercians chose to kill me as we marched. Of course they would be slaughtered themselves but by then the damage would be done. I laughed inside at myself. I knew who would kill me already and it was not a Saxon.

"Sound the buccina!"

The Roman horns were blown and we began to march across the damp sand towards the gate. Bors and Kay began to chant to help the men keep the beat. We all knew to start on the same leg. Speed was not important but a solid front was.

The path to the gate was, as I recalled, just wide enough for five men. We could have marched with a much wider front across the wet sand but that risked losing order when we tried to change to an attacking formation. With just Bors, Kay and three others before me I would be clearly visible by the time the sun came up. The tide was almost racing out now but it meant we were now walking on wet, soggy sand and, with our armour and weapons weighing us down, we began to sink a little deeper into the soft sand. It slowed us down.

The helmet I wore gave me good protection but also afforded me a good view ahead. It was well designed. I saw the stone walls of the fortress, now lit by the morning sun, lined with armed and helmeted men. I could hear their shouts. This was what usually happened before armies came into contact. It helped to bolster the defender's confidence. Behind

## Saxon Bane

me the men I led began to take up a different chant, "Rheged! Rheged!" It seemed to help us march across the wet sand. It helped us to keep time. The two sides were challenging each other. The difference was that the men I had had fought before and won. The Saxons had been sitting behind their walls for years.

Bors must have seen something for he shouted, "Arrows!" We were less than a hundred paces from the walls but the height of the archers meant they had a good chance of hitting us. Our shields came up as one. I hoped that Morcar, directly behind me would be able to cope with the standard and the shield; he would need concentration and coordination. Arrows and stones from slingshots pinged off the metal helmets and cracked off the wood. I heard no cries of pain. I felt something strike my helmet. It made a loud noise but nothing more. Then I heard the whoosh of arrows as Daffydd ap Miach marched his archers up behind us and they began to strike the enemy hard. The enemy arrows slowed a little. It takes a brave man to willingly stand in the path of arrows unless he has a shield and fine armour. We had both. The arrows were an annoyance.

Kay shouted, "Path!"

The going became easier as we started up the path. It was steep but it was firm under foot. The warrior on the right had the comfort of the wall while the one on the outside would see, hear and smell the sea just a pace or two from his feet. I braced my shield for the path meant we were below the warriors on the walls. They would begin to try to hit us with rocks and anything else that they could drop. That required no skill and everyone within the walls would be drafted to help repel us. I heard a cry and the warrior next to me fell to the floor. I caught a brief sight of his head which had been crushed by a rock. It looked like a ripe plum had been pulped. Then his place was taken by the next warrior, this was a Saxon I did not know. I began to count my steps. We had estimated that it would be a hundred footsteps to the gate. I had decided to draw Saxon Slayer when we were just thirty paces from the gate. It would raise the spirits of the men. The counting helped me to hide any fear I might have had. The cracks and cries made it obvious that we were losing warriors. We had expected this. No one attacked such a fortress without heavy casualties. I hoped that Fiachnae mac Báetáin and his men had secured an entrance into the fortress or all this could be in vain.

I counted seventy and drew my sword, "Saxon Slayer!"

There was a huge roar as the men around me heard my cry and the chant began. "Wolf Warrior! Wolf Warrior! Wolf Warrior!" It became faster and our speed towards the gate became much quicker.

Bors screamed, "Gate!" As he smashed his war hammer against the wooden beams the rest of the warriors raised their shields and Penda led forward his axemen. We might not be able to use a ram but we had strong men with mighty weapons; they would have to do. The cover of shields was not complete for one of the Mercians fell, transfixed by a spear. Another warrior took his place.

Soon there was a cacophony of noise as the axes and hammers struck the gate and stones, rocks and spears crashed down on our shields. I knew that they would be preparing boiling water and oil to use. I was just grateful that they had not had the foresight to prepare them before else we would now have been burned, boiled and beaten.

I raised my shield slightly and risked a look at the gate. I could see daylight where there should have been wood. There were cracks and chips in the ancient doorway. The warriors wielding their mighty weapons were attacking the gate as though their lives depended upon it.

Suddenly I heard a loud cry from beyond the gate. I hoped that it meant our men were within the walls. I risked a shout. "Our men are inside! Just a few more blows. We fight for Rheged!" I was rewarded by a huge cheer and felt a surge of pressure as they all pushed forward.

I saw Bors pull back the hammer. "Give a man some room!" he shouted and gave the gate one almighty blow. The gate shattered open. We did not wait but poured through. The press of men was like the water behind a burst dam. It had only one way to go; through the gate. All sense of order was gone. We raced to close with any Northumbrian foolish enough to stand against us.

One warrior, braver than the rest, hurled himself at me. He barged one of Penda's men out the way; the Mercian tumbled down to the water below. I just reacted. I braced myself behind my shield and as his whole

## Saxon Bane

body struck my shield I angled it away. He tripped over a dead warrior and fell at my feet. I stabbed down at him.

Even as I withdrew my sword a spearman thrust his spear forwards. My shield was at my side and my sword still being drawn from the dead warrior. The metal head scrapped noisily against my metal throat protector. Morcar jabbed at the spearman with the wolf standard and the metal spike went into his eye, killing him instantly. I turned to Morcar, "Thank you, nephew!"

A space cleared before me and, mindful of Hogan Lann's words, I paused to take stock. The courtyard was filled with small, individual, combats. I saw Hibernians ahead of me and knew that they had gained entry. Behind me I saw Dai leading fresh men of Gwynedd to boost our numbers.

"On! Let us finish them!" I could not move swiftly because of my injured leg. Marching in time was not a problem but trying to run uphill to get to the keep was not easy. We were gradually left by others as they surged past us. Morcar kept by my side. I saw that he held a dagger in his left hand as well as his shield. Lann Aelle had taught him that.

I saw a knot of warriors trying to rally. "Morcar bring the standard. Stay on my right and keep the wolf banner held high."

One Northumbrian was keeping my men at bay. He had a long pole and, at the end was an axe head. It meant he could swing with impunity. He was protected by a hedgehog of spears. Even as I watched I saw one of Bors' men lose his head. It bounced and rolled out of the gate and into the sea. I had fought against warriors like this and knew that the only way to tackle them was to time your run well.

"Morcar, put your shield on your right arm and hold the standard like a lance. When I say run keep with me."

His voice trembled a little as he said, "Aye, Warlord."

I could not run for long distances but by launching off my good leg I could cover the ground to the man so long as I timed it right. I saw the axe head begin another swing. "Now, Morcar!"

We took everyone by surprise as we burst through the warriors who were falling back. The warrior with the axe looked in horror as we closed within his swing. The spike on the standard knocked a surprised Northumbrian away and I stabbed into the unprotected stomach of the axeman. I pushed it all the way through until it ground along his spine and out of his back. Twisting the blade I withdrew it as he fell down dead. My men fell upon the spearmen as though they were not even there.

By the time we reached the door of the building, the defence was effectively over. Our men were dispatching the wounded. We had won.

It felt strange to revisit the scene of one of my more famous exploits. The last time I had been within these walls I had been a young warrior and now I was returned as an old one. Myrddyn shook his head when I greeted him. "They did not seal up the tunnel. Perhaps they did not know we had used it. If we are going to garrison this then I think we should stop it up."

I agreed. I saw King Fiachnae mac Báetáin approaching. I could see from his weapons and the blood on his armour that he had been in the thick of the fighting. I grabbed him by the shoulders, "Hail Fiachnae mac Báetáin of Din Guardi!" it soon became a name famous throughout Britannia and Hibernia.

He looked embarrassed. "Our task was easy. We just crept through empty corridors and then fell upon those intent upon killing you. The honour should go to you, Lord Lann, Warlord of Rheged."

"No, my friend, this day is yours." I pointed to his bent and broken sword. "I would choose a Saxon weapon. Most of them are better than yours."

He smiled, "I can see that now." He turned to his men. "Let us arm ourselves with some decent swords now. Today we begin to become warriors like those of Rheged!"

Everyone cheered. It was as though we had won the war but Myrddyn and I knew that this was just one step on the way to victory. As I sheathed my sword I watched as the Hibernians plucked weapons from the still warm hands of the dead Northumbrians. I saw one pick up the mighty axe which had almost taken off my head. I hoped that the warrior who would wield it had more luck than the Northumbrian.

Saxon Bane

# Chapter 15

We had many days to consolidate our hold on the land. Hogan Lann, King Cadwallon and Lann Aelle led columns of equites who flooded north and west to eliminate pockets of Northumbrian resistance. They spared the civilians but slaughtered any warrior who stood against us. By the time that Gawan's riders returned we had secured the whole of Northumbria north of the Tineus.

King Fiachnae mac Báetáin and Penda revelled in their victories. The armoury of the fort provided all of their warriors with better helmets, shields, armour and swords. We had an army which was better equipped than any on the island.

Myrddyn and I explored the fort with Morcar and Morgause. There were treasures hidden which were beyond gold. We found maps and writings which made Myrddyn's eyes widen with delight. It was a veritable treasure trove.

It was when we were exploring that I came to know Morgause a little better. I had taken her to be little more than a child but, as we explored the cellars and hidden places I discovered that she had see more than twenty summers. She was a woman.

"My mother made us all appear younger than we were. She knew that it would protect us. She had been descended from a long line of those who worshipped the Mother." As she said that she had looked at me with a shy look. "She told me that some of our ancestors had lived in Rheged."

*Wyrd*! The gods and spirits moved in strange ways. Who would have known that chancing upon that monastery would have led to such revelations? I could see why my nephew was so attracted to her. I looked at her as she helped Morcar to reach the high awkward places. They giggled together. I could now see that she did not look like the people of Mona. There was a different look to her.

## Saxon Bane

I drew Myrddyn to one side. "The women of the Mother cult, are there many left?"

He shook his head. "No, Morgause and her sisters may be the last of them. The Romans feared them and tried to wipe them out. They crucified them, burned them or sealed them in their caves. It is that way with many people. They fear what they do not know."

"You do not fear them?"

He laughed, "Of course not. There is much to learn from Morgause. It is good to have an apprentice again."

For a while Gawan had trained with Myrddyn and he had learned much but when he had married they had drifted apart and Gawan had ceased his studies. Myrddyn had understood but he had missed his young companion. Now he had Morgause and also a little of Morcar. It explained the spring in his step.

It was as we ascended the stairs to the main hall that I suddenly had a thought. "Myrddyn. Where is the treasury? We found weapons and we found writings and maps to delight you but where is the treasure of Northumbria?"

Unusually I had taken Myrddyn by surprise. I suspect it was the presence of the young witch which had distracted him. We descended again to search for hidden passages and doors but there were none.

The only survivors of our attack had been the old and the servants. We sought out the old steward. He looked to be ancient, even to me. He had no fear in his eyes as he was brought into my presence. When you are that old then death might be around any corner anyway. He looked me proudly in the eyes.

"Have you served here long?"

He stared back at me and never blinked. "I have worked here since before the days when you slew King Morcant Bulc of Bernicia."

I smiled at his impertinence. "So you are Bernician?"

"Bernician, Saxon, Northumbrian- they are all just names. I am who I am."

"Good. I like your honesty and your lack of respect does not upset me old man. What does upset me is a lack of truth so answer truly or it will go ill for you."

He chuckled, "I have outlived my sons and two wives. I think I will outlive you Warlord but I will answer you truthfully for men say you are honest and I was sad when King Urien was murdered. Ask your questions."

"Where is the secret room with the treasury?"

He laughed aloud. "The treasury has gone! King Aethelfrith was a greedy man and when he left to war in the south he took it with him. He had five wagons filled with the treasure it had taken years to accumulate." He shrugged. "Perhaps he took it with him to his grave."

"Perhaps he did. And thank you for your honesty. Will you stay on here?"

He shrugged, "Where else would I go?"

After he had gone and we had told the others of the treasure Hogan Lann asked why I was so concerned with treasure. "You do not care over much for gold, Warlord."

"I still do not care for gold but whoever has that treasure can buy arms and an army. Had it been here then we would have known that the Northumbrians could not use it to raise a bigger army. Now we are in the dark."

"Perhaps Aethelfrith did hide it."

"Then someone will know where it is. Until that day we seek the treasure."

Gawan's riders arrived the next day. It was one of the boy riders. "Warlord, the Northumbrians are gathered south of the Dunum. Your son says there is a mighty host. He says there are East Angles with the Northumbrians." I saw the concentration on his face as he tried to remember every word my son had told him.

"You have done well. You will be a fine horseman soon." I left him beaming as I sought the others.

King Cadwallon looked up at me after I had told them the news. "You know this land better than I; how long will it take us to reach there?"

## Saxon Bane

"Two, perhaps three days for the whole army but I will send the horsemen south today. Horses will cover the distance quickly. There is a fine Roman Road to the south. They can deny the Northumbrians the crossing of the river for the bridges are few and far between." Although there were only a handful of bridges across the river it was quite narrow in places and we had crossed greater ones before using boats as bridges and swimming the horses across. If Hogan Lann and his equites were there they could counter any advance which King Edwin might make.

Hogan Lann nodded his approval. He turned to the scout. "And the land between here and the river, is it free from warriors?"

He smiled, "Lord Gawan Lann cleared away the few that we found."

"Then we will leave now and reach there as soon as we can." He turned to his squire, Garth ap Daffydd. "Find my captains and tell them we ride. Prepare my mount."

I grabbed his arm as he turned to go, "Hogan Lann, be careful. King Edwin is wily. Do not fall into any of his traps."

He looked hurt. "You have trained me too well for that, Warlord." He smiled and said, "We will hold the rivers for you, never fear."

King Cadwallon nodded decisively too. "And I will go with Hogan Lann and take my banner south. It is important that King Edwin and the Northumbrians know who it is who comes to do battle."

We left Gruffydd ap Miach with thirty of the older warriors to guard Din Guardi. Gruffydd was a dependable warrior. I would have left Bors or Kay but I knew that I would need their leadership qualities before we had wrested the land back from Edwin. Thirty men could hold the castle against any enemies until we had defeated Edwin. Then we would garrison it properly. Myrddyn had pointed out that the men of Dál nAraidi were fierce fighters and allowed no obstacle to slow them down but they were wild and uncontrolled. Bors and Kay had iron control over their men.

We found carts and ponies in the fort and we used those to transport spare weapons. Daffydd's men had carried their hundreds of arrows on their horses but the carts meant that they could travel with Hogan Lann and help my sons deny the crossing to the Northumbrians.

## Saxon Bane

And so we headed south with a little over six hundred men. We were far too big an army to worry about any enemies and it was a pleasant march. I began to plan as we rode south. Lann Aelle and Pol had gone with Hogan Lann. I would not have their agile minds to augment mine. Kay and Bors were fine warriors but they did not understand strategy. I could have used Myrddyn but the old man was still preoccupied with talking with Morgause. Penda and King Fiachnae mac Báetáin found that they had much to talk about and so I ran through the different plans in my head. I used my own arguments against myself.

The Northumbrian army would be spearmen and other similarly armed warriors. They had learned to use archers but I had no doubt that my own bow men would negate them. They did not use horses. King Edwin would choose somewhere to fight where we would break ourselves upon his serried ranks of spears and shields. He knew the strength of my equites and he would make sure that they could not use their speed and armour to defeat him. I would need to employ guile if I was to outwit him. The two elements Edwin would not be expecting were Fiachnae mac Báetáin and Penda. Penda's banner would worry him and the sight of the wild men from Ulaid would unsettle him. I had to make him believe that I had more men than I actually had. If I could defeat his mind before the battle started then the actual battle would be easier.

Bors and Kay would be my rocks. Their men would not move. I would make him attack and batter himself upon their shields and swords. I would use my allies, as the spirits had told me, to draw the enemy out so that Hogan Lann and his equites could destroy them.

We camped south of Dunelm on that first night. We camped close to an old Roman fort. The land was littered with them. This had been the frontier. I was now but ten miles or so, as the crow flies, from the place I had been born. Saxon Slayer's home was not far from here. It was *wyrd*. It was like the sword was coming home. Perhaps the sword knew that my life was ending. Was it supposed to return to the hole in the ground? I would have to ask Myrddyn, when his mind was not on young witches.

## Saxon Bane

We had pushed hard so that we would have an easier second day. I wanted us fresh and ready to fight as soon as we closed with the Northumbrians.

Morgause prepared the food for the leaders; the men would fend for themselves. She had a delicate touch with herbs and wild fare. She had picked wild garlic and thyme as we had headed south and she had used that to season three old hares we had trapped in the dunes up by Din Guardi. I watched her as she carefully took every bone from the dead animals' bodies and then using the flat of Morcar's sword she beat them flat. She rolled the small pieces of meat around some wild mushrooms and sorrel she had collected and cooked them in a pot with some honeyed ale. The smell was a meal in itself.

As we sat eating the meat, which melted in the mouth, she questioned us about our plans. I saw Myrddyn smiling at the young girl who appeared to be so interested in such manly and warlike matters. Nanna and Delbchaem would never have dreamt of asking about warfare. That was the domain of the warrior.

"You will fight with this King Edwin?"

"We will."

"But what if he outnumbers you?"

"Undoubtedly he will outnumber us. He gathered a huge army to meet with King Cadwallon and he will have gathered more men as he came north."

"Then how can you fight when you know you will lose?"

Myrddyn laughed, "Child, we will not lose. Lord Lann is a fine stratego and I am a powerful wizard. Besides we have better warriors here than King Edwin has. You will be able to watch the army of Gwynedd destroy that of Northumbria."

She cocked her head to one side as though to examine my face, "But you have seen neither his army nor where he will fight."

King Fiachnae mac Báetáin said, "I am curious about that too, Warlord. You knew Din Guardi and what to expect but you know not where King Edwin will stand."

"But I do."

## Saxon Bane

With the exception of Myrddyn they all stared at me as though it was I who was the wizard. "How? Have you second sight?"

"No, Penda. He will have his men on a piece of high ground. His rear will be protected by higher ground and, probably a wood so that if things go awry he can escape. The ground on his flanks will protect him too. If he can he will have a piece of water before him."

Morgause's eyes widened, "How do you know this?"

"Because if I was Edwin that would be what I would do to face my army."

Penda stroked his beard, "And if he does not?"

"Then he will be defeated even quicker."

We left as soon as we could, the next day. We did not have far to go. We could almost see the sea in the distance. The Roman Road we travelled headed west towards the crossing of the Dunum. Since the Romans had left no one had built a bridge closer to the coast. I wondered why.

Tuanthal and his horsemen awaited us at the bridge. "Hogan Lann and the rest of the army are further east. They are shadowing King Edwin. He has a mighty host with him."

"Where did Gawan find him?"

"They were just twenty miles north of the Roman fort at Eboracum. He has many hundreds if not thousands of men, Warlord. There are warriors there from King Raedwald's army of the East Angles."

Then Edwin too was using his allies. "Where are we camped?"

"Where the river bends and the cliffs rise to the north."

I remembered the place well. There had been a settlement there years ago. "The river is narrow there."

"Aye Warlord, Hogan Lann thought that we would be able to retreat north if we had to."

He was right. We could use the horses to swim an army across and there were many trees to make a raft and ferry them. "Good." I summoned Ard.

"Choose twenty warriors and guard this crossing."

## Saxon Bane

The warrior was disappointed but all of my warriors knew better than to argue. I did not want to head south and find the bridge held against us. He looked at the small Roman fort which guarded it. "We will set about improving the fort. We may have need of it."

As I headed south east I reflected that my men were so confident that they were already planning on a future here in the east. I hoped that they were not being premature. We needed to defeat Edwin first.

Hogan Lann had set up camp on the bluffs which were some four hundred paces from the small river. It gave a good view towards the south east. It was noon when we trudged in. While the weary warriors rested I rode with Myrddyn and Hogan Lann to see the Northumbrians for myself. We took fifty of Hogan Lann's equites with us. As we rode he told me more of the enemy's dispositions.

"There look to be almost two thousand warriors. Many have mail. As soon as they saw Gawan and his warriors they halted. They keep attempting to send forward warriors to shift us but we just move out of their way and then return when they try to move the rest. They are moving in short but slow bursts. The horsemen make them stop but, with the hills at their backs and the spears to their front we can do little to hurt them. They have managed just thirty miles in the last couple of days." He smiled, "Little brother has done well."

"I am proud of you both. I approve of where you have the camp but I wish to move it." He nodded and waited. I peered into the distance and saw the hills rising in the distance. "He is keeping close to the moors."

"He is. How did you know?"

"It stops us from outflanking him. He will only head west, towards the bridge when he reaches the river. He can use the river to protect one flank and there is a great deal of swampy ground to the south of the river. I do not want him to reach the river. If we have to then we will try to force him across the plain towards the west. There we can use your horse to our advantage. If he has any sense he will avoid that but you never know. He might make mistakes."

"You seem to know the area well."

## Saxon Bane

"I should, we campaigned here when I was young and this is where we rescued Prince Ywain and Myrddyn tended to the Saxon wounded. And I was born less than thirty miles to the west. When we reach Gawan I will decide where we are to camp. I have a surprise for King Edwin. Tell me, has he scouts out?"

"Not that we have seen but he will know the land."

"That does not worry me. We know the land too." I pointed to the west. "I hunted close to here as well as searching for lost sheep. This is my land now!"

The flat plain before us allowed us to see the Saxons long before we were close to them. They were a dark stain against the green hillside. The Roman Road up which they travelled would have allowed them to make good speed had they not had Gawan's horsemen threatening them. By the time we reached Gawan, it was mid afternoon.

"Welcome father." He grinned. "We have found Edwin for you."

"You have done well." He did not look tired. It was good to be young. "I want you to stop them going north for a couple of hours. Use Hogan Lann's horsemen to help you." He nodded. "We are going to set up a camp there," I pointed north, where the hills begin to edge east. I will send a rider to you when you are to withdraw." I reached out and touched his arm. "Do not take risks. We cannot afford to lose a single warrior and I would like both my sons in camp tonight. All we are doing is allowing me and the rest of the army to frighten him."

He laughed, "They are too slow to do us any damage." He was a typical horseman with a low opinion of foot soldiers.

We rode back at a full gallop and I explained to Hogan Lann and Myrddyn what my plan was. "The Hibernians and the Mercians will be tired. They will not appreciate another forced march."

"They chose to be my allies and they will obey my orders. Besides they can rest tonight."

Surprisingly they did not complain overmuch and we moved to our new camp site remarkably quickly. Although it was only eight miles away it still took us until close to dark before we reached my chosen site.

## Saxon Bane

The men began to slump to the ground. I had the buccina sounded and they all stopped to watch me.

"I want every single warrior to collect enough wood to make two fires. I want two thousand fires burning by the time the moon is up." If they were surprised they did not show it. There were plenty of scrubby hedges and trees around and soon the evening was filled with the sound of axes and blades.

"Hogan Lann, send for Gawan."

By the time Gawan arrived all of the fires were blazing and the men were taking advantage of the fires to cook themselves some hot food. I gathered my leaders about me. "I want all of the fires kept burning all night."

King Fiachnae mac Báetáin asked me, "Why?"

"When King Edwin's scouts follow Gawan they will report our camp. They will see two thousand fires and assume that our army may be four or five times bigger than it is. I want the Saxons to fear our numbers so that when we attack they will be waiting for us to send in reinforcements who do not exist. He will keep a reserve. He outnumbers us by two to one; we have to outwit him."

Morgause and Morcar busied themselves preparing food for Myrddyn and me. We had our own fires. I was not exempt from my orders. As usual the mushrooms they had gathered smelled delicious but I was fated not to enjoy a hot meal that night. They had just been served up when Aedh found me.

"Warlord, you need to come. We have found a prisoner, a Northumbrian scout."

I looked ruefully at the steaming mushrooms. "You can have my share, Myrddyn."

"I will keep you some, Warlord." Our cook added as I went towards my horse.

"Thank you Morgause but I do not know how long I will be. Morcar I will not need you. Make sure you eat too." I quickly followed Aedh. He led me to a huddle of warriors about half a mile from where our camp fire was. Penda and Gawan were there along with Hogan Lann. Two

## Saxon Bane

Mercians held a Northumbrian by his arms. The knee of one of the Mercians was in the middle of the prisoner's back so that he could not move while the other held his hair so that his head was pulled back. His arms showed the pressure of the strain they were under.

I wondered why he was still alive. Penda glanced at me and then put his dagger under the warrior's tunic. He lifted out an amulet. Hogan Lann said, "We would have despatched him immediately had not one of Penda's men seen this."

"And what is it?"

"It marks the warrior as one of the oathsworn of Aethelfrith. He is one of Oswald's warriors."

I nodded my understanding. I went close to the warrior so that I could see his eyes when he answered my questions. "Why would an oathsworn of the brothers serve their enemy, King Edwin?"

"You are my enemy!" He tried to spit but the knee behind his back and the hand on his hair meant that he just dribbled down his beard.

I laughed, "You are as helpless as a baby and we have all night to discover the truth." A sudden thought struck me. "Where did you find him?"

"He and three others were leading six horses around the camp." Penda shrugged, "My men had to kill the others for they fought well. This one fell from his horse and banged his head. He is no horseman."

Gawan frowned. "Why would they bring two spare horses and why were they trying to get around our camp?"

The answer came to me suddenly. I remembered the other spy we had captured. He had spoken of spies. There was a spy in my camp. We had searched after Carac but not discovered any. With over a thousand men it would be easy to hide one especially as we had Mercians and Hibernians with us. I nodded to Aedh who pulled out a very thin blade. He placed the blade in the fire.

"Where were you to meet the spy?"

His eyes flashed the answer before he could control himself. "What spy?"

I shook my head. "You will tell us. You will suffer pain first but you will tell us."

"I do not care if you torture me. I swore an oath to King Aethelfrith and I will do all to protect his sons." He tried to raise his head but he was held so tightly he could not. He grimaced, "You will die, Warlord. Even if you kill me, then you will die."

Hogan Lann and Gawan exchanged a worried glance. "They were trying to get to you."

"Then they failed for I am safe here and unless this man has more skill than Myrddyn then he can do me no harm."

"Myrddyn may be in danger!" The apprentice wizard, Gawan, ran towards my camp fire some half a mile or so away.

I nodded to Aedh who took the blade from the fire. "If aught happens to my friend then you will go to the Otherworld piece by piece and over many days."

"Do your worst. I will not talk."

There was a hiss and a scream as Aedh applied the blade to his right eye. The smell of burning flesh filled the air.

"I will not speak," croaked the Northumbrian.

"Let me have him." There was a menace in Penda's voice I had not heard before.

Suddenly one of Gawan's men raced up to us. "Myrddyn is dying and your nephew has been wounded!"

I set my face to a mask of stone. "Find the names of these spies!"

Saxon Bane

# Chapter 16

Gawan was tending to Myrddyn while two of his warriors bound Morcar's head. "How is he?"

"I am stunned. That is all."

I looked around, "Where is Morgause?"

Morcar became anxious, "She is gone!"

"Find her. Have the camp put on alert, Lann Aelle." My nephew had just arrived and he would seal off the camp and prevent the escape of this killer.

Hogan Lann and I knelt by the wizard. His life was now in Gawan's hands. "Can you save him?"

"I know not. I think he has been poisoned." He pointed to the fallen dish of mushrooms.

"Morgause!"

Morcar shook his head, "It was not her. It could not have been. There must be some mistake. I ate the mushrooms and I am not ill. Gawan you are wrong. Perhaps his heart gave out, he is old."

I whipped around to face my nephew. "I am older and he had dreamed his death. This was not it. And do not lie to me nephew. I can see that only one person has eaten the mushrooms- Myrddyn. Do not try to protect the witch or we may think you had something to do with it."

"How can you say that? I loved the old man!"

I was angry and I turned from him, "Gawan, save him."

"Brother, find his leather satchel. There are potions inside which will help us." Hogan Lann raced off. "Father, find me a dish and some water."

It gave me something to do. By now Tuanthal and the Irish king had joined us as well as Bors and Kay. I grabbed a dish and poured some water into it.

## Saxon Bane

"Bors and Kay, Morgause is somewhere in the camp. She is one of the spies of Oswald. Find her and bring her here. I want her alive so that she may tell us what she used to poison him."

"I tell you she is innocent!"

We all ignored his ranting. Hogan Lann handed the satchel to Gawan who took out three small earthenware jars. He opened one and sniffed it. Seemingly satisfied he poured the contents into the bowl and mixed the black powder with the water to make thin grey slurry.

"Hold him and keep his mouth open." Hogan Lann and I held his head and I used my other hand to open his mouth. His breathing was laboured and light. He was dying. Gawan poured the disgusting looking liquid down his throat. "Keep him upright and close his mouth." My son pinched his nose.

I watched the throat of the wizard as his body forced the liquid down. There was a moment or two when nothing happened and then his body began to convulse. Gawan took his finger and thumb from the wizard's nose. "You can release his mouth now."

Suddenly, like a dam when the earth is moved, he vomited the grey slurry and everything else which had been in his stomach. He retched for some time until half eaten mushrooms appeared. He continued to retch until just a thin white liquid came out. I looked at Gawan. "Is that it? Is he safe now?"

"No, we must now give him plenty of water and then milk."

Milk! Where would we get milk from? King Fiachnae mac Báetáin nodded, "Leave that to me. I saw some cows as we headed here. I'll get you the milk if I have to carry the beast here on my back."

Gawan forced some water down the wizard's throat. This stayed down longer but eventually the white liquid returned. It took three draughts of water before the wizard stopped retching. "We have a chance now." He suddenly turned to Morcar. "You were closest to her. Did you see what she put in the mushrooms?"

"I tell you she is innocent she could have done nothing like this."

I grabbed Morcar with two hands and shook him. "Tell me what she put in the food!"

## Saxon Bane

His eyes were wide with terror. "I just saw her putting in the usual herbs and spices."

I believed him. "Where is her leather satchel?"

Even though we looked it was gone. I had had no doubts before but now it was confirmed. She was a spy and she had fled. Saxons would not have stopped to take her satchel.

Gawan sniffed the mushrooms which had fallen to the floor. He then looked at the vomit. "I am guessing but I think it is a poison called arsenicum. It is a deadly poison. He looked at me. It is the same smell as we had when Lupus was poisoned."

"What is the antidote?"

"There is none!" It was like a death knell sounding. "But there is hope. Myrddyn took a small quantity of arsenicum each day. He made it himself from various plants. He even used the pips of apples." Suddenly I remembered how he had always been hoarding apples. I had thought it was to ferment them to make drink but he obviously had another purpose.

Fiachnae mac Báetáin returned with a jug of milk.

"I am indebted to you, my friend."

He nodded, "If I can help to save the great wizard Myrddyn then my name will be remembered. It is enough."

Gawan poured it, drop by drop down the throat of the wizard. I think we all held our breath for, as the empty jug was placed on the ground, we all breathed a sigh of relief.

We all turned as a handful of warriors ran up. It was a bloody Penda and his men. "That Northumbrian spy was a brave man."

"Did he speak?"

"Aye before the end he just wanted to die and he told us all. The four of them were to hide to the west of the camp and await a girl and a man who would join them." I turned and glared at Morcar. Morgause was the only woman in the camp; this was the final nail in her coffin. "They were expecting the sword, Saxon Slayer, too. You were the target as well as the wizard."

I shook my head. This was *wyrd*. Had we not captured him and killed his companions then I would also lie stricken with the poison for I would have eaten them. The difference was that I had not taken the precaution of consuming this poison before. I was no wizard. I would be dead. Suddenly all fear left me. The spirits would make my death when they chose; it was completely out of my hands. The dream I had had and Myrddyn had dreamt would happen and I could nothing about it. I now had to make sure that Myrddyn lived.

Gawan said, "I will sit with my old master. He will not die on my watch. Get some sleep, father for tomorrow we will have to fight."

"You still intend to bring them to battle?"

"Aye Penda. And I need no sleep. I have slept my last sleep." Hogan Lann gave me a worried look. "Tell me Penda did he say anything about Oswald and Oswiu?"

"Only that they were close by."

Lann Aelle, who had just returned whipped his head around as though he might see them.

"They will not be that close, Lann Aelle, but Morgause will be heading to reach them. Tomorrow morning, Aedh, put your best tracker on her tail."

"I will Warlord, Osgar ap Gruffydd is the best we have. He can find tracks on stones."

"Good. I will sit with Gawan and Myrddyn. The rest of you get some sleep. Tomorrow we fight." Morcar nervously waited close by. "That means you too, Morcar."

"I still cannot believe that she did this but you must believe I knew nothing about it."

"Then your heart blinded your eyes and your mind. We will talk in the morning. Prepare my sword and armour before you go to bed."

"Yes Uncle. Sorry."

When he had gone Hogan Lann asked, "Do you believe him?"

"It doesn't matter. Tomorrow will be the most important day in my life. The dream I had in the cave will come to fruition in the morning."

"Then get some sleep."

## Saxon Bane

I smiled. "I promise you that I will sleep as soon as the battle is over and King Edwin is defeated. I will not sleep until I have spoken with Myrddyn." I did not want Hogan Lann questioning me any closer. He was too clever and might deduce what I wanted to remain hidden. "You know the plan for the morning?"

"Aye. And I am glad that you will sit on the knoll and watch. I will assign some warriors to watch over you."

"That is not necessary and you will need every warrior you can get. Do not worry I will have Morcar and Gawan and Myrddyn will be close by. And remember Hogan Lann, tomorrow, when King Edwin is defeated then you will be Warlord. Know that I love you and trust you as I do your brother Gawan here. Along with Myrddyn you are the closest men to my heart."

Hogan became agitated, "Father, this is not like you. What is wrong?"

I smiled, "Nothing is wrong. I have just cheated death and I realised that I do not tell those that I love how I feel often enough. It is a failing in me."

Seemingly reassured he said, "Then I will go to my bed."

I sat with my hand on Gawan's shoulder. We watched as Myrddyn's chest rose and fell. "Thank you, son, for saving Myrddyn's life."

"It is too early to say."

"He will not die. He has told me of the death he dreamed for him and this was not it."

"I do not know how I would be able to handle a dream of my own death. At least you will have warning when he dreams of your death." There must have been something in my face which gave me away or perhaps it was the fact that Gawan was fey too. His eyes widened. "He has dreamed of your death."

I could not in all conscience lie to Gawan. He too had dreamed in the cave and the spirits spoke to him. Perhaps I would speak to him when I was in the Otherworld. I nodded.

"But you need to tell us who and how so that we can stop it."

"If I had told you then you and Hogan Lann might have made me stay close to the fire and be guarded by warriors. If you had then I would have eaten the mushrooms and you would be mourning me. If it is meant to be it will happen no matter what you do. We cannot change what is ordained." I took off my baldric with the ornate scabbard and handed it to Gawan. "Keep this until I am dead. There is a chamber at Civitas Carvetiorum. I want you to place it there. Myrddyn will show you where."

He began to rise. "This has gone far enough. I will fetch Hogan Lann."

I shook my head. "You cannot, for the spirits speak with you. If you break this confidence then they will no longer communicate with you."

"But why?" He held the scabbard up.

"Because the sons of Aethelfrith want the sword. I cannot deny them that but without the scabbard then perhaps it will not be as powerful. Now hide it. Dawn is coming quickly. Remember you cannot speak of this."

I did not ask him where he secreted it. I did not need that information. I looked down at Myrddyn. "Well old man, I had hoped to speak with you before I went to the Otherworld but unless you wake soon it will be my spirit to whom you speak. I know not if you can hear me but you have been the greatest friend a man could have. With you at my side I feared nothing. I do not fear this death which approaches like a galloping horse. I would change the manner and the hand if I could but that is beyond my control. Watch over my family when I am gone. I know that you will but I ask you as a friend and not as Warlord. I will die easier knowing that my sons, daughter and my wife will have the protection of the great wizard."

Gawan appeared and stared around, "I heard voices. Who were you talking with?"

I waved my hand around. "My home, my land, my Rheged and my friend, Myrddyn." He smiled and sat next to Myrddyn stroking his forehead.

Poor Gawan was so tired that he eventually fell asleep. I moved him away from Myrddyn and covered him with a cloak. I had been lucky in my sons and was confident that they would not follow the route of Prince Ywain and change when I died. Myrddyn would see to that.

## Saxon Bane

The buccina to rouse the camp sounded even though it was still dark. We were preparing early for battle. Morcar joined me with my armour and sword. He looked as though he had not slept. He suddenly peered at me through reddened eyes; he had been crying too, "Where is your scabbard?"

"I will not need it today. You will have my banner and I will hold my sword aloft. I want the enemy to see me and know I live yet." I used Saxon Slayer to point at the hillside in the distance where the Northumbrians were already gathering. "That is where the enemy will see me and they will come for me."

As he began to dress me he said, "You will be the bait."

"We will be the bait. That is why there will be no warriors near us. I want the Northumbrians hatred of me to make them become careless."

I was almost ready. Morcar slapped his head. "I have forgotten the armour for the throat."

"It matters not. I will not have to fight today. This day I just have to look like a Warlord."

Gawan heard the noises and awoke. "You let me sleep."

"You needed it and look, the wizard lives still."

The sun had risen above the eastern hills when my captains rode up to me. "We are ready."

"I know, Hogan Lann."

"Are you sure you want no guards?"

"Remember, I am the bait. They must think I am vulnerable and come for me. You must strike hard and go for King Edwin. Take the head of the snake and the beast will die."

I walked up to Pol and clasped him by the hand. "Today, my old squire you will achieve true glory. You need to take your equites now if you are to be in position before the Northumbrians move."

He knelt, "It is an honour to serve you." He sprang lightly onto the back of his steed and led his hundred warriors away to the west.

Lann Aelle also knelt, "I too had better follow. I do not have as far to ride but it would not do to be late. I would not wish to let you down, uncle."

"You can never let me down Lann Aelle; you are just like your father. You are like a rock on which I can stand. You are totally dependable."

He left and headed after Pol. I turned to Bors, Kay and Daffydd. "You have the hardest task today. You must hold the enemy until Hogan Lann can launch his attack. I have no doubts that you will do so well. You truly are great captains and you two are a credit to your fathers." Bors and Daffydd stood a little straighter.

Kay said, "If they pass us it is because we are dead!" I nodded for I knew he meant every word.

King Fiachnae mac Báetáin and Penda exchanged a glance which showed that they had not seen such affection from warriors for their leader before. "And we may not be of Rheged but we will not let you down."

"I am glad that spirits sent me to speak with both of you. It is *wyrd*. Remember it will appear hopeless but follow the plan and we will prevail."

They both nodded and, clutching their protective amulets, left. King Cadwallon looked down at Myrddyn. "I hope the old wizard pulls through. Wyddfa and Gwynedd need him. He is our link to the past." He came to clasp my arm. And I am pleased that you avoided the witch's poison. We could not do without the Warlord."

"You are a great king, Cadwallon. Your name will go through history as the warrior who defeated King Edwin; this I swear."

He mounted his horse and rode off to join his men. They would be behind Hogan Lann, hidden by a fold in the land. They were the surprise I hoped the Northumbrians would not be expecting.

There was just me, my sons, Morcar and Myrddyn. Hogan Lann was about to speak when Aedh galloped up and he looked distressed. "Warlord, it is Osgar; he has been murdered. Someone slit his throat with a poisoned blade."

Hogan Lann smashed one hand into the other. "That witch!" He glared at Morcar. "I will have her crucified when I find her."

"Have you put another scout on her trail?"

"Aye, but he is no Osgar."

Saxon Bane

"Mayhap he will become one. Now you need to be in position too, Aedh."

"I am sorry about, Myrddyn."

"It was not your fault and he lives still. Take care."

"I will my lord!"

Aedh was like Pol. He was a member of my family. Hogan Lann shook his head. "Things are going wrong, Warlord. Perhaps we should not have begun this adventure."

"It was not of our choosing, Hogan Lann. It was the spirits. When you are Warlord they will speak to you and I will smile at the problems it causes."

He laughed. "Then I look forward to your smile." He glared at Morcar. "Cousin, protect the Warlord. His life is in your hands this day!"

The knoll upon which we waited suddenly seemed empty. I could see the spearmen with their fine banners standing some four hundred paces below me on the plain. I saw Hogan Lann leading his fine equites, as they spread out further to the east. I watched as Tuanthal joined him with his horseman who had been screening the army. I watched as Hogan Lann pointed toward me. Tuanthal put spurs to his horse and galloped up the knoll to join us.

"Your son sent me. King Edwin advances close to the hillside. He is coming in a giant wedge."

"Excellent. It is as we expected. You have done well my old friend. You have come a long way from the young warrior who rode ponies and delivered messages to King Urien for me."

He laughed, "Those were fine days. I miss many of the warriors who fought with us then."

I nodded remembering how close he and Garth had been. "Aye, we have both lost friends. Hopefully, today will not be one of them."

I caught a glimpse of the young pony rider from all those years ago as he trotted back to join his men. I hoped he would be safe. His lightly armed horsemen would have a difficult role this day. Morcar sat on his horse behind me. I mounted Nightstar. This was a warhorse. I hoped I would not need him but if I did then I knew that he would fight as hard

Saxon Bane

as any warrior. Saxon Slayer suddenly felt as light as a feather in my hand. I held it aloft and a shaft of sunlight caught it. It must have been a coincidence, else it was the spirits, for the Saxons suddenly headed for the gap between Hogan Lann and my spearmen. They had taken the bait!

My son had spread out his squires in front of his heavily armed and armoured equites. The advancing Northumbrians would just see a thin line of lightly armed horsemen and a few spearmen. There would appear to be no archers and none of the deadly warriors encased from head to foot in iron. Edwin would think it was as the previous day and we were trying to slow him down. He was pushing onto the river.

This was the first battle where I was just an observer but I had an excellent vantage point. I could see the whole battle unfolding before me. It was as though I was in the hall at The Narrows and this was a map in front of me. We had just one reserve of horsemen. They were away to the west. Tuanthal's younger brother Ardle led them. I hoped we would not need them. Everything else was planned. Ardle was there in case Edwin outwitted me or the spirits were precocious.

As the Northumbrians closed I could see King Fiachnae mac Báetáin visibly retraining his men. They were desperate, from what I could see, to hurl themselves at the advancing armoured giant. I saw Penda's banner between Kay's and Bors'. They would be resolute but I worried about the Hibernians. Suddenly the sky above my men became black as Daffydd and his archers showered the enemy with barbed death. It was as though someone had hit the whole of the advancing wedge with a hammer. It faltered and then stopped. The second and third arrow storm seemed to punch them back as they regrouped and reformed the wedge. It was too much for the men of Ulaid. They screamed their war cries and raced forward to engage with the enemy. It was a disaster. We had barely begun to whittle down the enemy numbers. In an instant my reckless allies had made victory almost impossible. My death would be in vain!

At first, the wild charge seemed to succeed and punched a hole into the side of the wedge. There were, however, just too many Northumbrians and the men of Dál nAraidi might have had better swords than before but they deigned to wear armour. The Northumbrians began to flood around the sides of the Irishmen and cut into their ranks. The shocked warriors did not fall back, they fled. I knew, as did my son, that fleeing warriors run until they feel safe. They would run until they reached the Dunum!

I heard the buccina sound as Hogan Lann tried to remedy the situation. He led his horsemen forwards to hit the Northumbrians who were pursuing the fleeing Hibernians. Ironically it was the lack of armour which saved the men of Dál nAraidi. They were able to outrun the heavily armoured Northumbrians. It was with some relief that I saw the banner of the king rally his men behind those of Bors. Daffydd's arrows continued to fall. Hogan Lann and his equites had saved our new allies. My fingers tightened around the hilt of Saxon Slayer. Could they extricate themselves?

I saw the dragon standard of Rheged and could hear its wail as Hogan Lann led the finest equites west of Byzantium. They thundered magnificently towards the disorganised Northumbrians. It was then I saw King Edwin's trap. He had many men hidden in the hills and the woods. A red and green mass of humanity poured down on to Hogan Lann's exposed flanks. The two forces of Saxons lapped around my son and his men to engulf them. When I saw the standard fall I knew that he was in danger. King Cadwallon was coming to his aid but he might not be in time. Pol and Lann Aelle would, even now, be approaching the rear of the Northumbrians but they would be too late to save the next Warlord of Rheged.

I dismounted, "Gawan, take Nightstar and order Ardle and the reserves to go to your brother's aid. Lead them, my son, and save your brother, the next Warlord of Rheged."

"But Myrddyn?"

"I will watch him."

He smiled, "You take care, father. I will be back."

He sprang into the saddle and galloped off. Nightstar was quick and the reserves just a few hundred paces from us.

"Morcar, keep the wolf standard flying high. Let the enemy know where we are."

## Saxon Bane

I watched as my son led our handful of reserves bravely towards the Northumbrians who had now totally surrounded Hogan Lann, Bors and Kay. I could do no more. My plan had been good but one mistake had ended any chance of success we might have had. I would be an impotent spectator. I could do nothing.

I looked down at Myrddyn. I thought I had detected a movement behind the closed eyelids. Was he coming round? I had done all that I could to help my son. The battle was now out of my hands and my work was finished. I had to help my old friend. In the absence of a scabbard I stuck Saxon Slayer into the ground. I knelt and wet the wizard's face with water. Miraculously I saw his eyes flicker open and then close. I poured a tiny amount of water into his mouth. There was a movement and I felt his fingers as they touched the hem of my byrnie. His eyes fully opened and I saw a smile begin to appear upon his lips as he saw me. Suddenly the smile was replaced by a look of fear. "Morcar!"

I turned to see Morcar stab down at me with a dagger. I put my hand up to protect myself and the blade burned as it slashed down my arm. He pulled it back and changed the angle of attack. He thrust it towards my neck. Then he twisted the knife and I felt it slip between my armour and leather byrnie to sink into my shoulder. I had had worse wounds but this one burned as though he had heated the dagger in the fire first. I punched Morcar with all the strength I had in my left hand. I saw him fall backwards. I tried to rise to my feet but I had no strength in my legs. I sank to my knees and began to roll backwards.

My nephew rose and grabbed Saxon Slayer. He sprang on to the back of his horse. Even though I knew he would be the one I had to know the reason. "Why Morcar? Why?"

"I will be king! I am not content to serve another. I will either rule or have nothing! You were a fool who sacrificed everything for another. I am not a fool and I will be King of Rheged! I have Saxon Slayer!"

He wheeled his horse around. I tried to go after him but I could not move my legs. Suddenly the sky was above me. Myrddyn's face appeared. "Why, Myrddyn , why?"

## Saxon Bane

He looked at me sadly. "You knew it would be him, Lann. You expected this."

"I will just rest awhile and I will feel better in a moment."

He shook his head and I saw a tear appear. "No, my old friend; that was a poisoned blade. I can smell the poison. This is your time. You are dying"

I nodded, "Watch over my family."

He smiled, "I heard you when I was in the spirit world. I will do all that you asked and more. Go with honour my dear friend. You have done more than the spirits expected of you and they will be waiting for you in the Otherworld e'en now. Go with your head held high for no man could have done more than you did."

He knelt forward and kissed my forehead. I tried to speak but it all became dark and the pain stopped. I was dying. I had thought I would die in battle defending Rheged from the Saxons. Instead, I was slain by my nephew. I was being sacrificed so that Rheged could rise again. I was content.

There was blackness as in my dreams and then I heard my mother calling me from afar. Why could I not see her? Suddenly the sky became blue and I saw my mother and father. Aideen was with them and there was King Urien dressed in his armour. I was lifted to my feet by my parents and I looked down and saw that I was wearing gold. King Urien said, "Welcome my Warlord of Rheged. Welcome to the Otherworld."

Saxon Bane

# Part 2

## Hogan Lann-Warlord of Rheged

# Chapter 17

I am Hogan Lann and when King Edwin sprung his trap I thought that I had lost the battle which my father had so carefully planned. When the Hibernians had attacked I saw the hands of the gods putting challenges in our path. I had thought to save the day by rescuing the wild men of the west. We had carved and scythed a path deep into the heart of the Northumbrians but that now worked against us. We were being pressed tightly together. When I saw the wave of Northumbrians pouring down from the hillsides I saw that King Edwin had planned as carefully as we had. He looked to have as many men on the hillside as before us.

Before all movement was impossible I roared, "Wedge!" Llewellyn, the standard-bearer, began to drop back as my heavy horses moved together to give mutual protection. A spearman stabbed at his right hand and the dragon standard of Rheged fell. I could almost feel the wave of horror which came over my men. If the standard fell then the battle was lost. Llewellyn was a mighty warrior and he leapt from his horse and swung his mace to demolish the head of the spearman who had dared to stab him. He picked up the standard and waved it one handed. It began to wail and the Saxon warriors closest to him fell back in fear. He regained his mount and dropped into the space behind me. Once we had the continuity of horses and shields we could begin to defend ourselves once more.

I hoped that King Cadwallon would soon be joining me. The surprise of his sudden appearance might just carry the day. We had to use our strength and power to move on. If we stayed still then the hordes of

## Saxon Bane

humanity pouring from the hills would overwhelm us. Our powerful mounts would have to carry the day.

"Rheged! Charge!"

It was little more than a fast walk but our heavily armoured horses moved inexorably forwards. I held my sword behind my shield in my left arm and I levelled my lance. I punched at each face I saw and then withdrew it. Even those who had a face mask on were felled by my triangular shaped lance. Its head had been forged and tempered by the best smiths we had and was superior to the flimsy metal it encountered. Those at the front of the wedge all held lances and we drove all before us. Amazingly we suddenly began to pick up speed as the Northumbrians fell back and fled the field. I wondered why and then I saw my brother, Gawan, leading the reserves into their flank. Bors and Kay were leading the spearmen in a controlled charge but racing ahead of them were King Fiachnae mac Báetáin and Penda screaming savage war cries as they closed with the Northumbrians.

I stabbed at the nearest heavily armed warrior and my lance struck him in the face and then shattered as another warrior struck the wooden shaft. I cast the wooden haft aside and picked up my mace. I swung it and finished off the job started by my now broken lance.

The wedge had now become a line as the Northumbrians began to flee. Our squires, riding lighter horses began to outstrip us but they were just as deadly as we were; their swords raining death on unprotected backs. Then King Cadwallon was next to me and our two dragon standards were side by side. The wailing standard of Rheged inspired fear in our foes and they started to discard weapons. I saw that they were heading up into the hills. The wild charge down the hill had isolated warriors who were now faced by heavy armoured horsemen. My father's plan would have worked completely and we would have cut them off but for the premature attack by King Fiachnae mac Báetáin and his men. We would win the battle but King Edwin and many of his men would escape. Our heavy horses would not be much use in the woods which rose steeply to guard the escape route of the Northumbrian. My father had been correct about King Edwin's choice of battlefield. Just one mistake was going to stop total victory; the mistake of an ill disciplined ally. My father would be Warlord for a little longer.

   I slowed my mount down. He was a fine warhorse as were all my horses but it did not do to push them too far. A broken warhorse would never recover. I pushed my helmet back to allow cooler air on to my face and to afford me a better view of the battlefield. The equites and squires led by Pol and Lann Aelle approaching from the south had joined with Gawan and closed the circle around the Northumbrians. The spearmen were eager to join in the slaughter and they would soon be despatching those pockets of oathsworn Northumbrians and east Angles who fought to protect the lives of their lords. I could see the movement up the slopes which marked the fleeing Northumbrians. I could just make out the standards which showed where King Edwin and his bodyguard were. There seemed to be many Northumbrians still behind them. The king had moved swiftly to escape capture.

   Gawan reined in next to me. His bloody sword showed that he had fought this day. I clasped his arm. "A timely arrival little brother."

   "It was father. He saw the problem and sent me to bring the reserves."

   I turned to view the knoll. "I cannot see him now."

   Gawan laughed, "You know how his leg aches. I daresay he is sat with Myrddyn. The view from the knoll would show him that we had won. He has fought his last battle as Warlord."

   "No, brother." I pointed to the hillside. "King Edwin lives still. He will make it to the Roman fort at Eboracum and from there he can sail to King Raedwald and safety."

   "Even so his army in Northumbria is finished."

   King Cadwallon reined in next to me. "A great victory!"

   "But not the one my father planned. If the men of Dál nAraidi had not attacked early then none would have escaped."

   Cadwallon smiled, "They fought well and their ferocious attack, whilst premature, broke the backs and the hearts of the Northumbrians. They were beaten from the moment that you and your horsemen charged."

   Why could these two not see what was clear to me? They were younger I knew but it should have been obvious that my father had planned the perfect battle. It would have been the battle to end this war once and for all in this fertile plain. Now we would have to winkle out pockets of Northumbrians. We had had them all before us for one brief moment in time. The net had been closing as my father had planned. One thing was certain. I would tell my father that he would be Warlord no longer. I would still need his advice but I would not risk his life again. I shook my head in wonder at his plan. Had we all done as he had ordered then we would have won. Perhaps the spirits had been wrong to send him for our new allies.

I pointed up at the hills. "Our foot can pursue them that way as well as the squires. Let us take Tuanthal and his men, head south and cut them off when they head for Eboracum."

"A good plan."

"Llewellyn, the signal."

My standard-bearer sounded the buccina and the commanders of horse joined me. "Pol and Lann Aelle, we will take our men south. Have your squires pursue the Northumbrians along with the foot. Tuanthal, join with us. Aedh, take your scouts and find where the Northumbrians will emerge from this high ground and watch them."

Aedh waved his acknowledgement and then he and his scouts flew like the wind to head south.

Cadwallon gestured to the spearman most of whom were now half way up the hills. "And those?"

"Tuanthal send a rider to pass on the orders to the king, Bors and Penda. They are to keep their swords in the backs of the Northumbrians"

"What about the Warlord?"

I laughed, "He said he needed sleep; he and Myrddyn can sleep the day away and young Morcar can watch them."

We had lost equites. Not all were dead but it was just over one hundred and sixty equites who followed me south. I left a handful of my equites, the ones whose horses had been injured, to gather the wounded and take them back to the knoll. If Myrddyn recovered then he would be able to heal them.

## Saxon Bane

We were going only slightly faster than the few Northumbrians who had taken that route but we were saving the horses. It was a slow pursuit but we caught them, gradually. We killed all those that we caught. There was no point in being merciful. Northumbrians were like rats; if you left one to breed then there would be a dozen within the year.

We paused near to the stream called Cod Beck and watered our horses. There Aedh's riders found us. "The leading warriors are less than ten miles from Eboracum. King Edwin is amongst them. We have seen his standard."

"Then we must hurry."

Before we could move I heard a commotion behind me. I saw Scanlan, one of the equites who had been wounded. He was not in armour and he was riding a spare horse. "My lord! My lord!" His voice carried over the vale as he urged his horse on towards us.

His face showed his distress even before he reached us. My mind ran through the problems which might have caused it. Perhaps we had been attacked by a second force of Northumbrians. It could be a trick of King Edwin's. It could have been that some had made a stand on the hill. It is what I might have done.

"My lord!" He leapt for his horse and abased himself. "The Warlord has been murdered. He is dead and Myrddyn says you are now Warlord."

I felt the whole world spinning. It could not be true. I stared at Gawan whose face showed his distress. "I should never have left him!" My brother's voice sounded like the wail of the dragon standard.

I shook my head. "You obeyed orders. No warrior is wrong if he obeys orders." I turned back to Scanlan. "Who did this? Saxons?"

He looked up the distress clear on his tear stained face, "No, Warlord; Morcar, your cousin."

There was a stunned silence. This was treachery of the worst kind. He was family; he was of our blood! We had taken in that arrogant youth and my father had tried to make a man of him. His repayment had been an untimely and treacherous death. I looked to Gawan, "We must return."

Saxon Bane

King Cadwallon said, "But you are Warlord. King Edwin remains at large."

I clenched my fists in anger but I heeded my father's words when he had spoken to me in the solar. He must have known then that his time was short. All of our recent conversations came flooding back and I realised that he had been preparing me for this moment. Every word he had said had been measured; he was telling me how to lead. I was now Warlord. I needed to think before I spoke. I forced myself to breathe a little slower. "I will just take Tuanthal and his men. I am sure that the warriors I leave can complete the task. Pol, you and Lann Aelle command the equites in my absence."

"We will, my lord." Both of my father's former squires showed that they were trying to contain the emotion that they felt. They had grown up as I had in the shadow of the greatest warrior Rheged had ever produced. I suspected my face looked the same as theirs.

I saw Cadwallon's face soften as the news of my father's death sank in. He too, as his father before him had been trained by the Warlord of Rheged and he was now gone. Just his shadow would remain. "You are right, Hogan Lann, and I am sorry for your loss."

I felt the anger come again and I fought to control it. My words came out tight and cold, "It is Rheged and Gwynedd which has lost more for he was ever the hope for a free Rheged. I fear that dream lies on that knoll along with my dead father."

I whipped Star's head around and dug my spurs in. I regretted it immediately. My horse was not the cause of my father's death and he did not deserve ill treatment. That was down to a witch and a treacherous cousin. Both would pay. Gawan and Tuanthal appeared on either side of me.

"I am sorry I left him, Hogan Lann." Gawan's face was filled with pain and something more; was it guilt?

I said nothing for I was still angry. I was not angry with Gawan but I knew that if I said anything then it would sound as though I was criticising him. I meant what I had said. He did right to obey orders and no-one could have known of Morcar's treachery. I had seen no sign of it. He had deceived me. How had he deceived Myrddyn and my father?

"I have served your father for longer than almost any. He would not want any blame placed at anyone's door. He would say it was *wyrd*. He would say that it was meant to be." Tuanthal and Aedh had served my father since he had held the Castle Perilous. He knew him.

I noticed a guilty look on Gawan's face. What was he hiding? What did he know of all of this? I shook my head. I was becoming suspicious and I had no right to be. I knew that my brother was innocent. I could not allow Morcar to make me mistrust everyone. "Tuanthal is right. Did you not notice that since his midsummer vigil he had changed? He had a dream in the cave which affected him greatly. Perhaps he dreamed this."

"Then Myrddyn, too, must have known of his imminent death."

Gawan nodded. "Of course he did." I saw the hesitation on Gawan's face. "Last night as we watched Myrddyn he told me that Myrddyn had dreamed his death and he was ready for it." I saw that he was becoming upset. "He gave me the scabbard for Saxon Slayer. I am to ask Myrddyn where the hidden chamber lies at Civitas Carvetiorum. I am sorry I should have spoken but he swore me to secrecy. He said it was ordained by the spirits. I was torn, brother. I wanted to tell you but I had sworn an oath."

My poor little brother was about to break. I saw why he had had the guilty look on his face. It was because he thought he had let me down. I suddenly realised that I was the head of the family now. I not only had my own sons and children to care for but the rest of the family too. I had to be careful with Gawan; I did not want him to break. That thought made me think of my stepmother. She would need help too for her heart would lie broken when she found out. I would have to tell Myfanwy. Her world would be destroyed.

"Brother you need not reproach yourself. Tuanthal was right. Father knew it was coming and he faced his death like a man. He was the true Wolf Warrior. He sent you away to save what he loved, his family and Rheged. He always put himself last. He kept everything inside. I think the only one who peered into his heart was Myrddyn and it will hit the old man hard. It will be harder for the living to bear the loss."

We rode in silence for a while. I did not know what the others were thinking but I knew that I was regretting not having spoken to him more. I now remembered all the times we had sat in the solar and he had spoken to us. Now I knew that he was aware of his death it became even more painful. I wished I had told him, when he was still alive, how he was the greatest man I had ever known. If I could be half the warrior, the Warlord, and the father that he had been then I would be a happy man. As we passed over the battlefield which was already covered in the magpies and crows feasting on the dead I smiled, ruefully. This had been his victory. He had planned to perfection and used all of our skills and warriors. Nothing had been wasted. Had he been leading then perhaps the disaster of King Fiachnae mac Báetáin and his wild warriors might have been averted and we would have had a complete victory. That was not our doing. That was *wyrd*.

There were a knot of warriors gathered around the knoll. These were the wounded warriors who had not the energy to pursue and they were the scouts sent by Aedh. Our father's body lay covered with his old wolf cloak. He had not used it for years but it had always accompanied us when we were on campaign. It marked him for who he was. Next to him lay the wolf standard. Both would accompany him to the Otherworld. Neither would go to war again. I looked for his sword. Saxon Slayer was nowhere to be seen.

Myrddyn struggled to his feet as we approached. He looked pale but his eyes were sharp. The wizard was back. "Where is Saxon Slayer?"

"Morcar took it."

I looked at Gawan. "Then you hold something valuable." I smiled at Myrddyn. "Father gave the scabbard to Gawan for safe keeping."

"He knew Morcar would kill him. He saw it as I did in a dream. At first, he did not believe it but after Morcar's abduction the youth changed. Your father saw it clearly the day that he announced that you would be Warlord. Morcar was the only one who did not celebrate."

"If he knew then why did he not do something about it?"

## Saxon Bane

"Because, Warlord, he was the sacrifice. He had to die so that Rheged could live. His time was over. You cannot change what is planned for you by the spirits. It was *wyrd*." Suddenly the old man's voice became thick with emotion. "You do not think that I enjoy losing my dearest and my oldest friend, do you? I walked the length of the country to serve him and I serve him still. I will serve you as I served him for I can see him in you." He turned to Gawan, "And in you. The best of the Warlord lives in you both. You, Hogan Lann, are the Warlord and the leader and you, Gawan, are the one who will speak with the spirit world. Together you are more powerful than you father ever was and that was why he needed to die. His time was done. The day of the Wolf Warrior is over."

I pulled the cloak back. He looked at peace. "How was he killed?"

Myrddyn pulled the byrnie to one side and there was a narrow cut. "There, he was stabbed."

I could not believe that such a tiny wound had killed a man who had suffered much worse before. "But that is just a tiny scratch. He survived much worse wounds before now."

"Aye a scratch from a small blade but the blade was tipped with Wolf's Bane. It was poisoned and deadly; a scratch would be enough to kill. The witch knew her poisons. It was chosen to kill the Wolf Warrior. He was the last of the Wolf Brethren."

"The witch."

"The witch, aye. And there I blame myself for I was blinded by her. She used her own witchcraft to blind my senses and I saw what I wished to see. She and her sisters are more dangerous than Edwin or the sons of Aethelfrith. It was she who poisoned the mushrooms and when that failed Morcar had to take matters into his own hand." He looked at Gawan. "Had your father not sent you then you too would lie dead here. The spirits saved your life. Remember that."

Aedh galloped up. "Have your scouts found anything?"

He nodded grimly, "Aye death. I found the headless corpses of my men close to Stanwyck. There were some of Oswald's men there."

"How do you know?"

"My men killed two of them."

Myrddyn shook his head. "I was blinded by that young witch. This has all been carefully planned."

"By Oswald and Oswiu?"

"Oswald is the cunning one. This was planned from the moment we set foot in Dál nAraidi. He worked on Morcar as the weakest vessel and then used his witch to ensure that his plan succeeded. He has done all of this to get the Saxon Slayer. With that weapon he can win over the Saxons of Northumbria. We have helped them by destroying Edwin's army."

"And what is in it for Morcar?" I found it hard to believe that my cousin had changed so much. "He is no Saxon."

"But he would be a king and a king of Rheged ruled by Saxons is better than being no king at all."

Gawan showed his disbelief too. "Is he that shallow?"

"I fear he is. Raibeart was a good leader and a loyal brother but he was not a good father. He indulged his son." Myrddyn smiled, "Something you could never accuse Lord Lann of. You two were treated in the same way as every warrior he trained and he made no allowances for your blood." He covered the face with the cloak.

"Do we bury him here?" As much as I wanted to take my father home I knew that it would take too long and the body would have begun to decompose long before we reached his wife.

"No, your father saw his tomb. We will take him there."

"Where is it?"

"In the dream cave at Wyddfa."

"But his body…"

"You remember when you were in Constantinopolis, Warlord?"

"I do."

"There were books and papers there about the Egyptians who mummified their dead Pharaohs so that their remains were preserved. I read them and I believe that I can do that for Lord Lann."

I did not want to know the details but I knew that it would please my mother to see his face one more time before he was buried. "How long will it take?"

"We cannot leave until tomorrow."

"And Aedh, can your men pick up their trail?"

"They can but with a head start like that they could be anywhere."

"You cannot find them?"

His face hardened. "I will find them, never fear, Warlord. I am just saying that this will not be quick."

"It does not need to be. We just have to find the sword and avenge the Warlord. There is no greater quest. We have a leader to bury first. Tuanthal gather your men we will leave tomorrow. I will ride to King Cadwallon. He can command until I have found Morcar and the sword."

"I will come with you."

Myrddyn shook his head. "No Gawan. I need you to help me."

My brother paled, "But why?"

Myrddyn spread his arms. "Because when I die I wish you to preserve my body. You will need to watch what I do so that you can repeat it for me." His eyes bored into Gawan, "I have dreamed my death too."

Saxon Bane

# Chapter 18

It was nighttime when I caught up with King Cadwallon. My men and I had changed horses so that we could make a fast time but even so it was late when we arrived. The king and the rest of the army had surrounded Eboracum. "He is within the walls of Eboracum with five hundred of his warriors. We have him trapped. He cannot escape, Warlord." My captain of spears bowed.

I suddenly saw Bors and the others in a different light. I was used to commanding but now I had supreme command. Even King Cadwallon would follow my orders.

"We have won a great victory, Warlord."

"But at too great a cost." I told them all that had befallen us."

King Fiachnae mac Báetáin looked distraught. It was almost as though his father had died. "This is my fault. If my men had not disobeyed their orders then the Warlord would still be alive."

King Cadwallon said quietly, "But this Warlord is still alive and I think that Lord Lann would not have this any other way. Is that not right Lord Hogan Lann?"

"Do not upset yourself. My father knew he would be killed by Morcar. It was *wyrd*; it was meant to be. He sent us all away so that only he would be hurt by Morcar. He was a great man with a vision I can only dream of."

"Nevertheless I will train my warriors now so that they are as disciplined as yours."

"Good for we will need them before too long. We have many enemies to defeat."

I looked at their expectant faces and noted that they were all tinged with sympathy. I did not need sympathy. I needed revenge. I forced my mind to clear so that I could focus on the task in hand. I was going to leave them.

## Saxon Bane

"I am here to tell you that I go to bury my father and then seek his killer and return Saxon Slayer to its rightful home. I will just use Tuanthal and his men. I will not take away any of the equites. Aedh is already hunting Morcar."

Penda looked worried. "But what of King Edwin and the Northumbrians? What of the alliance?"

"The alliance continues. You do not need the Warlord here. Eventually, Edwin will surrender and we will have won."

"Suppose he does not surrender?"

"Then he will fight and lose. Either way we win."

King Cadwallon grasped my arm. "You are right, Warlord. Go and bring his killer to justice. When Edwin is finished then we will return to Wyddfa and pay homage to the warrior who saved Rheged."

"Thank you.

I took just Garth ap Daffydd with me. He was my squire and almost ready to be an equite. This would be a good test for him but I needed someone I could trust and, outside of my brother and my captains, he was the only one. Oswald had spies in our camp and our army. They did not wear a sign. As Morcar had shown it could be anybody. We took spare horses from my hundred. They were fresher than the ones we had ridden hard.

Garth talked all the way north. Part of it was to keep me awake but he was also as shocked as any by the treachery. He had grown up in the fort at The Narrows. As the grandson of Miach the archer he knew of the traditions which ran through our army and our warriors. He had known Morcar for my father had placed him with me to test his suitability as an equite. Morcar did not have what it took to be an equite. He had been a good rider and a good swordsman but he did not work well with others. He was intolerant of the mistakes of everyone else yet he saw not his own flaws. Worse than that, he was loath to help anybody. His enlistment had been brief and I wondered what my father had planned for him. That was the trouble; I had not spoken to him when I had had the chance and now the chance was gone forever. I would not be dreaming in

## Saxon Bane

the cave. I was a little jealous. Gawan would speak with our father again and I would have to make do with second hand voices.

I was suddenly aware that Garth was watching me. "Sorry, Garth, what did you say?"

"I was just asking, Warlord, where would Morcar go?"

"That is a good question and I have been wracking my brains for an idea. It will be to the west. Hibernia or Manau would be most likely." At the back of my mind was something which my father had said early on in the campaign. How Morgause had two sisters and the Saxons had put them in different villages. Now that we knew that Morgause had been placed there by Oswald then we knew that the Saxons we had captured belonged to him. At the same time, there were at least two more villages on the west coast with two more witches. I could now see the clever plan. Morcar must have been seduced or suborned in Hibernia. I had no idea how. He had been the spy the captured Saxons had spoken of. He had been passing information to his new masters and would have known our route. Oswald had laid his human caltrops well. Had we not stumbled upon Morgause there were two more opportunities. There were two more witches in my land and they would need to be dealt with. If I left them then their evil would grow and multiply.

"King Fiachnae mac Báetáin should be able to help if they have gone to Hibernia."

I knew that Garth was just filling the silence and making conversation but he had stumbled upon something. "He will not be in Hibernia any longer. He knows that we now have an ally there. He will not risk us following there. He will need somewhere he can hide and defend. He will either be on Manau or the west coast. Well done, Garth!"

Although he looked pleased I could see that he didn't know what he had said that had brought that reaction. "We will follow then?"

"As soon as we have changed horses we will try to pick up his trail."

"And your father's body?"

"The wounded warriors will be a fitting escort for the Warlord of Rheged. The Wolf Warrior may not have his wolf brethren with him but he will have noble warriors who are true of heart."

## Saxon Bane

It was the middle of the night when we reached the camp. Tuanthal had many guards around the perimeter. He was taking no chances. The captain of the guard awoke him when we arrived. By the time he had joined us I had reached the fire and there I found Myrddyn huddled under a cloak. His hooded eyes flashed open when I approached. He looked drawn.

"We will leave first thing, Tuanthal. The wounded warriors and some of your older horseman can accompany Myrddyn and," I paused as though saying the words might repeat the deed, "my father."

"Will we have enough men?"

"We do not seek an army. We seek a snake and a witch. It will be enough."

He half turned and then he smiled as he said, "You will be as good a Warlord as your father. It will just be a different Warlord."

He walked to the other side of the fire and lay down. I looked back at Myrddyn whose eyes had searched my face as I had spoken with Tuanthal. There was an unspoken question in my head. Had he finished his grisly task of mummifying my father? He seemed to know it for he nodded and said, "It is done."

"How…?"

He chuckled, "Your father asked me that many times. I find it easier reading your brother's thoughts but it will improve as time goes on. Like your father I am aware of the passage of time."

"Why did you not tell me you had dreamed his death?"

"Because that was your father's decision and it was a good one. All the decisions you made were for the best of reasons. Had that idea of his death been in your head you would have made the wrong ones for the right reason." He closed his eyes and lay back. "All things are written before we are even born," he said, enigmatically.

I lay down next to my brother and tried to sleep but I was a death beyond sleep. My mind seemed to be filled with unanswered questions and I found myself wondering if I had done things differently would we have had a different outcome. It was too complicated now. When it had just been our small army led by my father it had been easy to make

## Saxon Bane

decisions and to do the right thing. Now we were allied to the men of Cymru, Hibernia and Mercia. We had to think about their men and their leaders. As the Irish had shown they were not always predictable. Would things ever be the same again?

I must have slept but I did not remember it. I opened my eyes and saw the sun peering over the hills. No one spoke as we broke camp. We had a cart we had used for arrows and I hitched Nightstar to it. My father's warhorse could carry him home. His days of fighting were over and he would be given his freedom when we had buried the Warlord. I helped Tuanthal and Gawan to reverently place the body in the cart and cover it with the wolf cloak. Gawan looked dreadful. My father, by contrast looked as though he was still alive. Perhaps that was where the legend grew that the Warlord did not die but sleeps waiting to come to the rescue of Rheged. His face was just covered with the wolf cloak and men wanted to see the face of their Warlord. The followers of the White Christ had their saints and their relics. That day the idea of the Warlord of Rheged, the Wolf Warrior, became our relic. Whatever Gawan and Myrddyn had done for my father had worked. Myfanwy could look at the body and see the man she had loved.

Myrddyn then placed some amphorae with him. I went to ask and Gawan said, "Don't ask!"

Myrddyn looked at me sadly, "It is your father's organs. We shall bury them with him." I shivered at the thought of what my brother and the wizard had had to do. They both had a courage I could only dream of.

Our route would be shared for a while. We were both heading west. Aedh and his men had picked up the trail. There would be little point in thrashing horses to death. The weather remained fair and it was unlikely that the signs would be washed away. I was convinced that Morcar would have sailed for Manau but we could not afford to overlook any possibility.

As we passed Stanwyck all of us looked to the site of my father's birth and his first fight with Saxons. How ironical that he had died so close to his place of birth, the place where he had killed his first enemy and yet had died at the hand of a blood relative.

## Saxon Bane

Once we had crossed the high divide the road headed south. The scouts came back and told us that the trail was going towards the coast. "They camped at the deserted church."

Myrddyn suddenly became interested. "How far away is the church?"

"A mile away, perhaps two." I could see that the scout was desperate to know the reason why but he was afraid to ask.

"Captain Tuanthal, guard the Warlord until we return. Hogan Lann, Gawan come with me."

Everyone was mystified but we trusted the wizard enough to follow. We spied the church before we saw it. It stood high above the river and looked to have been the centre of a small community. The cross still stood atop the small bell tower. We saw the evidence of the Northumbrian's camp fire. Myrddyn dismounted and took a box from the back of the saddle.

"Follow me." I looked at Gawan and he shrugged. "Gawan does not know what I am about to do Warlord. Your father does. He and I discussed this before he died."

When we reached the church we saw that the roof had gone and anything of value taken. Myrddyn handed the box to me and then dropped to his hands and knees. As he did so I examined the box. It had an equite on the top with the dragon standard; yet the box looked old and weathered. How could that be?

Myrddyn moved around the stone floor cleaning as he went. Suddenly he shouted, "I have it! Come here with the casket." I gave it to him and he placed it on the floor. He took out a knife and ran it around a line of dirt. He patiently scraped it all away until I saw that it was an inset stone. He put his eye close to the middle and began to pick at it with his knife. Suddenly I saw two more lines in the stone. He scraped away the dirt and then prised up a piece of metal. He smiled up at me. "Here, Warlord, use your strength for something useful. Lift this stone."

I pulled but nothing seemed to happen.

"Use all of your strength. The future of Rheged may depend upon this."

## Saxon Bane

I do not know if it was the words he used or something else but the stone began to rise. Once it was clear I moved it to the side and a damp musty smell came from beneath the hole.

Myrddyn picked up the box. It fitted almost exactly into the hole. He dropped it in and then, using the hilt of his dagger, pushed it away from view. If you looked down the hole appeared to be empty. Then he replaced the stone. He rubbed dirt and soil back into the cracks and then stepped back, seemingly satisfied. It was as though the hole had never been there. He rubbed his hands and smiled.

"Now, Myrddyn, the explanation."

"Your father and I found the box at Civitas Carvetiorum. Inside was a message from Brother Osric. Your father was far-sighted and knew that Rheged might not always survive. This is a message for one of your descendants. If they come here and dig this up it will lead them to Civitas. The map showing them where the treasure is to be found is in the box. Now that Gawan has given me the scabbard of Saxon Slayer I will place it there too. It will show your descendant that this is to help Rheged."

I shook my head. "Should the scabbard not be with Saxon Slayer?"

He looked at me sadly, "I have dreamed of the death of Saxon Slayer. It will not need its scabbard where it is going."

"Tell me and I will save the sword!"

"How can you save what you do not have?"

"Besides," added Gawan, "if you change the future then you may be destroying Rheged. The spirits will not let us down."

"Your brother is right. He is learning rapidly. The story is already written and we are just acting it out. Trust your heart, Warlord and your brother."

"But whose descendant will it be?"

"That I cannot see. I know the face of the warrior but he did not wear a name in my dream. He looked like your father, as you do. Watch over your children and tell them of their past and their future for they are intertwined. What we do now will affect their lives and their futures. They need to know about this deserted church on the estuary. They should tell their children. I know not how many generations this will take."

By the time we reached the men and the wagon Gawan and I were deep in thought. Tuanthal and Aedh knew better than to ask what we had been about. Myrddyn and his escort took the Roman Road south. "I will not bury your father until you are there."

I laughed, "Suppose we do not make it."

Myrddyn closed his eyes for a moment. "I have not dreamed your death yet." He pointed a bony finger at Gawan. "Remember, Warlord, your brother can dream too. Keep him close. Keep him safe."

Aedh and his scouts rode just fifty paces from us. There were now just eight of them. We had lost some to treachery and ambush and we had left some for the king. The ones we retained were the best. Tuanthal had kept forty resolute warriors too. With Garth, my squire, we were more than equipped to deal with Morcar and whoever else Oswald and Oswiu had waiting for us.

We found that the trail headed towards the south east. We were moving away from the village where we had found Morgause. I knew little of the coastline and the villages. This was all new country to us. We would have to move carefully and stealthily. We crossed the Lune and it became too dark to continue without losing the signs. We camped in a sheltered dell with a nearby stream for water. It was cold fare we ate. I wanted no fire. We had no idea how close or how far away the enemy were. Their fires at the church had shown us that they were lighting fires. The fact that we could neither see nor smell fires, meant that they were not close. However, I was taking no chances. Morcar knew our ways. Sentries were put around the camp and I found myself asleep as soon as I stretched out.

I did dream. It was not one of my father's dreams. It did not tell me of what was to come. It was just a vision, over and over of Morcar stabbing into my father's neck. I watched, unable to move as the wolf's bane dripped from the point of the cold dagger. I saw my father as his body shook and shivered when the poison took hold. I heard Morgause and Morcar laughing like demented foxes. And then I awoke.

## Saxon Bane

Gawan was awake and he was watching me. "You dreamt."

"A nightmare more like." There was something in the way he said it. "You knew."

He nodded, "I dreamed too. I have the gift, like Myrddyn. It is not as accurate as Myrddyn's but I saw that you dreamed of our father's death."

"And what did you dream?"

"I saw a sea and a whale rising from the sea. It opened its mouth and I saw Morcar. He was holding Saxon Slayer."

"That makes no sense."

"I know. Myrddyn told me that I had to interpret my own dreams. I do not understand it yet but I will look for a whale. As we are not close to the sea I will not look for it yet."

"What made the noise which woke me?"

"It was a couple of foxes."

I nodded, "The fox is the younger brother of the wolf. I dreamed of foxes." Something nagged at the back of my mind. It had been Morcar and Morgause who had sounded like foxes.

The nightmare did have one effect; it had made me wide wake. Perhaps that was my father at work for, as Gawan lay back I was suddenly aware of a slight noise and it was close. I slipped my sword from its scabbard and rose. Gawan knew me well enough to follow my actions. I walked to Tuanthal and shook his shoulder. When he saw the sword in my hand he too rose and grasped his weapon. We awoke all those around the fire. Soon we had twelve armed men. The rest were sleeping closer to the horses.

I scanned the outside of the camp. There was something missing; the sentries! "Alarum! We are being attacked!"

I sensed a movement and whipped around. My sword caught the edge of a spear which had been thrust at my side. A heartbeat later and I would have been skewered like a piece of meat. The warrior's momentum carried him forward and I punched him hard in the side as he came past. As soon as I hit cloth I knew he had no armour. He began to fall to the floor and I raised my sword and brought it crashing down on the side of his head. There was crunch and he lay still. I whirled around

## Saxon Bane

and two dark shapes were racing through the dark to reach me. I knew that I might not be so lucky this time. I reached down to grab the dead warrior's spear. Taking a chance I dropped to one knee and braced the spear against the ground. The first warrior ran on to the spear and I slashed my sword to rip into the unprotected thigh of the second warrior. They both screamed. The man with the spear stood looking at the wood coming from his middle and then fell while the second quickly pumped his life away.

   I stood and took in the scene. I could not see any other warriors close by. I knelt down and picked up the short seax the first warrior had had in his belt. I ran away from the fire to the horse lines. I reached there just as the warrior who had been trying to save them was slain by two Northumbrians. They did not see my stealthy approach. As they went to untie our mounts I stabbed one in the back with the seax and, as the other turned punched him in the face with the guard of my sword. He fell stunned to the ground. I needed prisoners. I stabbed him in the palm of his right hand and his left. I knelt down and cut the tendons on the back of both ankles. He would not move.

   I checked to make sure the horses were still securely tied and then ran back towards the firelight. My men were all awake now and the raiders were either fled or dying. Tuanthal, Aedh and Gawan all came running towards me. "We thought you, too, were slain."

   "No, little brother." I gestured to the skies with my sword. "The spirits sent the nightmare to wake me." I noticed that it was getting lighter. Dawn had broken. "I wounded a warrior by the horses. Bring him to the fire so that we may question him. Gawan, see to our wounded."

   I sheathed my sword and slipped the seax into my belt. We had been lucky. I knew we had lost men but it could have been far worse. Had Gawan and I not been awake then we might all be dead. As I stepped over the bodies of the first warriors I had killed I remembered how the Roman legions would build a camp each night to protect themselves. Perhaps we needed to do the same. We had become overconfident because of our successes.

## Saxon Bane

I examined the dead bodies. The warriors had no mail and only poor helmets. I could only see a couple of badly made shields. These were Saxons but they were not equipped like seasoned warriors. My guess, before we questioned the wounded prisoner, was that they were mercenaries. These were warriors without a lord who needed coin. That was a disturbing development; I had assumed that Oswald and Oswiu would be running out of warriors. Little by little we had been thinning their numbers. If they were hiring new killers, that would pose a problem. I needed to question the prisoner to discover the truth.

Aedh and Tuanthal were not gentle as they dragged the bleeding and moaning warrior to the fire. I saw that he was a young warrior. He had seen no more than eighteen summers. His beard was straggly. If he lived he would be crippled for life. I would offer him a warrior's death. Then I saw the cross of the White Christ about his neck. He would not thank me for that. We would just kill him when we had finished with him.

"Aedh, take some of your men and see if you can pick up their trail. They may have come from the main camp."

I reached down and ripped the cross from the warrior's neck. His eyes opened and I saw fear in them. I dangled the cross before him. "You have one chance to have this returned to you before I kill you; you answer my questions. If you do not then I will throw this into the fire and you will not see the White Christ after I kill you." His eyes widened in terror. He tried to raise his hand but the pain was too much and I saw him wince.

"Where did you come from?" I waved the crudely made cross in the direction of the fire.

"Manau."

"Is that where you lived?"

He shook his head. "No, we are West Saxons and we followed our lord, Aethelred, to fight against the Welsh. He died and we became bandits when we were left far from home." Now that his tongue had been loosened he could not wait to tell me all that he knew. Perhaps he hoped to be spared. "Eorl Oswald paid us to become his warriors and he took us to Manau."

"That is where he has his men?" He nodded. "How many does he have?"

He shook his head, "I am not sure. There were thirty of us who were brought on the ship to find you."

"How did you know where to find us?"

"The Welshman with the sword told us."

I shivered, "Saxon Slayer?"

He began to smile, "Yes that is it. How did you know?"

I ignored his question. "Where is this Welshman with the sword?"

"We left him and the woman who has the golden hair like a sunset with the ship at the coast."

"South or north?"

"South. A day's ride."

"Thank you." I put the cross into his maimed hand and nodded to Tuanthal. Even as the youth smiled my captain of horse ripped his blade across his throat. "They must have some horses close by."

"Where would they get horses?"

"I have no idea but at least we have a direction for Morcar now and we know that he is with Morgause and they still have the sword." As I stood and looked at the wrecked camp, an idea came to me. "And we know that Oswiu and Oswald are not on the mainland."

"How do we know that?"

"Morcar still has the sword and I think that the boy would have mentioned them. He told us the truth."

Saxon Bane

# Chapter 19

The attack had cost us dear. We had but twenty-four warriors remaining. With Gawan, my squire and my two captains that left less than thirty of us. As we headed down the clear trail which Aedh had found I spoke with Gawan about what we might face. Tuanthal and Aedh were great warriors but their minds were not as sharp as my little brother's. He had, like our father before us, the ability to see into the dark places of other men's minds and discover their plans.

"I think, Gawan, that they are using their father's treasury to buy back the throne. Remember we could not find it at Din Guardi. It explains why he was able to hide in Hibernia. He bought the protection for the two of them."

"That would make sense. If you wish to be king then no price is too great to achieve that."

"As our treacherous cousin proved."

"Perhaps the flaw was always within Morcar. We did not know him much when he was growing up. We were too busy becoming warriors and serving Rheged. He was indulging himself with his father's treasure."

"Was our father wrong to try to make a man of him?"

Gawan got that faraway look I often saw on the face of Myrddyn. "It was ordained. It was meant to be."

There was some comfort in knowing that everything was decided by the spirits.

The followers of the White Christ had so many rules to follow it was a wonder that they ever got out of bed in a morning. "Will they still be at the ship?"

Gawan closed his eyes. I was not sure if he was doing what Myrddyn did or if he was just trying to be like the wizard. "They will want to know if their attempt on your life succeeded. We found but four horses. I think they were to take the message back. The warrior told you it was a day's ride away. It would have taken them longer to walk."

"You are saying that if we hurry we can reach them before they leave."

I saw a brief moment of indecision and then he nodded. "Yes."

"Aedh!"

My captain of scouts galloped back to me. "Yes, Warlord?" It felt briefly strange to have this warrior whom I had grown up with deferring to me but I had to get used to it. I was now Warlord.

"Is this trail clear? Could we go faster? My brother and I believe that Morcar and the ship will be waiting for the return of these killers."

Enlightenment dawned, "Aye Warlord. We will go like the wind and leave you signs if we deviate from a straight line."

The scouts all had the fastest and most agile horses we possessed. They galloped off and I rode next to Tuanthal. "We are hoping to catch Morcar on the beach with his ship. We must brook no delay if we find him. We need to risk all and stop the sword from leaving these shores. The heart would go from Rheged if word got out that we had lost Saxon Slayer to the men of Northumbria."

"Fear not, Warlord, my men are keen to avenge the murder of the Warlord." Resolution and conviction were in his words and eyes. He had served with my father as long as any. I knew he would have given his life for my father without a moment's hesitation.

I was feeling more hopeful having seen the state of the mercenaries we had fought. If that was the best they had then I could take them with a handful of warriors. However it could be that the brothers had better warriors who they would have with their boat to guard Morcar and the precious sword.

The land through which we were travelling was flat. It meant the journey was easy but we could not see very far ahead. High hedges and trees were close to the paths and trails we took. We were not moving along Roman Roads. These were tracks made by animals and hunters and they wound around obstacles. I hoped that Morcar had not laid an ambush. This was perfect country for ambushes. We rode with our

## Saxon Bane

helmets tied to our saddles. We needed our eyes and ears to find the enemy before they found us. It was, indeed, our noses which smelled the sea before we saw it. The trail dropped down a bank and there, at a tree we saw a mark in the bark. We were to head west.

When we came upon the river we knew that we must be close to an estuary. Despite our need for speed I had to slow us down. Aedh and his men might be hiding ahead and watching for the ship. It proved to be a wise decision for one of Aedh's scouts suddenly stepped from the trees and held up his hand. We all stopped instantly.

He spoke quietly, "Warlord, the ship is in the estuary. It is one of the small Saxon ships with a dozen oars."

"Any sign of Morcar?"

He shook his head. "There are eight warriors on the beach."

I dismounted. "Leave the horses here. Tuanthal, leave five men with them."

I carried my helmet and my sword. I did not think I would need my shield. I knew that Aedh and his scouts would have bows. They would be our best attack. We trotted down the track and then our guide waved us to drop down and we crawled the last few paces to the small bluff overlooking the estuary. I was glad that I had carried my helmet else it might have alerted the Saxons on the beach to our presence.

I slithered next to Aedh. He began to whisper to me. "The ship is just twenty paces from the banks. It must either have a low draught or the water will be deep there." He nodded with his head. "Occasionally one of the Saxons walks over here and looks to the north. We hide when he does that." I could see that the men on the beach were just waiting. I could not understand why they did not have someone watching from the bluff where he could have given them early warning of either the other men or us. It was extremely careless of them not to have someone hidden in the woods to keep a look out.

I rolled on to my back to look at the sky. We still had some hours of daylight. I slipped down the bank to join Tuanthal and Gawan. Aedh soon joined us. "Tuanthal, how many of your men can swim?"

"Six or seven I think."

## Saxon Bane

"Good. I want them to go back along the trail and find some driftwood. I saw some trees damaged in a spring storm. I want them to float down to the ship and board her." I saw the question forming on his lips. "Do not worry I do not send them to be slaughtered. Aedh and his archers will attract the attention of the men on the beach. Aedh, I want your archers to wound them. We will then attack when our men clamber aboard the Saxon ship."

I looked around their faces, not for approval, but to detect any flaws. There appeared to be none for they all nodded their agreement.

The selected men went upstream and I left Gawan to watch for them as they floated down. When he saw them closing with the boat I would order our attack. We had been lucky to find them still so close but I was worried that we had seen neither Morcar nor Morgause. We went back to watch for the swimmers. I was not certain how long the ship would remain there. I supposed that the eight warriors leaving the beach would be a sign. Aedh had his men with their arrows notched already. Suddenly Gawan appeared like a wraith at my side. He pointed up stream. I saw what looked like branches drifting down the river. Had I not known there were men with them I would have been fooled into thinking it was natural.

"Ready Aedh?" He nodded. I waited a heartbeat or two to allow them to drift closer to the Saxon ship and then I said, "Now!"

They were good bowmen and four of the eight men waiting on the beach were struck in the legs by the arrows. The others stood and looked around for the danger. As Aedh and his archers loosed again I rose and led Tuanthal and his men down the bank towards the Saxons. We ran silently for I did not want to make it easy for them to see us. That was when I saw Morcar. He was at the stern and was hacking through the rope holding the anchor. He knew us too well and the arrows descending from the dark skies told him all he needed to know. He was holding Saxon Slayer! Oswald had not yet got his hands upon it. Three more of the watching Saxons on the beach were down. Two of them looked as though they were dead.

## Saxon Bane

The unwounded warrior was wading through the water in a desperate attempt to reach the ship. Suddenly there was a twang as the rope parted and the ship began to drift away from the shore and out to sea. I wondered why the oars were not being used and then I heard a splash and watched as two of the swimmers we had sent were hurled back into the water, dead. They had used the crew to repel our attack. When the oars began to move I knew that our plan had failed. They might be undermanned but, with a sail they could escape. Morcar himself stood at the tiller. I was close enough to see the grin on his face. He shouted something but I could not hear it.

I turned to Tuanthal and shouted, "Kill the prisoners!" I wanted the Saxons on the boat to know their fate if they were caught.

Tuanthal had seen all but two of his men killed and he was not in a merciful mood. They all died. We watched the small ship, propelled by just four oars and under a shortened sail as it headed northwest. He was going to the island of Manau. We had lost the sword.

There was little point in leaving the river. We would not reach Deva any quicker. We were exhausted. Instead, we camped. We buried our dead and cast the Saxons, stripped of clothes, arms and valuables into the river. Their bodies would return to the sea.

"Brother, why did you strip the dead?"

"We will need to follow Morcar into the nest of vipers. I will need to take men who look like Saxons if we are to blend in."

"That is dangerous. It is not only Morcar who knows you but also Oswald and Oswiu. Perhaps it should be me."

"You are a good warrior, Gawan, but this will need something more. This will need a killer. I will choose only those warriors who can be as ruthless as me."

Gawan looked angry. "It was my father too! I can be ruthless."

I hated to do it but I grabbed his damaged hand and held it before his face. "This can hold a shield but if you were fighting with your bare hands then you would lose. I do not intend to lose my little brother as well as our father and his sword. Besides you need to plan how we defeat Oswald and Oswiu. Father and I did not realise the danger they represented. Now that we have hurt King Edwin they might be in a position to gain Northumbria and all our work and sacrifice will be in vain. I need your mind and not your sword to work out how to defeat Aethelfrith's spawn."

I could see that his quick mind had assessed what I had said and found no flaw in it. "Very well but will you not be able to kill the two brothers when you have the sword?"

"If I can I will but my priority is the sword and then to kill Morcar. I am now Warlord and I have a responsibility to Rheged. I cannot risk all, just to avenge father and kill those two. That may have to wait for another day."

The next day everything took longer than I had planned. The river crossing was difficult and the journey south was hard; the rains came and drove into our faces. It was late evening when we reached Deva. The commander there was an old warrior called Angus. He had served with my father and only his damaged leg had stopped him from marching north with us. He broke down when I told him what had befallen the Warlord.

"I have lived too long. There is none left now who fought in Rheged. All of my brothers in arms have fallen."

"We will fight again, Angus. We have fought a great battle and Edwin is a spent force."

He gave me a sad smile. "It is not good to be the last soldier."

"You aren't. There are captains like Tuanthal and Aedh yet serving Rheged."

He laughed, "They were young boys when I was fighting in the shield wall around Dunelm, Warlord. To me, they are young boys still."

I began to understand my father a little more. He had seen all of his comrades die, some violently and some, like his brother Raibeart, silently in their sleep. His days of fighting had been over since the battle of Wrecsam. His last fight had been against the Irish giant, Calum. But in sacrificing himself for Rheged he might have saved our land. He had fought again knowing that he would die.

## Saxon Bane

"I need a message sending to The Narrows. Have we any of the messenger riders here?" We used young boys riding fast ponies to take messages from one part of the land to the other. Eventually, they became scouts, horsemen or, if they were particularly gifted riders then squires and ultimately equites.

"Aye Warlord, I will send for one."

The land between Deva and The Narrows was as safe a piece of land as you could find. The rider would be there by morning for there were no dangers along the way and it was a Roman Road. Hopefully, a ship would reach me within a day or two.

Just to be sure I sent two boys with the same message. Morcar's lead was a long one. I needed to find him before he left Manau.

Angus provided a good feast for my brother, my captains and me. We told him of Morcar's perfidy and where we sought him.

"But you do not know if he is there?"

"No, we saw his ship leave and head northwest."

He nodded. "That would be Manau. I think you may be right. Those who travel the seas speak of the island being conquered by Saxons. As it never seemed to concern your father we did not worry about it. I have a fisherman who knows the island well. I can send him to spy out the land for you if you wish. If I send him this night he could be back here when your ship arrives."

An idea suddenly came into my head. "How many men can the boat hold?"

"I am not sure. Let me think." He rubbed his beard, "With just him he could carry four men. Why? Are you thinking of sending your warriors with him?"

"Send for him please, Angus."

Angus looked perplexed but he went to the door of the hall and shouted down the corridor. I turned to Aedh. "Pick your best two men. Make sure they can speak Saxon. You and I are going to Manau."

Aedh looked delighted and leapt away from the table to find his men. The reaction of Gawan and Tuanthal was exactly the opposite; they were appalled. "You cannot do this, brother. It is far too risky!"

## Saxon Bane

"Listen to Gawan, Warlord. He is speaking sense. If Myrddyn were here he would say the same."

I looked at them both. "As Warlord, I have to listen to your advice but I do not need to heed it. Now listen to me. It will not be a risk. We will go in disguise. We will pretend to be Saxons and we will find the sword. I will not try to take it until you arrive with the ship and the men, Tuanthal." They both looked dubious. "Think about this. We gain a day! All we will need to do is to hide on the island until you arrive. The fisherman can guide you to the same place he drops us."

When Angus came back he had with him a much younger man than I expected. He had the gnarled hands and weather-beaten face of one who worked at sea. "This is Aed. He and his father used to fish off Manau until the Saxons there attacked their boat and killed their father. He hates them."

"Aed, would you take me and three of my men to the island of Manau?"

"I will and I will join you on the island if we are to kill Saxons."

"No, I just need you to drop us, come here and then guide my ship and my men back there."

I saw Angus smiling. It was a strange smile as, over the years, he had lost teeth in combat. "Just like your father! He was as impulsive as you are. If he had an idea then he acted on it. The land is in good hands, Warlord. If I was ten years younger I would come with you but I would just hold you up."

"And I would take you." I turned to the fisherman, "We will meet you by the boat." Aedh returned with the two warriors he had selected: Geraint and Daffydd. "We need to change into Saxon attire. As soon as we are ready we will sail."

After I was dressed as a Saxon we headed to the boat. Gawan accompanied us and said, "You will not let me come with you but I can give you this potion. It is Belladonna. It may help you. If you wish to make someone sleep, then add two or three drops to their drink. If you wish to make an enemy unconscious, you must use six drops and to kill them half of the bottle. You may find it useful. Remember you are fighting a witch as well as our cousin."

I clasped his arm, "Thank you brother and I will return."

He laughed, "Angus is right, you do sound like father."

The boat looked far too small to me but it was my decision and I had to look confident. I began to climb into the boat. Aed held up his hand and said, "You are Warlord of Rheged on the land but on my boat I am king. You will need to sit where I tell you and do exactly as I say."

Aedh began to bridle. "He is right Aedh. It is his boat and we are not sailors. Put us where you will, King Aed."

He smiled. "You and this one are the biggest." He pointed to Geraint. "Sit in the middle next to the mast. You will raise and lower the sail." He pointed to Aedh. "You are the same size as me. Sit in the stern and the other one can sit in the front. You will find a piece of canvas there. Rig it on those metal hooks. You will be the driest and it will stop the boat from filling with water."

We sat where he told us and the boat tipped, alarmingly, as we all climbed on board. Amazingly it did not capsize and Aed looked happy. The men at the side of the river pushed us off.

"Good luck Warlord!"

"Hoist the sail." Aed pointed to me. I looked at Geraint who grinned and put a rope in my hand. He had a similar one and he began to pull. I copied him and the sail rose and then filled. There was a piece of metal on the side of the boat and I did as Geraint did and wrapped it around. "Good. Later we will need to move the sail around to catch the wind but we will wait until the wind changes for that. The Allfather is with us today for the wind blows from the south. We will fly over the whitecaps."

I turned to look at the land but my brother and the others had disappeared into the gloom. We were on our way across the sea to Manau. I had never been there and knew nothing about it but the spirits had deemed that we go there and I was in their hands still.

While we were still in the river the boat moved steadily but it was not uncomfortable. Daffydd, at the bow had the cosiest nest for he could shelter beneath the canvas. I wondered if I should exercise my right as Warlord for such a privilege but then I remembered Aed's words; he was king. He had placed us where he wanted us to sit. I saw the grin on his face as we left the estuary and he pushed the steering board over. The wind caught us and we seemed to jump like a warhorse over an obstacle. I gripped the mast and the side in fear.

Aed laughed. "I told you she would fly."

Soon I had no time to worry about the speed as Aed reset the sail a number of times until he was satisfied with its tautness and our speed. My hands became redraw and I found the saltwater and spray flying from the bows made me desperate for a drink. I was, however, gratified with the speed with which we flew across the water. When dawn began to break I saw a dark shape in the distance. It was a grey smudge. Aed looked serious as he said, "There it is, Manau; the island of the Saxon killers!"

We half lowered the sail so that we would be harder to see from the land. "There is one main settlement on the eastern coast. I will take you around to the headland on the southeast coast. It is only a short journey to the place of the Saxons. They do not keep watch from the high places. They may have homes and farms across the island but I think there is only one place where they have a wall and warriors. It is on the eastern side of this island. I know the place well for it was just offshore from their fort where they killed my father. I go nowhere near there now." I could hear the bitterness in his voice. We had something in common; those on the island had been responsible for the deaths of both of our fathers.

With the lowered sail it took us some time to close with the island but it allowed me to watch the island grow larger. I felt the hairs on the back of my neck begin to rise. The island appeared to look like a whale rising out of the sea! It was Gawan's dream. The sword would be here! The spirits had not lied to us and I was meant to come.

Saxon Bane

# Chapter 20

Daffydd kept a close watch on the shore. There might be no watchers but I was sure that there were shepherds and fishermen. If they saw us being landed then they might pass that news on. We were a fishing boat but once we landed then anyone who saw us would become curious. We had to be invisible. We had to become Wolf Warriors just like my father and his men had been. *Wyrd*!

Once we had cleared the headland then we raised the sail again and the wind took us close to the small cove. We edged into the beach which was a mixture of sand and shingle. "Bring my ship back here and we will be waiting." As my men scrambled and splashed ashore I clasped his arm. "I will reward you when we return."

"My reward will be the death of the Saxons and to avenge my father."

I jumped into the icy water and watched as he skillfully turned his small boat and headed due south. When he raised the sail he would not be seen. I wondered how he would manage his sails on his own but he seemed like a more than competent sailor. He would manage and we had more important things to think about. It was now daylight and we had to get out of sight as soon as possible.

Aedh and his men quickly checked the small beach. There was a path, of sorts, leading up from the beach. The cliff was not very high and it was not rocky as they were on Mona. I nodded to Aedh who led his warriors towards the stony trail. I daresay it had been used by people collecting shellfish. I could see many discarded shells amongst the shingle and sand. I wanted us to be away from such paths as soon as we could. Aedh pushed on ahead. He would pause, briefly, every few steps and sniff the air. Then he would hurry on. It was not far up the slope but we went carefully. He waved us down as we neared the top and he slithered along on his belly. He disappeared and the three of us made our way up to join him. When we reached Aedh we could see the land rising away to the north. There was the hill which had made me think that the island looked like a whale rising from the sea. It seemed to dominate the whole island. It was a few miles away. A tendril of smoke drifting from the northeast showed us where the settlement was. The fact that we could see and smell the smoke meant it was not far away.

Satisfied that there was no one in sight Aedh got to his feet and sprinted towards the undergrowth some fifty paces from us. It was obvious that there were no roads to be seen. I doubted that the Romans had ever visited here. Aedh waved us forward. We were moving across earthen tracks made by the feet of man and animals. We headed northeast towards the distant smoke. We found a deep valley and a stream. The stream flowed from the west. The valley clearly headed inland. Aedh turned to me. "Warlord, we will take this valley."

I frowned. It made no sense. This valley would take us northwest, away from where we wanted to go. However, Aedh had been my father's most trusted scout. "Why?"

"This gives us good cover. If you notice the stream is neither deep nor wide. It will soon rise to a place which may be higher than the settlement. It is always easier to peer down into a place and observe those within than to look from below where you can be easily seen."

I smiled and nodded. "I am sorry for my questions Aedh. You are right."

He shrugged, "We are used to sneaking around. It is in our blood. You are used to fighting off hordes of Saxons. Your father would have asked too"

We made our way up the narrow, rocky valley. We had to watch our footing for there was no trail here. It was dark under the canopy of trees and bushes and we all slipped into the water more than once. As soon as he could Aedh led us across the narrow stream to the other side. The only trail down here was one made by animals coming to drink. We would not meet any Saxons in this dark place. I noticed that, as we began to climb, the path became lighter.

We paused at the top and listened. We could hear nothing save the sounds of the birds. Using the moss on the trees as a guide Aedh led us through the woods. He kept us moving towards the fort Aed had told us about. There was a path once more; this one had been made by the feet of men. It would lead somewhere. The trees along the path were not close together and we came out into patches of sunlight before being plunged into darkness again. Suddenly Aedh waved us to the side. Something was coming. We dived into the undergrowth. I found myself lying next to Aedh under a hawthorn bush. I watched as he grabbed some damp soil and smeared it on his face and hands. I did the same until he grabbed my hand to still it.

I could hear nothing. I looked at Aedh who just held his hand up as though I ought to be patient. I wondered why for I could hear nothing and then I knew what he meant. We could no longer hear the birds. Someone was coming. As I put my hand on the ground I felt the vibration. Feet were coming down the trail.

When the voices spoke they seemed to be almost next to me and I had to fight myself to remain still. "It is a waste of time if you ask me."

"Well no one asked you. The Prince told us to check it out and check it out we will."

"But it was one little fishing boat! You know what? I bet he was fishing!"

"Tadgh you are a real comedian! The fishing boat was heading away from the island. It was not fishing."

"Well what do they expect us to find?"

"Listen, you half wit, we have captured that sword, Saxon Slayer. The Welsh won't like that. That new warrior thinks that they will come to get it. In fact I heard him telling the two princes that he expected someone to come in the next few days."

They were moving away but I heard the first voice give a lascivious laugh, "I wouldn't mind a piece of that woman he brought with him."

"I wouldn't go near her, my friend, I have heard she is a witch!"

I could not hear what Tadgh thought of that for they disappeared. We remained still for some time until Aedh gestured for us to rise. "We know now that the sword, the witch and Morcar are here. What we need to find out is where they are being kept."

## Saxon Bane

Aedh shook his head. "But not down this path. We will have to break trail. If three warriors use it then there may be others."

As he led us away I marvelled at his skills. I had heard the voices of two men but I could not have been able to tell how many men had passed.

We went to the east. It was hard going for there was no path and Aedh was trying to avoid leaving evidence of our passing. I followed in his footsteps and his men made sure that there was no sign left behind us. After a while we emerged from the woods. Aedh pulled us back in almost immediately. There, not far away, was the wooden wall guarding the Saxon village. We hid behind the trees as we assessed it. Aedh pointed to the nearest large tree and Geraint scrambled up like a human squirrel.

When he descended he spoke quickly and quietly. "It is the Saxon village. I can see, beyond, the masts of at least two ships. The village has a wooden wall all around and is on a low hill above the water. I can see just a shallow ditch."

I had brought us here but I had not thought how we could get into the village. The fact that Aed's boat had been seen meant that they were now wary. We would not be able to just march into the village as though we were visitors. They would examine every face even those dressed as Saxons. I was too well known. I would be recognised. I had to change my plan. What would my father have done? I smiled to myself. He and Myrddyn would probably have flown in. But I had no Myrddyn here. Then I cursed myself. I had Gawan. Myrddyn had been right; we were two halves each making up one whole. He might have a damaged hand but here I needed a mind and not a warrior. I would have to think for myself.

Aedh pointed to a high point beyond the settlement. "I think if we can reach there we might be able to spy on them."

It took one of my father's old warriors to come up with the solution. "Lead on, Aedh!"

We edged back through the undergrowth until the land began to rise. Aedh seemed to sense which way to go and, after we had left the security of the undergrowth he found a patch of scrubland which dipped away from the village. We remained hidden. The climb to the vantage point was over a rocky weed ridden piece of ground but it brought us up behind the small rise. Three of us bellied up to it while Geraint sat at the bottom watching the trail we had just used.

Although we were at least four hundred paces from the west wall we could see clearly the fort and the sea beyond. I took in that there were just two Saxon ships. One was the one which had evaded us and the other was of similar proportions.

"How many men would you say the ships could hold Aedh?"

"There are just eight oars on each one. If we assume that they have two men to an oar and the same number of passengers then thirty-two."

"I think that there can only be double that number within these wooden walls. I cannot see any other ships. Count how many warriors you see and keep your eyes open for Morcar and Morgause."

We saw Oswald and Oswiu long before we discovered where the two fugitives were. The sons of Aethelfrith were in the large wooden hall. We saw them emerge when three men entered the gate. The three men pointed south and shook their heads.

"They must be the men who were seeking us, Warlord."

"Aye, and it looks like they found no trace of us. Well done. Aedh."

The five of them went down to the water. I saw a conversation take place with much waving of arms, especially from Oswiu. Eventually, a warrior ran to the warrior hall and returned with ten warriors. They climbed aboard the ship we had seen on the mainland. It began to pull away from the land. Daffydd asked, "Are they leaving?"

"No, I think not. I suspect they are going to sail around the island and make sure we are not here."

"So far I have the thirteen warriors on the ship and I have counted another twelve who are in the village."

We watched until late afternoon. Worryingly there was no sign of Morcar or Morgause but we did see, coming from the north, a line of warriors who had been hunting. There were ten of those. When they entered the compound there was a cheer and another five warriors emerged from the warrior hall.

"Forty warriors all together."

Just as Aedh said that my attention was drawn to a small hut which was just inside the gate. Morcar came out when he heard the cheering and, draped on his arm, was Morgause. I saw that he still had Saxon Slayer around his waist. He was assiduously ignored by the warriors who had just returned. I found that interesting. Morgause put a small jug into the large amphora which was outside the hut. When she carried the dripping jug towards the hut I knew it contained water. They returned into the hut once more.

When the ship returned, just before dark we had managed to gather the numbers of all the warriors and others in the village. There were only five women and four children. They appeared to have few slaves. We counted only six. Either they had another ship or they had arrived at the island on overcrowded boats.

Once the sun dipped behind us we watched as they shut and barred the gates. They had torches lit close to the two ships and we saw a deck watch of four men on the two Saxon vessels. Once the gates were slammed shut another four men became the sentries. They had one on the main gate; a second on the small gate to the west and the other two looked to be patrolling around the walkway.

When it became too dark to see anymore we slithered down to the bottom of the small rise and headed back to the undergrowth. We needed somewhere we could talk and sleep undisturbed. Eventually, we made it back to the small valley we had first used. It was some distance from the village but there was water and we could sleep safely.

Geraint and Daffydd went up and downstream to set traps and alarms to protect us while we slept. I sat with Aedh and we ate the food we had brought with us. "What is your plan, Warlord?"

I laughed, "What you really mean, Aedh is, have you any plan at all?"

"No, Warlord. You are your father's son and you both have the same kind of mind. You will come up with something that, perhaps, others would not think of."

## Saxon Bane

He was right, of course. My father and I had studied in the east at the court of the Emperor. We had learned that there were many different ways of approaching a problem.

"The key is the sword. Now that we know it is kept close to the gate then we can get to it quickly." Aedh just nodded and chewed. "It will be just as hard or as easy to get in and take the sword as to get in and destroy the Saxons."

His eyes widened a little. "You are thinking of fighting Oswald and all of his men then?"

"I am. It all depends how many men Tuanthal brings." I chewed and reflected. The warriors with Oswald were not the best I had ever seen. Even if Tuanthal only brought twenty warriors with the three I had with me we would be more than a match for the Saxons. The key would be surprise. There was almost no ditch and only four sentries. If the gates were held and if we could contain the warriors within the hall then we might succeed. I would have to ensure that Morcar and the sword were both captured.

I realised that Aedh was looking at me with a bemused expression on his face. I smiled, "I am resolved. When Tuanthal comes we attack and we rid ourselves of this den of rats so close to our land."

"Good. It will be an ending then."

Saxon Bane

## Chapter 21

I woke stiff and hungry. As I threw some water on my face I chastised myself. I was getting soft. I needed to become a warrior once more.

"I want Geraint and Daffydd to wait for Tuanthal at the cove. It could be any time in the next two days." When the two scouts came Aedh explained what they should do.

"We will, Warlord."

"When they arrive then bring Captain Tuanthal and his men to the hill above the village; the place we watched from."

"And where will we be, Warlord?"

"We will be watching there to ascertain more precise numbers and to try a little mischief." I turned to Geraint. "If we are not at the hill then tell Tuanthal to wait for us."

"I will, Warlord."

We separated and Aedh and I retraced our steps. We knew the places now which were dangerous and we went more carefully there. At other times we were able to move quicker. We made it to the small rise and settled ourselves down to watch.

"You have a plan Warlord?"

I nodded, "The beginnings of one." I pointed to the hut used by Morcar and Morgause. "You see the amphora by the hut?" he nodded. "I intend to sneak down there and put the belladonna which Gawan gave us into the jar. It will either kill them or make them sleep. Either suits us."

"But how will you get the poison into the jar. It is close to the gate."

"I do not know yet. We need to watch for something which might help us."

It was a long slow morning as we peered down into the village. The only ones who appeared to leave through the gate were the slaves and a couple of women. They went to the northern part of the shore where we saw them gather shellfish. When it was slaves who went foraging then

## Saxon Bane

two guards went with them and watched. They looked to be our only chance.

In the early afternoon we saw the brothers. They went to Morcar's hut. He and Morgause came out. There appeared to be a heated discussion. One of the brothers, he looked younger than the other, and I took him to be Oswiu tried to hit Morcar at one point. I saw Morcar's hand go to Saxon Slayer before Oswald intervened. Morgause must have said something for Oswiu retreated a little. Then the four of them left and walked down to the ship. They all boarded and it left. It went in the same direction as the previous day and headed south.

Aedh said, "They are looking for us again."

"Will Geraint and Daffydd be safe?"

"You know where they are but I would defy you to find them if we went there. They will not be discovered."

"I have an idea. Let us go to the northern beach where they collect shellfish and see what transpires."

I could see, from Aedh's face that he thought it a bad idea but I was Warlord. "Then follow me and keep low."

There were plenty of gorse bushes and, by crouching, we were able to make it into the rocks close to the beach where we had seen them collecting shellfish. We both drew our swords and laid them next to us in the sand.

"How do you know they will come again this afternoon?"

"I am guessing. We saw no hunters going out. Unless they have vast quantities of food laid in then they will have to use what is around the settlement. They will want shellfish which is fresh. When the tide turns again they may come for more." I shrugged. "If they do not come then we will try again in the morning when we know that they will come."

He nodded and we settled down to watch. As the tide began to recede I became more hopeful. It seemed likely that they would come when the tide was on its way out. The wait became more tolerable as I anticipated a result. We saw the four thralls come down. They were carrying large baskets which, I assumed would become heavy as they collected more shellfish.

## Saxon Bane

The reason why the guards were necessary was answered when the two guards followed them. The women had been waiting by the water's edge. The guards gave them crude knives. Obviously the slaves were not to be trusted with weapons however small. We had both missed that in the morning but it gave us a chance. They would need to collect the knives back from the slaves before they returned to the settlement.

The women worked quickly. Their hands plunged into the water and after they had used the knives they would put their catch into the basket. Three of them worked in the water whilst the others clambered around the rocks hacking off mussels, barnacles and oysters. Either there was little game on the island or the Northumbrians were lazy. The two guards then began to drink from a skin. I assumed it was a potent brew for they appeared to enjoy it.

Gradually the thralls filled their baskets and one by one they returned their knives to the guards and then headed back to the settlement with their baskets on their heads. Soon there was but one left. She was a young girl of no more than fifteen summers. As she drew close to the two guards I saw them exchange a look. My mind began to work out what would happen next. "Be ready to follow me, Aedh." He nodded.

One of the guards held out his hand for the knife. As she handed it over the other grabbed her other arm and dragged her beneath the rock on which they had been sat. I knew from our observations that they were out of sight of the guards. The other warrior joined his friend. I heard a muffled shout.

"Now Aedh!"

We raced towards the rock. He went one side and I the other. I did not pause, I hurled myself at one warrior and threw my arm around his neck. I knocked him from the girl. I landed on top of him and my weight took his wind. Before he could recover I ripped my sword across his throat and he bled to death. Aedh did the same for the other. The girl was shocked and I jumped towards her and put my hand across her mouth.

"Ssh!" She nodded her acquiescence. "What are your people?" She looked confused. "Where were you taken?"

"Rheged!"

I was relieved beyond words. "I am the Warlord of Rheged. Will you help us? We will take you home."

"I will. Will you take my sisters too?"

"We will take all of you." I turned to Aedh. "Put on the dead man's clothes." We stripped the dead and we dressed in their clothes. Both men had had hoods and we put them up. "Now then…?"

"Ciara."

"Now then Ciara, I want you to pretend that the men violated you. Pretend to weep as we go through the gate. Can you do that?"

"I can."

"Say nothing to the others but we will come back. That I promise you."

She leaned up and kissed me on my cheek. "You saved me from more pawing and groping. I am grateful." She pointed to one. "He is Aella and he," she pointed to the other, "is Egbert."

"Thank you Ciara. You are brave."

She put the basket on her shoulder and began to move towards the gate. I took the wineskin and held it to my mouth and put the other arm around Aedh. It hid our faces and made us look drunk. Ciara's tears sounded real but had no effect on the guards.

"You two horny bastards will come a cropper one of these days. Hey, Aella, I am talking to you."

I affected a slurred voice, "Ah go play with yourself, you queer."

They must have bantered before for the guard merely laughed. And then we were inside the settlement. Aedh began to urinate against the gate. One of the guards said, "Dirty bastard!"

While they were watching him I poured the belladonna into the amphora. Just then the guard said, "Here, watch out, the Princes are back."

I looked up and saw the ship returning. I staggered towards Aedh and said, "Shit, I have left my knife on the beach. Egbert, come and help me find it."

The guard laughed, "You had better hurry up then, we intend to bar the gates when they are back inside."

## Saxon Bane

We staggered drunkenly towards the rock. When I was sure that we were out of sight we scurried back up the hill. Aedh made sure that we leapt from rock to rock to avoid leaving tracks. When we reached the safety of our lair Aedh began to laugh.

"You are the Warlord's son. Only you or Lord Lann himself would have tried that!"

I shrugged. "Men see what they expect to see. Our problem now is will those men be missed."

We peered over the rise and watched the Northumbrians with Morcar and Morgause walk from the ship. When they reached the gate Oswald said something to the guards and they ran back to the ship. They returned carrying something, we could not see what but it took two of them to carry it. When the two guards were through the gate it was closed. With luck the two guards we had killed would not be missed until morning or even later. I hoped that, by then, Tuanthal would have reached us.

The night was not an easy night. We heard the sounds of screaming coming from the village. We could not work out what was going on. Our vantage point did not allow us to see inside the huts and they had no fires burning outside. Worried by the noises we took it in turn to sleep. I had the last watch before dawn. When Aedh roused me dawn was just breaking to the east. His face was grim.

"What is it Aedh?"

"Come and see."

We slithered over to the rise and looked down at the village. The sentries were on the gate still but there, on two spears just before the gate were the heads of Ciara and Daffydd. Now we knew what the screams had meant.

Back in our dell a mixture of emotions raced through me. We had caused the death of a young girl and I felt guilty. I was also angry at their treatment of her.

"What of Geraint?"

Aedh shook his head, "There is no sign of him."

"He may be dead and Tuanthal may be waiting in the cove for us. Obviously the drugged water did not work. It may be they have not drunk of it yet. We will have to return to the cove and wait with Geraint. I think the girl will have told them that I am on the island. They will hunt us as soon as it is daylight."

Nodding, Aedh rose and led the way. Having made the decision there was no time to lose. There was a danger that there could be warriors waiting for us at the beach. My first quest as Warlord looked to be heading for failure. I had failed to build a camp and allowed the mercenaries to kill irreplaceable warriors, I had allowed Morcar to escape and my vanity had caused the death of an innocent girl and a fine young warrior.

When we reached the cove it appeared deserted. Aedh frowned. "Even had they been seen they would have left signs. I can see no evidence of a struggle. Wait here Warlord whilst I search."

While my captain of scouts searched I peered out to sea. Why was Tuanthal not waiting in the cove? What other disaster had befallen us?

I heard a noise and whipping my sword out turned to face the danger. It was Aedh and he was carrying an injured and soaking Geraint. "I am sorry, Warlord, we failed you and it was my fault."

I could see that he was upset but I needed him to be calm so that I could gauge the size of the disaster. "Just tell me what happened Geraint."

"We were watching for the ship when we saw the Northumbrian boat coming around the headland. We went to our hiding places." He pointed to the cove. "I had a rocky perch and Daffydd hid in the trees. "They fooled us. They had sent four men through the woods. I knew nothing save I heard a noise and then I saw them dragging my friend towards the top of the cove. Seeing that there were just four of them I tried to get to my friend but I slipped on a slippery rock and tumbled down the far side of the cove into the sea. My leg was trapped between some rocks and it took me all night to escape."

I could see that his leg was badly gashed, "Aedh, see to his leg. It was not your fault Geraint, it was *wyrd*."

While Geraint was attended to I returned to watch for the ship. It was not quite the disaster it could have been. They would have questioned

## Saxon Bane

Daffydd before killing him and that explained the screams. They would have done the same with the girl. Now that it was daylight they would search for us. We had not hidden our trail from the vantage point. It would take them some time but they would find our tracks and it would not take them long to work out that we would be where they captured Daffydd.

I waited, as patiently as I could until the wound had been bound. "They will follow us here."

"I know."

"And we have nowhere to go. So if we are to be here then let us make it hard for them. Geraint, come and watch for Captain Tuanthal. Aedh let us lay some traps for them."

I knew that warriors give up too easily if there is no hope. The traps would not save us but they would slow down the enemy and buy us a little time. They would also make them wary. I had seen the despondency on Geraint's face and I knew that Aedh would take the loss of one of his best men hard.

We hurried back to the valley we had used. The lack of tracks meant that they might not be aware of its existence and would be wary. It was narrow and had many natural dangers. We just used them. We made a trip with some hemp line and a pile of rocks. We moved some of the rocks in the water so that they would make an unstable platform. We littered the valley with pitfalls and traps. We worked as long as we dared and then headed back to the cove. Here we had slightly more time. We used caltrops to direct them towards hemp lines to trip them. Aedh cut stakes close to the trips. If they fell on them then they would be hurt. We used the wild blackberries to make impenetrable barriers which forced them towards our traps. Once we had used all of our resources we returned to the cove and Geraint.

"Any sign of the ship?"

He shook his head, "None."

In the far distance I could hear dogs. Of course they had dogs, we had heard them in the village. They would be upon us sooner rather than later. The dogs would follow our trail they would have the scent of

## Saxon Bane

Daffydd's clothes to guide them. When I heard a howl of pain I knew that the dogs, at least had found one of the traps. I had hoped it would be a warrior.

"They will be here soon. Geraint, can you make it to the beach?"

"Yes Warlord, but I would rather fight here with you."

"You will be more use down there so that you can direct Tuanthal and his men up here. Besides, your leg would slow you down. Captain Aedh and I can move quicker if we are not worrying about you."

Geraint reluctantly hobbled down to the cove. Drawing my sword I led Aedh to the bushes which were close to the path and the top of the rise. We waited. I spoke quietly, "I think my time as Warlord will be a little brief."

"Do not say that yet, Warlord. We do not know what *wyrd* has waiting for us. When he was younger your father had many close calls such as this one. We deal with one problem at a time."

We could hear the dogs and the cries of pain drawing closer. Soon all of our traps would be gone and we would have to face Oswald and Oswiu's men alone.

It was the dogs which reached us first. They were not big dogs but they were fierce. There were four of them. They leapt at us even though we were hidden in the hedges. Although they were slain with ease they had marked our ambush. Ten warriors emerged from the woods. I saw neither of the brothers or Morcar with them.

"Ready, Aedh?"

He grinned, "I was born ready, Warlord."

Just then we heard Geraint's voice, "The ship! It is here!"

We had a chance but we could not just run down to the beach. We would be cut down before we had gone eight paces. To my horror, I saw another ten warriors emerge just two hundred paces from the first ten.

There was nothing for it; we had to attack, even though outnumbered! I had a seax in my left hand and, roaring, "Rheged!" I charged the first knot of warriors. I took them by surprise. I sliced down over the top of a shield and my sword, made in Byzantium of the finest metal there was, split open the helmet and head of the first surprised warrior to die. As blood and brains splashed across the face of the second warrior I ripped the seax across his throat. My momentum carried me forward and I was able to get inside the shield of the next warrior and I ripped my sword into his middle. I pushed his body hard and it rolled into the path of a fourth warrior who stumbled; it was a fatal fall for I brought the sword down onto the back of his neck and decapitated him. The other two warriors facing me fell back in fear.

Suddenly I heard, "Warlord!" I turned and saw two dead Northumbrians but Aedh was clutching his side as he fought off the other two. Blood was pouring from the deep wound.

I roared a challenge and hurled myself at them. One half turned and I stabbed him in the chest. As the other raised his sword to finish off Aedh I swung my sword and cut him almost to his backbone. I did not hesitate. I picked Aedh up over my shoulder and ran towards the slope. The two who had fled from me were now joined by the other ten. Perhaps the spirits or my father gave me strength but I pounded down the slope towards the welcome sight of my ship edging into the cove. How I did not fall I do not know but I managed. Geraint was urging them on and I saw Aed with his fishing boat, also filled with warriors. A spear was suddenly hurled at me and flew over my shoulder. The mistake would have been to turn around and I kept on running grateful that I was now on the flat beach for I was tiring quickly.

Tuanthal must have had archers with him for I saw a shower of arrows fly over my head. I heard cries and thuds. The arrows had struck home. I fell to my knees and Aedh rolled on to his back. Geraint ran up.

"Get some bandages."

"No, Warlord, there is no point. It is a fatal wound." Aedh lifted his tunic and I could see him cut deeply. Even if we stitched him he would not survive. "It has been an honour to serve you and your father. I go now to tell him that Rheged is in good hands."

He winced as he turned to face Geraint. "Watch over my scouts and my family, my friend."

Geraint nodded, "I will Captain. It has been an honour."

## Saxon Bane

I took his hands in mine and place my sword between them. "Go to the Allfather and the Otherworld. You are a true hero of Rheged." He was smiling but he said nothing for he was already dead.

Tuanthal raced up to us and dropped to his knees in the sand. "No, not Aedh too?" I nodded. "Then I am the last and I have lived too long." He stroked the hair away from his friend's face.

"There will be time for that later. Now we have a sword to find. It is what Aedh would have wished. We will take his body with us and bury it close to my father. They should journey together." I turned and saw the eight Northumbrian survivors scrambling to safety. "It will take them some time to get to the fort. We will sail there by ship."

Tuanthal said, "We will attack?"

"Aedh and I had planned it that way but now we go by ship but we must be swift."

We clambered aboard and Daffydd a Gwynfor quickly got us underway. I put every warrior on the oars as we laid on every uncia of sail we had. We needed to get back before the brothers found out that we were coming for them. Riding a ship was not like riding a horse. You could not take a short cut and you suffered the whims of the sea, tide and the wind. I knew that Daffydd ap Gwynfor was doing his best but it seemed to take forever to round the headland despite the men rowing as though their lives depended upon it. There were out to avenge deaths as we all were.

Saxon Bane

# Chapter 22

As the men rowed, now with even more urgency, I asked Tuanthal about his voyage. "How many men do you have?"

"Using the fishing boat and this ship we have forty warriors with us."

I looked him in the eye. "And the delay?"

He looked distraught, "The captain could do nothing about it. It was a combination of tides and the wind. We seemed to be pushed back by the gods."

"Do not distress yourself. This was meant as a test for me. We will find out if we have passed when we reach the village."

As we rounded the headland I saw that someone must have reached the settlement already for one of the Saxon ships was preparing to leave. "I want every archer aiming at that ship. Kill as many as you can."

We slowed down as the archers left their benches to loose their arrows. I saw men fall into the water but whoever commanded them used shields to protect them.

"Head for the other ship." I saw the last of the warriors we had fought. They were racing to get to the gates before they closed. As soon as we bumped next to the ship I said to Daffydd. "Keep ten warriors on board and follow the Saxon ship. I want to know where it goes. Do not allow them to damage you."

"I will do so Warlord. And what of you?"

"We will use the other ship."

Most of the men had crossed the Saxon ship and were now preparing a shield wall. "Captain Geraint. Keep two men and hold this ship."

"I will Warlord." Then my words sank in. "Captain Geraint?"

"Captain Aedh promoted you with his dying breath; who am I to gainsay such a warrior."

I joined Tuanthal. We now had less than thirty men. "Are we too late for the sword, Warlord?"

## Saxon Bane

"I know not but I have the Saxon ship under watch and we can go after them soon enough." I pointed to the two forlorn looking heads on the spears. "Besides we have two people to avenge."

The wall was lined with warriors but I knew that they would not prove an obstacle. My men were ready for revenge. The sight of Daffydd's head on the spear would make them fight through fire to get at those who had done this. I spied some timber which they were obviously using to repair their ship.

"Grab that spar!" I picked up one end and eight others helped me. "Keep the men from the walls." I turned to the men with me. "This is for Aedh, my father and poor Daffydd there. Rheged!"

We set off, not slowly, but at full tilt. I felt an arrow as it almost parted my hair and then I heard a scream of pain from the walls as the archer was slain. They had had no time to lift the bridge from over the shallow ditch and we hurled ourselves and the spar at the gate. The weight of my warriors and our speed crashed through the wood which was shattered asunder. As soon as we were through we dropped the spar and went into a defensive circle while we waited for reinforcements.

Tuanthal joined me. I turned to him, "Finish this Captain Tuanthal. Teach them a lesson!"

"Aye!" Roaring their war cry my men charged the defenders who were falling back to the western gate. I turned and went to Morcar's hut. I did not know what to expect but I had to know if the sword was there. I pushed my sword through the entrance and leapt in. What I spied when I entered was a shock. There lay Morgause. She was obviously dead and had been laid on a bed and flowers placed around her head. Of Morcar there was no sign. I walked up to the body and sniffed, for there appeared to be no sign of a wound. I could the white foam on her body which showed that the belladonna had worked. She had been poisoned but where was Morcar? And who had laid her out?

The answer was clear. Morcar had not drunk the water but she had. He had laid out his love. The questions now remained; where had he gone? Had he fled with Oswald or remained here on the island?"

## Saxon Bane

I left the hut and ran to where my men were fighting. "We have killed most of the Northumbrians." He pointed to the open gate to the west. "Some escaped."

I nodded. "There are some of our people who are slaves. Free them and enslave the others. Have those heads taken down." I pointed to the hut with the witch's body." I want that and all within it burned to the ground!"

"Where are Morcar and Morgause?"

"Morgause is within the hut; she is dead and as for Morcar? He is either fled on the ship or with the survivors. We will search the island first. Give me ten men."

"Warlord, you have done enough. Let…"

"Give me ten men and let me finish this!" I softened my voice. "I have to do this. He is my cousin, my blood."

He nodded and gave a slight bow, "As you wish, Warlord."

I stuck the seax I had picked up in my belt and put my sword in the scabbard. I checked that the fine dagger my father had given me at Yule was still tucked into my boot and I set off. At least not wearing armour would make the climb I was about to make a little easier.

The ten warriors lined up behind me. "We are going up there. Any Northumbrian you find, kill, but if you see Morcar then he is mine!" Their grim eyes showed their resolution and they all nodded.

We left through the gate at a trot. As we began to ascend the whale like hill we began to find discarded objects and wounded men. The wounded were slain out of hand. Perhaps there had been more warriors within the fort than we had counted for, unless the ship had been crewed by a handful of men, we still had quite a few warriors to kill.

One of the warriors shouted. "There Warlord! To the east!"

I looked and saw five warriors breaking away to head back to the sea. "Go after them!" I think they intended to make it to the second ship.

Five of my men ran down to cut them off. As we climbed higher we began to gain on the remainder of the warriors. I counted seven of them but none of them appeared to be Morcar. Perhaps he had escaped. We would kill these seven and then continue our pursuit.

## Saxon Bane

These seven looked to me like the mercenaries who had attacked our camp. I think their leader was with them. For there was a warrior with a long scar running down his cheek and he used a long Danish axe with two handles. His arms were ringed with battle amulets. The first of Tuanthal's men who raced eagerly forward found that the axe had a longer reach than he had thought. The axe took his head in one blow and it rolled down the hillside.

"You men take the others. I will deal with Scarface."

It looked as though he recognised me. "So you are the one they call The Warlord. You do not look like much to me and your body will afford few pickings."

"If you would wait awhile I shall sail back to Rheged for my armour." I shook my head. "No, that would give an even greater advantage than the one I have now."

He looked puzzled, "And what advantage is that?"

"I am a warrior and you are a piece of mercenary scum. I will have to wash my sword for a month to get the taint of you from it!"

I had annoyed him enough. That had always been my intention. I wanted him to be impulsive. He swung the axe at my head. He anticipated me moving backwards but instead I ducked and stepped closer to him. The axe flew over my head. I stabbed forward with my sword. He was a wily customer and he spun. Even so my blade scored a long cut down his side.

He stepped backwards and held the axe across his chest so that he could use both ends if he needed to. This warrior was experienced. I held up the sword. "See, it is tainted already."

He tried to catch me unawares by punching with the haft of the axe. I countered with the seax held in my left hand. The sharp edge cut across his fingers. I saw the ends of two of them fall to the floor.

"I will take you piece by piece if I have to. But you will die!"

"And when I kill you then you too will cry as your scout did when we gelded him."

The man was a fool. He was already a dead man walking but claiming to have tortured Daffydd meant it would be a slow death. He stepped back and swung again. This time I spun in the opposite direction to his swing and brought my sword across the back of his knees. It sliced through the tendons and he collapsed to the ground. I stepped over to him and wrenched the axe from his hands. He flinched as he waited for the death blow.

I laughed and sheathed my sword and seax. "You will not die so easily." I felt the edge of the axe it was sharp. I ripped open his tunic revealing his pale and dirty torso. "You shall die by your own weapon!" I dragged the edge across his midriff. It split open like a ripe plum. I looked over to where the warriors were despatching the dead. "No one touch this man. He will die slowly and the animals will feast on his remains."

"Aye, Warlord!"

"Kill me quickly, I beg of you."

"Had you honour then I would but you do not." I looked up at the peak of the mountain; it was some few thousand paces from me. It looked bare. My men had killed all of the others. "Search around here for any others and then take their weapons back to the fort." I handed the Danish axe to the leader.

"And what of you, Warlord?"

"I shall walk to the top of the mountain and spy out the land. Fear not there is no one left. They are all dead."

The leader's whining voice accompanied me all the way up the mountain. His sobs gradually subsided. Had he had any honour then I would have given him a warrior's death. I knew why I had treated him thus. Morgause had not suffered enough. I had thought that the poisoned water would have made them all sleep. Perhaps only Morcar and Morgause had used that water. Perhaps it was *wyrd*.

I remembered my father telling me that he found the walk to the cave at Wyddfa cleared his mind and helped him to think better. I knew I needed that now. I had only been taking these decisions for a few days and yet I had made many mistakes already. I had begged my father to retire and let me lead the warriors. He had been right to deny me that opportunity. I had thought I was ready and now I knew that I was not. It

## Saxon Bane

proved that he was a greater Warlord than I would ever be. He had been leading King Urien's armies since he had been younger than I was and he had saved Rheged. I could not even recover a sword held by a squire!

The air was much clearer as I neared the top. A few hundred paces from the peak I turned to look to the south east and my home. I saw a smudge that was Wyddfa. There would be my wife and my children. There would be Myfanwy. Myrddyn and my father's body, along with Gawan should be approaching St.Asaph by now. By the time we had finished and returned it would be time for the burial. I turned and began to clamber towards the top. I looked to the right and saw the mountains of Rheged. It was so close I thought I might be able to touch it. Would I be able to save it? Could I guarantee its future?

One thing my father's death had done was show me how much we relied on Myrddyn. Without him the land would be chaotic. He brought some order. It was not just his magic it was his wisdom and his foresight. When I returned I would learn as much as I could from this man. When I descended and rejoined my family I would ensure that he was protected as would my brother. Those two would be the most important men in my land. There were spies in my army and I needed to weed them out and find the loyal warriors.

As I stood on the windswept top I turned all the way around. There was Hibernia; would the brothers return there? Then there was Gwynedd; it was the rock we needed to help us rebuild Rheged. And there was Rheged itself. A rocky little landlocked island that looked somehow vulnerable from where I stood.

And then I saw the Saxon ship. It was heading for the Lune which I could see as clearly as my sword. There too was Daffydd ap Gwynfor following behind, the wind filling his sails. I almost jumped for joy. I knew where Aethelfrith's sons were going. When my father was buried I would pursue the brothers and Morcar. As I turned to climb down I wondered if the brothers had tired of Morcar and taken the sword from his dead hands. That would be a pity; I wanted to be the one who killed him.

## Saxon Bane

I do not know if it was my mood or the spirits but, as I descended I caught a movement some five hundred paces down the slope. There was a warrior left alive and he was moving cautiously and surreptitiously down the mountain. I was the only warrior left; I had sent the rest back to the fort. He was not one of my men and I would finish him off.

I moved stealthily but swiftly. The rest at the top had enabled me to get my breath back. I saw that the warrior held a sword. That, in itself, was surprising. It was easier to move down hill, as I was, with hands free. There was something familiar about the warrior and I wondered if one of Tuanthal's men had been a little tardy getting down from his search. It was when he half turned to negotiate a boulder that I recognised him. It was Morcar!

I began to move quicker and that proved to be a mistake. I set off a small fall of rocks which tumbled down to him. He turned round and saw me less than two hundred paces from him. He ran. I saw the direction he was taking and I took a route which would enable me to cut him off. He had been taught well by my men and he did not look back. His younger legs began to extend his lead. However, he could not resist a glance back at me. When he saw what I was up to, he jinked to the side. It was a mistake. His foot slipped and he rolled down the hillside a little. I ran directly for him.

He sprang to his feet and set off like a startled hare. As luck would have it he had landed on the path and he began to make good time. I stuck to my plan of cutting him off. I had no idea where he was going but, as he appeared to have purpose, I assumed that he had confederates waiting. His path took a sudden turn and he had the choice to begin running across open ground or continue along the path. He hesitated and I closed a little with him. He ran along the path. I hurled myself at him when he passed just below me. My shoulder hit him and we both rolled down the slope. The landing took the wind from me and, by the time I had recovered, he was racing towards me with the sword raised.

I rolled away and Saxon Slayer sent sparks from the rock it struck. I jumped to my feet and took out my sword. I knew that he was a good swordsman; Pol had told me that. He was also quicker than I was. The

## Saxon Bane

only things in my favour were my experience and right. He held Saxon Slayer but he had no right to it. I had to believe that the spirits were on my side and I would prevail. I held my seax in my left hand to parry the sword.

As luck would have it we were both on the same level. "I take it that it was you who poisoned the water and killed my love?" I nodded. He grinned and it was an evil grin full of malevolence and cruelty. "And you will die slowly for I have coated Saxon Slayer in Wolf's Bane. You will die as your father did. A fitting end for a wolf. I shall take the lion as my symbol for that is more regal." He slipped his own seax into his left hand.

"It seems to me that a dog would be more appropriate. You turned on your own family. What would your father think?"

He feinted with Saxon Slayer and there was a blur of metal. I barely parried the sword but his seax gouged a red line in my arm. I was too accustomed to fighting in mail.

"My father was a fool! He could have ruled Mona and been king. It is the richest part of Gwynedd but he would not. I begged him but he said that his brother was Warlord and that was enough! Well, it was not enough for me! I was born to be king. My mother was a princess! She was heir to Elmet! If my father had not been a weak warrior then we would have stayed in Elmet and fought for our land. I would be King of Elmet and it would be I who conquered Northumbria!"

He came at me again but I was ready for the sudden burst of flying blades. I countered Saxon Slayer with my seax and pushed hard with my own sword. As our faces closed I saw the poison glistening on the edge of Saxon Slayer. It was an uncia away from my hand and death. He grinned. "It is a deadly poison. I watched it make uncle look like a baby. When you are cut I will watch you die slowly!"

He swung again with the sword and this time, when I met it with the Saxon seax, the poorly made blade shattered in two. I leapt backwards as he crowed for joy. "Now what will you do?"

I slipped my hand down and took the dagger my father had given to me at Yule. I felt a surge of power as I held it. The blue stones were magical; they came from deep within the mountains of home. I felt more confident. I used my experience. I was going to head-butt him. However, I risked catching the poisoned blade and so I put my right foot between his and punched at his face with my sword. He fell backwards and rolled down the hill. The wound on my left arm was bleeding so much that it was making the hilt of the dagger slippery. My evil cousin was winning.

I could see his confidence as he advanced toward me, "Resorting to dirty tricks eh? Not like the behaviour of a warlord is it?"

"But stabbing your uncle in the back is?"

I could see that the barb had struck home. "It was his own fault. He should have made himself king!"

I looked in his eyes and saw pure naked ambition. "And this still would not have saved my father would it? He would still have died, and Gawan and me?"

He cocked his head to one side, "Probably. You are too weak. All of you are weak. I am the only one strong enough to rule."

"And what of you and your weakness? You gave in to Oswald and Oswiu too quickly."

"Ah that is where you are wrong. They were going to make me king of Rheged and Morgause would have been my queen. When we two had power then we would have used the cult of the mother to destroy Oswald and Oswiu and we would have taken over the kingdom of Northumbria. Did you know that Edwin is converting to Christianity?" I saw his eyes flick towards my sword.

As I expected he attacked again in a flurry of quickly moving blows. All he needed to do was to break my skin with the poisoned sword and I would die. He had, however, made the mistake of being below me so that I could jump up the hill away from his blows. He fell to his face on the ground. He expected me to strike while he lay prone and he rolled away to the side.

As he got to his feet I darted in with my dagger and scored a long cut on the back of his left hand with is razor sharp edge. "I think we are even now, cousin."

## Saxon Bane

"We will not be even until you have lost your love as I lost Morgause."

"Morgause? Your love? She was a witch and a whore!"

My insult was deliberate. I wanted the blood pumping around his veins and out of his hand. "You lie!" This time I did not meet Saxon Slayer with my seax but instead, I swung my sword with the whole weight of my body behind it. I swung from over my left shoulder and he held up Saxon Slayer to parry the blow. I drove Saxon Slayer towards him and he watched in horror as the side of the blade touched the wound on his left hand.

I sprang back. "What was that you said about Wolf's Bane? That it just needed to touch a wound and a man would die? How are your legs, cousin? How is your heart? Do your eyes still see?"

He tried to lurch towards me to strike once more but it was as though someone had pulled his legs from beneath him. He collapsed to his knees. The deadly blade was still held in his hand and he looked at it in horror.

"You will soon be with your witch in the underworld. You will not see Lord Lann for he will be in Mag Mell and you will not. You will suffer torment for all eternity while your father will try to understand why you gave in to the dark side of your character."

"End my torment now, cousin, I beg of you."

"Do you think me a fool? The moment I close with you then you will strike with the poisoned blade! The poison must have reached your mind already!"

His eyes flashed anger, "I will take you with me!"

He tried a sweep with the sword but he fell on his face and the sword flew from his hand. It stuck between two stones and the hilt vibrated. Strangely it sounded as though it was singing.

I stared at his dying eyes. "You will not take me with you for when I die I shall go to the Otherworld, I shall go to Mag Mell."

I walked over to the sword and watched the poison dripping, still, from it. Tuanthal and a handful of men raced up with weapons drawn. "Warlord, are you hurt?"

## Saxon Bane

They saw the blood puddling from my hand. "It is nothing but Morcar here has caused his own death. His eyes were still open but he could not speak. I walked over to Saxon Slayer and I drew it from the stone. It seemed to scream as it came from between the rocks. I wiped the blade on the grass and then raised it.

"I name this sword Caledfwlch. Saxon Slayer was the name my father gave the weapon. I have drawn the sword from the stone and it told me its name. The sword from the stone!"

The last thing Morcar saw, before his eyes closed and he died, was the sword. He had died by the sword, Caledfwlch. He had died by his own hand and that told me the sword was alive. It would not suffer to be used by those with evil in their hearts.

Saxon Bane

# Chapter 23

We left Morcar's body for the birds and the foxes. We trudged slowly down the mountain. I was weary. I had taken no pleasure in witnessing the death of my cousin. I remembered him as a child when we played at the Yule gatherings. I could not believe how much he had changed. I would give my children closer attention now. I would watch for those signs which would tell me they were becoming like Morcar and I would stop them.

As we descended Tuanthal asked, "Why did you rename the sword? Saxon Slayer was a renowned blade."

"Aye it was, but when my father found it he did not know its name. He named it for himself. The name has a history. It would have been named before." I told them of the combat and how the sword had stuck in the stone. I shrugged, "The name seemed to come to me. I will live with the name, for good or ill."

By the time we reached the devastated village it was almost night time. The Northumbrians who had survived were chained together and the few slaves we had freed were made comfortable. The bodies of the dead were burned and we set a watch. No one had seen any more Northumbrians and the freed slaves told us that we had accounted for them all. However, I took no chances.

I woke early and rose. Tuanthal stirred but I told him to rest. The guards at the gate let me out and I wandered down to the beach. I had much to think on. Since the murder of my father I had had no time to think. I had just had to react to what was happening. Now that the sword had been safely recovered I had time to reflect.

I walked to the water and laid the sword in the salty sea. I wanted every particle of poison washing off. When I took it from the water I rubbed it in the sand and then thoroughly dried it on my tunic. I felt better. The sword felt clean.

## Saxon Bane

Thanks to my father we had won. Rheged was free. However, we had paid a high cost. Not only my father but also Aedh and many other irreplaceable men had been lost. I needed to use the warriors and leaders that we had already. Northumbria was huge. It was far bigger than Mercia. Who would rule there? Should I leave The Narrows and take my family north to rule our old lands? Morcar would have done so but would my father have done that? I needed to hear Gawan's words. Myrddyn was correct; we were two halves of my father. I was not my father and I would need to do things my way but Gawan would be the voice which would show me the right way.

I saw the sun begin to rise over the sea to the east. It was a new day and I was decided. We would bury my father in the tomb that Myrddyn had built in the mountain. I would return to the east and end the war then, and only then, would we be able to sit around my father's war table and talk of the future and peace.

Appropriately, having made a decision, I saw a sail in the distance and knew that it would be Daffydd ap Gwynfor. We would be able to leave Manau. We could take the second Saxon ship to enable us to travel more comfortably. As I walked back into the village, now coming alive, I looked up at the whale mountain. Gawan's dream had come true. There was, however, nothing to keep us on this island. When we left it would revert to the wild and empty place we had always had as a neighbour.

"Tuanthal, get a crew for the Saxon ship and begin to load her. It looks like Daffydd has returned."

"Aye Warlord." He gestured to the village. "Do we burn this before we leave?"

"No, let us leave it. We do not want the island but there may be others who wish to live here. They will, at least, have a roof and walls to protect them."

By the time Daffydd had tied up we were ready to leave. My captain looked tired. I daresay he had had little sleep in his pursuit of the brothers. His face looked drawn and serious.

"Warlord we followed the Saxons to the estuary of the Lune."

## Saxon Bane

I nodded and pointed up at the mountain. "I saw you both heading there from the peak of the mountain."

"Aye but what you did not see was the fleet of ships which were anchored in the river. The brothers have raised an army. There were many Saxon and Hibernian ships anchored there. I was lucky to escape undamaged. We should leave quickly before they return here."

"They will not be coming here." Now I knew why the brothers had sailed out while we watched. Now I knew why they had taken Morcar with them. They had been recruiting others to their cause and using the allure of the famous sword as bait. Once they had paraded him they did not need him any longer. They had not been searching for us when the ships had left. They were meeting with the other ships and chiefs. They had their own alliance. Oswald wanted his throne back. We had done the hard part for him. We had weakened King Edwin to the point of defeat. My dreams of a conquered Rheged had lasted hours.

"Warlord?"

"Sorry, Daffydd. You have done well and my mind was elsewhere. When the ship is loaded we sail home. Let us bury the Warlord and then face these brothers again."

It was not a speedy voyage but we all had much to reflect upon. Aedh's body had been placed at the prow and I stood with Tuanthal as we headed south-east. "The two of us were both boy riders for your father. I too had been a scout. I always wanted to be the horseman and ride to battle. Aedh never grew out of being a scout. He loved the freedom. He was a fine warrior and would have made an equite but he chose to go into the most dangerous of places."

"My father thought highly of both of you. He knew that he could rely upon you." I shook my head. "I was too full of the lure of the east and the armoured horsemen. I neglected what was best about Rheged."

"We could not have won without your equites, Warlord."

"I know but I will now be as my father was. I will command the armies. Pol and Lann Aelle can command my heavy warriors. I need to see the bigger picture."

"Then you are becoming your father. When we left Castle Perilous in the north he had to change. When he had commanded that lonely outpost with Garth, Aedh and me, he had been happy. When he was given command of the army of Rheged he had to change. Change can be hard, Warlord, but through change comes growth."

I laughed, "Why, Tuanthal, you have become quite the philosopher. You would fit in well in Constantinopolis. There they sit and talk just as you just did."

"I am a warrior and that is all." He looked at the darkening sky. "It will soon be winter and then another year will have passed. How many more will I see, I wonder."

I knew why he reflected upon death. He was going to the funeral of the last two of those he had grown up with. There was just my uncle Aelle left from the old days. It was the end of an era.

When we reached home we were greeted by Myrddyn and Myfanwy. Their eyes were drawn to the sword which still lay, without a scabbard, in my belt. My stepmother hugged me. "My heart was in my mouth when you stepped from your ship for you looked so much like your father. I thought he had returned from beyond the grave."

I could say nothing to that. It was, perhaps, one of the kindest things she could say but I knew that she had meant it. Myrddyn smiled. "That is why the Warlord will never truly die for he is there in Hogan Lann and in Gawan."

"Where is my little brother?"

"He and Brother Oswald are preparing the funeral. We only waited for you."

I turned as Aedh's body was removed from the ship. "And we have another captain to bury. Aedh fell."

Myfanwy's hand went to her mouth. "Not Aedh too?" It was as though naming him made her remember Morcar. "And your father's murderer?"

"Morcar is dead." She nodded and, as we walked up to the fort I told her of his death.

Myrddyn seemed satisfied. "*Wyrd*. That sword has powers far more ancient than even the Romans. We discovered much about it in

## Saxon Bane

Constantinopolis but I can see that there is more to it and it lives still. The sword killed the hand which stole it; how appropriate."

The next day would be the funerals. Everyone who wished to was allowed to attend. I had not been to the cave for many years and when I saw what Myrddyn had done I was astounded. "It is like one of the mausoleums in Constantinopolis save it is natural."

"This will endure long enough to pass a message to the future."

I looked at Gawan who shrugged. "You know how enigmatic he likes to be."

My father's body had been brought on a cart from the fort. The four of us, Tuanthal, Gawan, Myrddyn and I, lifted the body and carried it into the cave. Brother Oswald led the procession holding Caledfwlch. My mother walked before with a torch and my tearful younger sister Delbchaem followed. The warriors and the people followed.

I was amazed as we walked across the stone floor. Myrddyn's workers had polished it smooth. There was a niche in one side beneath a Latin inscription. We reverently placed my father's body in the niche and Brother Oswald handed me the sword. I placed it on the body and stepped back.

"Warlord, we are here to say goodbye and for you and your mighty sword to be reunited." Everything went silent. The mourners were united in silence and grief. From the dark recesses of the cavern came a steady drip of water. When the drip stopped it was as though the heart of the mountain had stopped. Beyond the cave there was a distant rumble of thunder and then the drip began again.

Myrddyn seemed delighted, "The spirits have spoken. This place is now a special place a holy place." He nodded at me.

I walked back to the body and took the sword from my father. I paused as I took it. I leaned close in to his face and whispered, "I swear that I will protect your land for you. Watch over me, father, for I need your help still."

I turned and faced a sea of torch lit faces. "I take this sword, Caledfwlch, which was Saxon Slayer and swear to continue to fight Rheged's foes."

## Saxon Bane

The silence continued and Gawan walked up to the body. I could see tears in his eyes. In his hands he held the old wolf cloak. I could see that others had repaired it and there was now a clasp with two beautiful blue stones holding it. He placed it on the body and then he too leaned in and whispered something.

He joined me and we watched as Geraint and Aedh's scouts marched in with his body. There was no niche made for the Captain of Scouts but they reverently laid his body on the ground beneath my father's.

They stood around with heads bowed as Myrddyn intoned, "Spirits of Wyddfa here is a brave warrior, Aedh of Castle Perilous. Let him watch over his lord until the end of time."

I know not how long we stood there but when I looked around there was just my family, Brother Oswald, Myrddyn and Tuanthal.

Myfanwy put her arm around Delbchaem. "Come let us go and feast. It is what your father would have wished."

As we walked into the storm filled afternoon I heard my sister say. "What did those words mean above my father?"

Brother Oswald walked next to her. "That is Latin. It said, 'Here lies Lord Lann, Warlord of Rheged: the greatest warrior in the west."

She nodded, "It is true and he would like that."

Myfanwy shook her head. "He would not like that for your father was the most modest man I ever knew. But I am glad that those words are there so that the whole world will know what they have lost."

Our plans to mourn Lord Lann were destroyed five days after he was placed into his tomb. The first of the scouts arrived back to tell us of the disaster of Eboracum. They had been sent by King Cadwallon to warn us of our imminent danger.

"Warlord we had the fortress surrounded but we found ourselves surrounded. The brothers Oswald and Oswiu came with their elder brother Eanfrith." I was about to ask a question when Myrddyn held up his hand. I heeded his advice. "At the same time a fleet of ships appeared in the river carrying King Raedwald and his men." He hesitated. I could see criticism in his eyes but he had been trained well by Aedh and he continued with his message. "King Cadwallon tried to break out south.

## Saxon Bane

King Fiachnae mac Báetáin led his men northwest. We had to fight our way to the high divide. The Saxons pursued us relentlessly. Captains Pol and Lann Aelle led attack after attack to drive back the Saxons but they were like the sands of the sea. No matter how many they slew more sprang up to take their place. We found an old Roman fort on the high ground. We took shelter there and they beat themselves against it for half a day before drifting back east. We brought the survivors over the divide. King Cadwallon and Penda have gone to Wrecsam and Lord Lann Aelle is bringing the survivors here."

I patted him on the shoulder, "You have done well, now rest."

He half turned and then he said, "Someone said that Captain Aedh had died."

"He did."

The man looked despondent. "Then the last alliance has failed and we will drown in a sea of Saxons."

"No it has not. This is a setback only. We will return stronger from this. The sacrifices made by Lord Lann and Aedh will bear fruit in the future."

I looked around at my little brother who seemed to have grown in stature since we had buried our father. "Send for my uncle, Lord Aelle. We need to make plans."

I saw Tuanthal nod and leave the hall. Myfanwy smiled, "It is good that we laid in so much food for the funeral feast. We will now need it to feed your army, Warlord."

I kissed her on the head as she left. My father had chosen well. "Brother Oswald, we had best prepare maps again. We have a campaign to plan."

When they had gone there was just Myrddyn and Gawan left. "Who is this Eanfrith?"

"I had heard the name, Hogan Lann, but I thought he was insignificant for he was not with his father at Wrecsam. We have much to discover."

The remnants of our mighty army drifted in the next day. It was a sorry sight. I could see, from their numbers that they had lost heavily. There were but four scouts who remained. Daffydd ap Miach was at the head of a mere forty archers. Of Bors and Kay there was no sign. Pol and Lann Aelle led in sixty equites and barely ninety squires. They were all that remained.

I embraced Lann Aelle and then Pol. "Bors and Kay?"

"They live. Bors took his forty men to Deva whilst Kay headed north. He had only thirty men with him."

"Come let us go to my hall." It was a sparse looking hall as the eight of us sat around the table. "Tell me all."

Pol and Lann Aelle looked at each other. Myrddyn banged the table. "Come! This is the Warlord! Speak the truth and do not hide anything. If you do so then we shall surely lose!"

Pol nodded at Lann Aelle who sighed and began to speak. "We were looking at the fort and not to the west. King Cadwallon was sure that Edwin would surrender soon. It was almost a party atmosphere. A few days after you left the scouts to the south reported a fleet arriving in the river. King Cadwallon sent Pol and I to investigate with Daffydd's archers. While we journeyed south a new army arrived, Saxons under this Eanfrith. He is a good warrior and a clever general. They drove a wedge between King Cadwallon's men and those under Bors and Kay. The Hibernians were also with King Cadwallon." He shook his head. "Bors told me that the king tried to attack the wedge with all of his army. At the same time King Edwin broke out of the fortress and attacked his rear. That was when Dai died. He was defending the standard. The Hibernians fled north." He shook his head, seemingly unable to go on.

Pol put a sympathetic arm around his shoulder. "Bors sent a scout after us and he and Kay began to retreat west." He gave me an earnest look. "It was the right thing to do, Hogan Lann, I mean Warlord."

"I know and there is no criticism intended."

"We turned and headed north as soon as we could. We found King Cadwallon and Penda surrounded by the enemy. We charged into their rear and there was great slaughter," he paused, "on both sides. With the armies of Mercia and Gwynedd rescued we headed west."

I think we might have escaped unscathed had we not been ambushed by Oswald and Oswiu. We were at low ebb and had crossed the divide when they fell upon us. We were lucky for most of those who fell upon us were mercenaries but even so their numbers meant that we could not defeat them. We fought them all the way to the Maeresea. They retreated when we reached the river. Kay went home as did King Cadwallon and Penda." He slumped back into his seat. "I am sorry we let you down, Warlord."

"You did not let me down. Tell me why did King Cadwallon send his best warriors to investigate the fleet? Surely scouts would have been just as effective?" They both shrugged.

Myrddyn spoke. "Now we know why the ships were waiting in the Lune. But what I cannot understand is this new alliance. It is disturbing."

"We shall have to begin again. The wolf warrior may be dead but his legacy lives on. We have suffered a setback, true but the heart of Rheged beats still in this room. I made a misjudgement when I pursued Morcar. I took myself away from the place where I was needed the most."

Gawan said, "No, you are wrong brother. You had to recover the sword. Had you not done so then Morcar would now rule in Rheged and we would never come back from the loss of the sword. This was *wyrd*." He smiled. "There are fewer of us who are left but it is like a wine which is distilled, we become stronger and more powerful."

I saw Myrddyn nodding his approval. "Before we begin to plan let us all visit the tomb of the Warlord. It will be good to go there and feel his spirit enter us."

We set off immediately, despite the weariness of our warriors. It was just the captains who accompanied us. As we ascended Lann Aelle asked, "Who built this tomb? I have no idea where it is."

Myrddyn chuckled, "You do; it is the cave where the Warlord and I would dream. I have just enlarged it somewhat." He looked at me expectantly. "I have kept the torches burning."

The day was a dark and dirty one with thick black ominous clouds. It felt almost like night time. The trees through which we climbed made it even gloomier. When we emerged from the forest we turned north and there we saw the tomb. As we turned we saw that the lights we had left burning around the bodies now made the wolf entrance seem to come alive. The eyes glowed, the mouth seemed to open and I smiled. The Wolf Warrior lived still. This was the sign. Rheged would rise once more.

Saxon Bane

# Epilogue

The full import of the disaster was brought home to us in the time between Yule and the first lambs. The Saxons had divided the land up. Eanfrith ruled Bernicia with his brothers and King Edwin, now a devoted Christian had conquered Rheged and Man. He now threatened Anglesey. If it were not for King Fiachnae mac Báetáin whose men constantly harried his northern borders we might already have been fighting. As it was he had bought us time. We could begin to build our armies up once more and the sword would go to war again.

We had much to do before we began to start again. We needed ships and we needed arms. Much had been lost in the disastrous battle and retreat. We used all of our money to send to the east for weapons. However, we could not buy men. We would have to rely on our new allies. And that was a surprise. They had not deserted us. In fact, the opposite had happened. They were as committed as we were and Penda persuaded King Cearl to ally Mercia with us. My father's dream and his vision had been good.

At the winter solstice, Gawan and I journeyed to the tomb. Myrddyn did not come. He told us that this was something for the sons of the Wolf Warrior. There were no torches burning when we arrived. We lit faggots and carried them within. Once the flames burned they threw their light onto the walls and I saw that Myrddyn had had the walls decorated with paintings. They showed the scenes of the battles in which we had fought and won.

We wandered over to the niche. Aedh had not been mummified, merely wrapped in bandages but my father's face looked alive.

I looked at Gawan. He nodded at our father and said, "We have much to do brother. I know why Myrddyn wanted us to come here alone. We are with the spirit of the Warlord. We should swear an oath now. He will hear it."

"You are right. Warlord, we swear that we will not stop fighting until Rheged is free."

Gawan stepped forward, "And we will be as one mind we two will become one."

We looked at each other and nodded. We said, "We are the Wolf Brethren!"

## The End

Saxon Bane

# Glossary

**Name-Explanation**
Acidus-acid
*Aidan-* one of Lann's captains
*Aedh-*Despatch rider and scout
Aelfere-Northallerton
*Aelle-*Monca's son and Lann's stepbrother
Aethelfrith-King of Bernicia and Aethelric's overlord
Alavna-Maryport
Artorius-King Arthur
Banna-Birdoswald
Belatu-Cadros -God of war
Belerion-Land's End (Cornwall)
*Bors-* son of Mungo
Byrnie – mail shirt
Cadwallon ap Cadfan- King of Gwynedd
Caedwalestate-Cadishead near Salford
Caergybi-Holyhead
Caestre- Chester (Deva)
Caledfwlch – Excalibur (in Welsh the name comes from *caled* "hard" and *bwlch* "breach, cleft"). Literally the sword from the stone
Civitas Carvetiorum-Carlisle
Constantinopolis-Constantinople (modern Istanbul)
Cymru-Wales
Cynfarch Oer-Descendant of Coel Hen (King Cole)
*Daffydd ap Gwynfor-*Lann's chief sea captain
*Daffydd ap Miach-*Miach's son
*Dai ap Gruffyd-*King Cadfan's squire
Dál nAraidi- Northern Ireland
*Delbchaem Lann-*Lann's daughter

Saxon Bane

Din Guardi-Bamburgh Castle
Dunum-River Tees
Dux Britannica-The Roman British leader after the Romans left (King Arthur)
Erecura-Goddess of the earth
*Einar*- A Dane serving the Warlord
Fanum Cocidii-Bewcastle
*Felan*-Irish pirate
Fiachnae mac Báetáin- king of the Dál nAraidi
*Fiachra*-brother of Fiachnae mac Báetáin
*Freja*-Saxon captive and Aelle's wife
*Gareth*-Harbour master Caergybi
*Garth*-Lann's lieutenant
*Gawan Lann*-Lann's son
Glanibanta- Ambleside
*Gwynfor*-Headman at Caergybi
Gwyr-The land close to Swansea
Hagustald- Hexham
Halvelyn- Helvellyn
Haordine-Hawarden Cheshire
Hen Ogledd-Northern England and Southern Scotland
*Hogan Lann*-Lann's son
Icaunus-River god
*Kay*- Captain of the north
King Ywain Rheged-Eldest son of King Urien
*Lord Lann*-Warlord of Rheged and Dux Britannica
Loch nEachach-Lough Neagh (Northern Ireland)
Loge-God of trickery
Loidis-Leeds
Mael Odhar Macha-King of Airgialla
Maeresea-River Mersey
Mag Mell- Welsh for heaven. This is reserved for those who have attained glory. Annwn was also a place of joy when one died.
Mare Nostrum-Mediterranean Sea

Saxon Bane

Metcauld- Lindisfarne
*Morgause*- witch
*Mungo*-Leader of the men of Strathclyde
*Myfanwy*-Lann's wife
*Myrddyn*-Welsh wizard fighting for Rheged
*Nanna Lann*-Lann's daughter and wife of Cadwallon
Nithing-A man without honour
Nodens-God of hunting
*Oswald*-Priest
Penrhyd- Penrith,Cumbria
Penrhyn Llŷn- Llŷn Peninsula
Pharos- lighthouse
*Pol*-Captain and Hogan Lann's standard bearer
Prestune-Preston Lancashire
Prince Pasgen-Youngest son of Urien
*Raibeart*-Lann's brother
Riemmelth- Prince Pasgen's daughter
*Roman Bridge*-Piercebridge (Durham)
*Roman Soldiers*- the mountains around Scafell Pike
Scillonia Insula-Scilly Isles
Solar-West facing room in a castle
Sucellos-God of love and time
Tatenhale-Tattenhall near Chester
*The Narrows*-The Menaii Straits
Tineus- River Tyne
Tomtun- Tamworth- the capital of Mercia
Treffynnon-Holywell (North Wales)
*Tuanthal*-Leader of Lann's horse warriors
Uí Néill – the largest clan in Ireland in the Dark Ages
Vectis-Isle of Wight
Vindonnus-God of hunting
*Wachanglen*-Wakefield
Wæcelinga Stræt- Watling Street (A5)
wapentake- Muster of an army

Saxon Bane

*Wide Water*-Windermere
Wrecsam- Wrexham
Wyddfa-Snowdon
Wyrd-Fate
Y Fflint-Flint (North Wales)
Ynys Enlli-Bardsey Island
Yr Wyddgrug-Mold (North Wales)

Saxon Bane

# Historical note

I mainly used four books to research the material. The first was the excellent Michael Wood's book *"In Search of the Dark Ages"* and the second was *"The Middle Ages"* Edited by Robert Fossier. The third was the Osprey Book- *"Saxon, Viking and Norman"* by Terence Wise. I also used Brian Sykes book, *"Blood of the Isles"* for reference. In addition I searched on line for more obscure information. All the place names are accurate, as far as I know, and I have researched the names of the characters to reflect the period. My apologies if I have made a mistake.

There is evidence that the Saxons withdrew from Rheged in the early years of the seventh century and never dominated that land again. It seems that warriors from Wales reclaimed that land. I have used Lord Lann as that instrument. King Edwin did usurp Aethelfrith. Edwin was allied to both Mercia and East Anglia.

There is a cave in North Yorkshire called Mother Shipton's cave. It has a petrifying well within. Objects left there become covered, over time, with a stone exterior. In the seventeenth century a witch was reputed to live there. I created an earlier witch to allow the Roman sword to be discovered and to create a link with my earlier Roman series.

The Saxons and Britons all valued swords and cherished them. They were passed from father to son. The use of rings on the hilts of great swords was a common practice and showed the prowess of the warrior in battle. The Irish were known for having poor quality brittle blades.

I do not subscribe to Brian Sykes' theory that the Saxons merely assimilated into the existing people. One only has to look at the place names and listen to the language of the north and northwestern part of England. You can still hear anomalies. Perhaps that is because I come from the north but all of my reading leads me to believe that the Anglo-Saxons were intent upon conquest. The Norse invaders were different and they did assimilate but the Saxons were fighting for their lives and it did not pay to be kind. The people of Rheged were the last survivors of Roman Britain and I have given them all of the characteristics they would have had. They were educated and ingenious. The Dark Ages was the time when much knowledge was lost and would not reappear until Constantinople fell. This period was also the time when the old ways changed and Britain became Christian but I have not used this as a source of conflict but rather growth.

King Cadfan was succeeded by his son when he was still alive and he retired to a quiet life. I have used this battle with the Mercians as the reason for that retirement. It was also about this time that Aethelfrith was killed in battle. His sons, Oswiu and Oswald became famous and outshone their father and Edwin. At the time of my story they were in Ireland. Their assassination of Lann and the theft of Saxon Slayer are pure fiction. As both of them were canonised after their deaths their people thought highly of them. I am writing from the viewpoint of their enemy. One man's freedom fighter is another man's terrorist. They were hard times. They did have a brother called Eanfrith. He died without becoming king and is a shadowy character.

King Cadwallon became the last great British leader until modern times. Alfred ruled the Saxons but no one held such sway over the country from Scotland to Cornwall in the same way that King Cadwallon did. Of course, I have him aided by Lord Lann the Warlord.

The practice of sacrifice was an old one in the pagan religions. There is evidence of it taking place even in the time of the Romans. The victim was usually a volunteer. It would not be a surprise for Lord Lann to know the identity of his killer but be willing to give his life for his country: Dulce et Decorum Est Pro Patria Mori!

Penda and the other kings, Cearl and Fiachnae mac Báetáin were real and contemporaries of each other. Fiachnae mac Báetáin is named as having been to Din Guardi. There is some confusion over the reigns of both Cearl and Penda. Some people think that they ruled jointly for a while. Certainly, Penda was the last pagan king of Mercia and he did defeat Edwin as well. His reign saw the ascendancy of Mercia and the demise of Northumbria. The theories about his age are laughable. It is said that he gained the throne at 50 and ruled for 30 years before dying in battle! I have accepted the 30 years theory but not his age. I have him as younger, in his thirties when he meets Lord Lann so that he dies in battle in his sixties. As with all my books I have researched as much as I can but I am a writer of fiction. I have chosen the facts to suit my story.

I stole the idea of the multiple fires to fool the Northumbrians from Genghis Khan- always steal from the best! He used them when fighting a superior force of Mongols.

Saxon ships were relatively small; it was the Norse and their Drekar or Dragon ships that created ships capable of carrying larger numbers of warriors.

Caledfwlch is the original name of Excalibur. Excalibur was created by the French and Norman writers but the legend of Arthur and his sword in what is known as the Dark Ages is Welsh in origin.

The Warlord and King Cadwallon will return and they will meet the Saxons once more on the field of battle.

*Griff Hosker August 2014*

Saxon Bane

# Other books by Griff Hosker

If you enjoyed reading this book, then why not read another one by the author?

## Ancient History

### The Sword of Cartimandua Series
(Germania and Britannia 50 A.D. – 128 A.D.)
Ulpius Felix- Roman Warrior (prequel)
The Sword of Cartimandua
The Horse Warriors
Invasion Caledonia
Roman Retreat
Revolt of the Red Witch
Druid's Gold
Trajan's Hunters
The Last Frontier
Hero of Rome
Roman Hawk
Roman Treachery
Roman Wall
Roman Courage

### The Wolf Warrior series
(Britain in the late 6th Century)
Saxon Dawn
Saxon Revenge
Saxon England

Saxon Bane

Saxon Blood
Saxon Slayer
Saxon Slaughter
Saxon Bane
Saxon Fall: Rise of the Warlord
Saxon Throne
Saxon Sword

# Medieval History

### The Dragon Heart Series
Viking Slave
Viking Warrior
Viking Jarl
Viking Kingdom
Viking Wolf
Viking War
Viking Sword
Viking Wrath
Viking Raid
Viking Legend
Viking Vengeance
Viking Dragon
Viking Treasure
Viking Enemy
Viking Witch
Viking Blood
Viking Weregeld
Viking Storm
Viking Warband
Viking Shadow
Viking Legacy
Viking Clan

Saxon Bane

Viking Bravery

**The Norman Genesis Series**
Hrolf the Viking
Horseman
The Battle for a Home
Revenge of the Franks
The Land of the Northmen
Ragnvald Hrolfsson
Brothers in Blood
Lord of Rouen
Drekar in the Seine
Duke of Normandy
The Duke and the King

**Danelaw**
(England and Denmark in the 11$^{th}$ Century)
Dragon Sword
Oathsword
Bloodsword
Danish Sword

**New World Series**
Blood on the Blade
Across the Seas
The Savage Wilderness
The Bear and the Wolf
Erik The Navigator
Erik's Clan

The Vengeance Trail

**The Reconquista Chronicles**
Castilian Knight

Saxon Bane

El Campeador
The Lord of Valencia

**The Aelfraed Series**
(Britain and Byzantium 1050 A.D. - 1085 A.D.)
Housecarl
Outlaw
Varangian

**The Anarchy Series England
1120-1180**
English Knight
Knight of the Empress
Northern Knight
Baron of the North
Earl
King Henry's Champion
The King is Dead
Warlord of the North
Enemy at the Gate
The Fallen Crown
Warlord's War
Kingmaker
Henry II
Crusader
The Welsh Marches
Irish War
Poisonous Plots
The Princes' Revolt
Earl Marshal
The Perfect Knight

**Border Knight
1182-1300**

Saxon Bane

Sword for Hire
Return of the Knight
Baron's War
Magna Carta
Welsh Wars
Henry III
The Bloody Border
Baron's Crusade
Sentinel of the North
War in the West
Debt of Honour
The Blood of the Warlord
The Fettered King

**Sir John Hawkwood Series**
**France and Italy 1339- 1387**
Crécy: The Age of the Archer
Man At Arms
The White Company
Leader of Men
Tuscan Warlord

**Lord Edward's Archer**
Lord Edward's Archer
King in Waiting
An Archer's Crusade
Targets of Treachery
The Great Cause

**Struggle for a Crown**
**1360- 1485**
Blood on the Crown
To Murder a King
The Throne

Saxon Bane

King Henry IV
The Road to Agincourt
St Crispin's Day
The Battle for France
The Last Knight
Queen's Knight

Tales from the Sword I
(Short stories from the Medieval period)

**Tudor Warrior series**
**England and Scotland in the late 14th and early 15th century**
Tudor Warrior
Tudor Spy
Flodden

**Conquistador**
**England and America in the 16th Century**
Conquistador
The English Adventurer

## Modern History

**The Napoleonic Horseman Series**
Chasseur à Cheval
Napoleon's Guard
British Light Dragoon
Soldier Spy
1808: The Road to Coruña
Talavera
The Lines of Torres Vedras
Bloody Badajoz
The Road to France

Saxon Bane

Waterloo

**The Lucky Jack American Civil War series**
Rebel Raiders
Confederate Rangers
The Road to Gettysburg

**Soldier of the Queen series**
Soldier of the Queen

**The British Ace Series**
1914
1915 Fokker Scourge
1916 Angels over the Somme
1917 Eagles Fall
1918 We will remember them
From Arctic Snow to Desert Sand
Wings over Persia

**Combined Operations series**
**1940-1945**
Commando
Raider
Behind Enemy Lines
Dieppe
Toehold in Europe
Sword Beach
Breakout
The Battle for Antwerp
King Tiger
Beyond the Rhine
Korea
Korean Winter

Saxon Bane

Tales from the Sword II
(Short stories from the Modern period)

**Other Books**
Great Granny's Ghost (Aimed at 9-14-year-old young people)

For more information on all of the books then please visit the author's website at www.griffhosker.com where there is a link to contact him or visit his Facebook page: GriffHosker at Sword Books